An Ark
On The Flood

By the same author:

The Work of Her Hands
Matthew Ratton

An Ark
On The Flood

Anne Knowles

St. Martin's Press
New York

To my own particular Ark,
and all who sail in her

Library of Congress Cataloging in Publication Data

Knowles, Anne.
   An ark on the flood.

   I. Title.
PR6061.N547A8   1985   823'.914   85-11722
ISBN 0-312-40920-X

First published in Great Britain by Methuen London Ltd.

First U.S. Edition

10 9 8 7 6 5 4 3 2 1

Chapter One

Milchester lay asleep in the cool dark of an April night: dark except for scattered squares of lighted windows here and there; silent except for the occasional rumble of traffic passing through, the sudden yowling of cats romancing, the clatter of raided bins in a pub yard where a fox was after pickings. At the town's edge where the fields began sheep huddled like grey rocks in the gloom, keeping their lambs close and their ears alert to the small noises of the night: something hunting down the stream, the rattle of the yard-dog's chain at a nearby farm, the stirring of branches in a sudden breeze. In one of the last houses at the edge of the town, human sleepers dreamed soundly in the quiet darkness.

Suddenly, somewhere down the long corridors of sleep, there was a bell ringing; urgent, imperative, demanding an answer. Rachel, in pursuit of it, blundered into wakefulness into a world that was still dark, except for the pale oblong of early morning sky where the window was.

Silhouetted against the grey was Tom's hunched shape, and as she watched it, it unfolded itself, rose and padded away from the bedside. Tom seemed able to answer these early calls as if on automatic pilot: would not have a bedside receiver in case he might answer it and fall instantly asleep again.

Rachel made herself snug in the warmth of his side of the bed and lay deliciously cocooned, the pleasure only faintly spiced with guilt at the possibility that it had most likely been her turn. Tom came back and swiftly began to dress.

'Are you awake?' he asked.

'Mm-mm,' Rachel nodded, sleepily.

'It's that cow Myrtle,' said Tom. 'Darned inconsiderate, I call it.' He moved to the bed, hopping on one socked foot while searching for the other, and gave her a swift kiss. 'I must go,' he said. 'I wouldn't leave your bed for another female if it weren't in the line of duty.'

Rachel grinned. 'Phone if you need reinforcements,' she said.

She heard him leave the house, registered with a mind still half asleep and drifting the slam of the door, an engine starting and briefly rolling then the clack of the outer gates. She pictured Tom with his coat collar turned up against the cool air, driving with his windows wide as he always did. 'So I can smell where I'm going,' he had told her. She had laughed, but he was right. Each place had its own subtle air, its own odours. They did not have to scream at you like the silage dumps at Topend, or the vast piggeries at Claybridge.

She had learned so much from him in the six months they had been married. He had revealed in her a treasure house of passion and affection that she had known existed, but which she had locked away like gold in a vault, because it had seemed to her that learning and practising the skills she was now well qualified in must be all-demanding, exclusive. With Tom she had found it possible to expand what she was: to be all that she had been and infinitely more. Her fears that in becoming part of someone else, she might become less than her skill and her pride demanded had dropped away from her like bud scales from the springing leaf.

She chuckled quietly to herself, remembering her doubts, her attempted rejection of him. 'What a young prig you were,' Rachel chided herself. She let her thoughts drift, and they swam, dream-like, with idle inconsequence. She saw herself walking along the passage at Stapleton House on her way to her first surgery with Malcolm Halliday, and recalled how people had reacted to this new young woman their vet had taken into practice with him. What traps and pitfalls she had had to be wary of, what suspicion and plain pigheadedness from some of the old farmers in the countryside round about. And what friendships too, and wide, demanding experiences she had found; and what growing affection for the Cotswold landscape and the people who worked it. This landscape she had also seen through Tom's eyes, in the paintings he had invited her to see, and they had given her her first insight into the sort of man he really was: had helped him win that long slow battle with her reluctance to become involved with him in any way other than professionally. 'Your paintings made love to me long before you ever did,' she had teased him.

'And did you find the main dish as much to your taste as the starters?' he had asked, not needing an answer.

So much had happened since that first nervous day's work with Malcolm. Even now she found it hard to accept: the sad fact of his death and the knowledge that she would never again see his grey shape striding towards her down Milchester High Street or stepping out of his car to join her on one of the lonely farms. People she met or worked for still spoke of him with regret, with affection, and with the sort of respect that has almost gone out of fashion. She doubted if anyone would speak of her in those terms. Perhaps, one day; but it would take a lifetime of work, and even then she felt she'd need to be safely dead before any of the farming people around Milchester would voice such an opinion. They made sure around here that you did not grow big-headed with praise. Still, she had learned to translate their reticent speech, and to recognise thanks behind the sparing words.

Even after all this time she occasionally woke thinking she was still in Stapleton House, and took a moment or so to bring herself back to reality. But Stapleton House stood empty now, waiting for new owners to move in. Rachel had not gone back there, except to drive past when she needed that particular road.

The house where she now lay, where she and Tom had set up practice together, was something of an oddity: a dumpy white building hidden behind a high wall that muffled the noise of the Gloucester-bound traffic. It really was an incongruous piece of architecture, set down in the middle of a farmyard that was a good few centuries its senior.

The original farmhouse had been Milchester's only bomb victim: a direct hit from a straying aircraft had reduced it to rubble and blackened angular ruin. The new house had been built as soon as possible after the war, with whatever materials austerity could provide and the building restrictions would allow. It was cement rendered, welsh-slate roofed and seemed to peer out of its metal-framed windows with a mixture of surprise to find itself in such a situation, and embarrassment at its Cotswold surroundings. It was the last house in the world Rachel would have thought Tom would buy. He had a painter's eye for proportion and pleasant line in building. He was no sentimentalist, and preferred the gaunt angularity of many of the Cotswold farmhouses to the tea cosy cottage up to its eaves in hollyhocks, but he would surely find nothing aesthetically pleasing in such an old place. Yet after he had shown her round, joking about it, saying it looked like a seaside villa cast up by a storm, she could see the sense of it. For one thing, it was nothing like the price of the available stone properties; for another it was in an ideal position near the entrance to the town, with plenty of space for cars to park, and plenty of privacy behind the original stone wall and wooden entrance gates, once surgery was over for the day.

Most of the original farm buildings had been ruined with the house; a few of their outer walls only remained to enclose the new one. But, with their backs to the upstart house, as if offended by its presence, stood a block of stables and a small barn which had once been one side of a further yard. The other side of that quadrangle had also been demolished, not by enemy bombs this time but by time, weather, and the increasing value of the stone and timber in them. In view of this Rachel had been surprised to see in what a state of stout repair the remaining buildings stood: slate roofs complete, unmossed and unsagging, windows whole, the timber in good repair. She was glad of it though, for it formed the boundary of the land that Tom had bought, and certainly no slates were going to come sliding down from that stout roof onto unsuspecting heads on their way to visit the vets.

The serge-grey of the morning sky through the windows was

paling to silver now. Rachel could hear the increasing pulse of traffic on the Gloucester Road, muted by the high walls, but insistent, reminding her that it was was market day. Pigs and sheep would be homing into Milchester, to be decanted in a bewildered protesting flood into the pens from which the buyers, sharp for a bargain, might view and consider them. George would be up by now, then, and putting on his boots. He never missed a market day.

Rachel had been in the house a week before she discovered George. The house was called Painter's Farm Cottage, after the vanished farmhouse which had belonged to the Painter family for generations. Perhaps it had been the name which had first attracted Tom to it, in spite of its architectural shortcomings. It had certainly amused him, anyway, the aptness of the name; and the walls of the house, which were plain and pleasant enough inside, were now hung with many of his own paintings: Cotswold landscapes for the most part, but seen with such unconventional vision and set down with such brilliance of colour and intricacy of form, that even now Rachel caught her breath at them.

So, to Rachel and Tom the place was 'Painters', and the 'new vets'' to the people of Milchester, though it was the establishment that was new, rather than Rachel and Tom Adams who were familiar enough figures in the Milchester landscape.

George, however, had not yet met Rachel, nor she him, and Tom had not mentioned his existence. Then one morning she had come home at first light after a complicated foaling at the Ashton Stud, in that mood which is beyond tiredness, filled with a light-headed energy which prevents sleep, even when the body craves it. She had made herself some tea, resisted the temptation to wake Tom, checked the day's appointments, and then wandered back outside again to walk the perimeter of their property in a pleasantly proprietal way. She walked along the inside of the high wall, down the wide passageway that led to the surgery entrance, across the paved area behind the house that had once been the flagged floors of the old kitchen and sculleries, right round the edge of the small piece of dug earth where vegetables were to be encouraged to grow,

11

and then up to the other side where the blank back wall of the barn blocked off the early sun. Between the end wall of the house and the beginning of the back wall of the stable a high planked gate stood shut. Rachel knew quite well that the land beyond this gate was not theirs: she had seen the plans, and knew the boundaries. But in that early morning mood she looked at the shut gate, with its latch hole high up in its solid wooden planks, and she wanted to see, out of pure curiosity, what was on the other side. She told herself she really hoped for a view of the sun coming up over the flat meadows that lay beyond, but really it was more childish than that; more unconsidered than that.

The latch went up, the gate opened with no protest, no unoiled creakings, and beyond it lay a passageway as narrow as the gate itself between the bulked sides of the two buildings, and the air between them was cool and blue. Beyond this was the sudden brilliance of new sunlight, silvering the wet grass. From roof-angle to wall a cobweb was down-hung with water-drops like an intricate necklace of crystal. It was so lovely, so enchanting in its sudden-ness, this view of the morning, that she could scarcely bring herself to move out into it. Then she laughed, and ran out onto the expanse of glittering grass, and spun round to take in all the glory of it . . . For a moment she felt fifteen again with all the light-headed, airy pleasure that balanced all fifteen's glooms and despairs. Marriage, responsibility, profession, years, all shed off her as she twirled and danced. Then in her enchanted, spellbound ears came the sound of a voice: a sharp, suspicious voice that said, 'Wodgerwant?'

Rachel turned feeling startled, guilty and decidedly foolish, to come face to face with a little man, weasel-thin and brown with small eyes, a large sharp nose and large hairy eyebrows that met across the bridge of it like two caterpillars at loggerheads.

'Who are you?' Rachel asked, playing for time in which to assemble her thoughts to clothe herself in her right mind again, to put on a little dignity.

'That's for me to know about you, I'd say,' the man remarked. 'Seein' as I live 'ere and you're a tres-passer.'

He was right, of course. She had no business to be where she was, and it was not his fault that she felt as if she had been dropped from a great height. He stood there, bristling at her. Had he begun to growl it would not have surprised her. His anger made him look very funny, though not to be trifled with – like an ancient Jack Russell terrier, probably gone in the teeth but still game for a fight.

'I am very sorry,' Rachel said, making no excuses for her presence. 'I am Rachel Adams, the vet, from next door you know.' She pointed behind her towards Painters.

'Thought as much,' the little man said, and stumped away without a word to vanish into the stable, leaving Rachel feeling foolish, with her mouth open, still not knowing who this was.

'I should have told you about George,' Tom had said, chuckling over her re-telling of her morning's adventure as they sat at breakfast.

'I thought those buildings were empty,' Rachel said.

'They often are,' Tom answered. 'George comes and goes. He worked on Painters Farm from a boy, did George. He was just a muck-shovel stable lad to start with, and worked his way up to have charge of all the horses, and there were about a dozen of those apparently, just before the war: heavy horses, Clydesdales, shires, half-breds. He was very well thought of by the Painters, and he deserved it by all accounts. Then he was called up in the war, and when he came back the farm was in ruins and all the horses dead or sold, and heavy horses on the way out, or so it seemed. Anyway, the Painters took him on again, and let him keep one old mare and a tub-cart to help about the place, and when old Mrs Painter died and left instructions for this house to be sold, and the main block of farmland, she left that barn and stables and a couple of acres in trust for George for his lifetime. After that it reverts to the family, for George has no-one to leave it to. He does a bit of dealing, in a small way, goes off round the horse fairs. He's a fierce little man, as you've discovered. He's got a face I'd like to get down on canvas, but he's never still for long enough.'

So that was how she met George. George would be up and doing now, his bed in the loft over the stables neatly remade according to the habit of years, his market dress of breeches, boots and long-skirted jacket carefully brushed. He had gone to market every week of his working life, except for those interrupted years in the war. Buying or selling, or just to keep an eye on the way of things, he had gone dressed exactly as he would be dressed now this morning. Anything else would have been unthinkable.

It was time to get up. There was no denying it. No putting it off any longer. Soon Mrs Partridge would arrive and start to clatter about in the kitchen. She still hadn't arranged the Painters' kitchen to her liking, and Rachel knew she still missed Stapleton House, with all its known and accustomed spaces that she had worked in for so long. Vi Partridge had been Rachel's friend and ally in that first year in Milchester: her good Gloucestershire voice and marvellous cooking had pulled Rachel back from many an edge of misery, weariness and sheer sense of failure as she had struggled to find her feet in Malcolm's practice. They had shared many a joke together too, and from her Rachel had learned a great deal, and greatly for her benefit, about the crafty, kindly, bigoted, generous, blinkered, eccentric, splendid characters that made up the Cotswold community in which she lived and worked.

Sometimes Rachel considered, guiltily, that Mrs Partridge was possibly something of a luxury. There were plenty of professional couples managing without an equivalent Mrs Partridge. Tom told her, when she spoke to him on the subject, not to be ridiculous.

'We both work darn hard,' he said, 'and so does Vi Partridge. There's enough work here for at least three of us. Would you want me to sack the dear woman to satisfy the stirrings of socialistic conscience in your beautiful breast?'

'No, of course I wouldn't,' Rachel had protested.

'Well then, be quiet will you, or I'll tell Mrs P you want to get rid of her.'

There was no denying the time now. The alarm clock began its insistent and totally unnecessary bleeping as Rachel rose and began to dress. She went downstairs, and had just switched on the kettle when she heard the gates open again, and the sound of Tom's car coming in.

She set a mug of tea ready on the table for him, and he appeared in the doorway, filthy and smelling of cow.

'Well?' she said.

'Twins,' he said. 'One of each.'

He sloshed himself off in the sink, and she held the tea for him to sip as he dried himself off.

'Lord, that's good,' he said. He gave her a great hug, and she could feel the coldness of the morning on him, and a mixed smell of soap, dampness and birth. It was a mixture she was well used to.

'You know,' he said. 'You're very beautiful. For a vet.'

Chapter Two

Leaving Tom to finish morning surgery, Rachel set out on the rounds. She drove through the narrow streets of Milchester, the little town all spruce and springlike and scrubbed by the pale sunlight of the early year.

The pavements were a-jostle with women in from the country for a day's shopping, having cajoled a lift in Landrover or cattle-lorry, or arrived by public transport from the once-a-week bus villages, whose passengers knew each other and each other's business, and whose conversation on the journey could bring a blush to the cheek – or at least to the back of the neck – of the young man driving them to and fro. Their shopping trips were social occasions as well as marketing expeditions, and were a breath of stimulating air away from the kitchen and the constant battle to keep straw and mud in the yards where they belonged, and not on the carpets and in the corners.

Many of these women Rachel knew. She had drunk tea with them and listened to their lives, watched them at work and called on them to help with the nursing of creatures that needed bringing into the warm and cossetting. You could stock a fair-sized holding, Rachel considered, with stock that farmers' wives and daughters had willed life into when their men had not thought it worth the battle.

She waved to one or two familiar faces as she drove by. Mrs Allerton and Mrs Croft from Hawkshill and old Mrs Briggs from Topend Cottage – the one whose cat had swallowed a beer-bottle cap – and there, loaded down like a packhorse already with baskets of shopping, Mrs Holder from Overbury, whose goats ran the gamut of capricious mischief, regularly damaging themselves or each other or some other creature on the farm, so that Tom and Rachel began to dread being called out to them for fear of what they would have found to do next.

Rachel had one call to make in town before she started the farm visits. Mrs Kyle's siamese had bad ears again, and Mrs Kyle was far too badly disabled to bring him to the surgery. Neighbours would have brought him of course, but Rachel liked an excuse to call. She liked Mrs Kyle. They had met when Tom was still living in the flat in Sheep Street opposite where Mrs Kyle herself lived, for on warm days Mrs Kyle would sit in her chair in the open doorway overlooking the narrow garden and quiet street, and Rachel had stopped once to speak, and the habit grew, so that on days when it was cool and the door was shut, Rachel would knock on it and go in and talk for a while.

Mrs Kyle got about very well in her wheelchair in her ground floor flat. She was a little shrunken woman, her shoulders hunched, her head held upright by a surgical collar, her hands and arms lying along the arms of the chair, thin as sticks and looking every bit as brittle. Yet birdlike as she seemed in her physique there was nothing beady or beaky about her personality. It was a whole, sound woman that looked out of those perceptive eyes and spoke from an agile and witty brain. Rachel had grown very fond of her, and worried because her door was always unlatched, night and day; and yet she was often alone, by choice, sending home-helps, neighbours and callers-in away to their own homes with the assurance that if she got burglars she'd make a noise like a dalek and terrify them. Once, on an infrequent bad day, she told Rachel that a knock on the head would be doing her a favour, but she seldom let such thoughts show through.

She looked shrivelled, heavy-browed, claw-handed, like a little crippled bantam hen, and her courage was as fierce. She had no time for sentiment, and was outspoken in her remarks to those who attempted to treat her as a Good Cause. She had indeed been a little wary of Rachel's approach at first, until she had seen Tom come out to claim her and had been assured that Rachel was okay. So neither Rachel nor Tom offered her any favours except the minor one of dancing attendance on her cat; but they had heard delicious reports of how home-helps and social workers had fled from her wicked sense of humour, these reports mainly from the woman who came in now to help her, and who could give as good as she got. The conversations between these two that Rachel had been party to were like the sparring of experts and were life's blood to Mrs Kyle, making a whole woman of her, acid intelligence informing her ridiculous body with a kind of fiery dignity.

While Rachel examined and treated the cat that morning Mrs Kyle talked rapidly, questioning, plucking news and information of the town, its inmates, its comings and goings, like a hungry child stripping berries from a bush. She cackled, commented and probed as Rachel regaled her with stories, and her withered face grew flushed with the pleasure of good talk. It was not gossip. She demanded no names; only wished to be part even at second hand of all that babbling, tumbling stream that was the life of the town.

A good while later, the reluctant cat's ears cleaned and dressed, Rachel drove on northwards out of the town, to where at the top of a slope just before the turn to Nether Leybourne stood Abel Cash's filling station, where she intended to call in for petrol. Although it was so short a distance out of Milchester, the little shack with its three pumps standing like space-warriors at attention felt curiously remote on its bleak eminence. It had the atmosphere of a staging post on an old coaching route; perhaps it stood on the site of some long-forgotten Inn. This worked greatly to Abel Cash's advantage, for motorists felt drawn to this scruffy little establishment as if to an oasis. Certainly, Abel's lit windows beckoned out invitingly enough on a bleak night if one was driving towards Milchester from the North through the windswept darkness and the tossing trees.

Now, its daytime shabbiness was washed over with April sunshine, and in the foot or so of poor earth between the walls of the shack and the cement of the forecourt a few daffodils were trying to look Wordsworthian in this somewhat unlikely setting.

As Rachel pulled up alongside the pumps, Abel came out from his shack and patted Jessica affectionately on the bonnet. He was one of the very few people to whom Rachel had admitted the name of her little yellow car. Malcolm, her old boss, had chided her – not with any great seriousness – for 'sentimental anthropomorphism'. Abel loved cars – indeed any mechanical vehicle – as if they were living creatures, and he greeted Jessica as warmly as if she were muscle and blood.

'Morning Mrs Tom. Morning Jessica.' Tom and Abel were old cronies. Rachel was Mrs Tom from the moment she had been introduced, and from Abel it was an odd sort of compliment; not implying that she was merely a possession of Tom's, more as if she had been grafted on to him.

She smiled to herself. That was far too horticultural an image for a man who was black-thumbed rather than green-fingered, but she could think of no mechanical equivalent.

'Morning Abel. Fill her up please,' Rachel said.

From behind the shack a lean, sandy-haired lurcher came trotting and made, with some interest, towards Rachel.

'Hello, Mick,' she said, and rubbed his ears while he pressed himself against her, waving his long fringed tail and sighing with pleasure. Mick was a dog who kept aloof from strangers, but he knew a friend when he saw one.

'He's lame, Abel, did you know?' Rachel asked.

'It's nothing much,' Abel said, his eye on the pump gauge. 'Twisted it, I expect, galloping about.'

Mick delicately lifted one forepaw and nibbled at it. Rachel could see places where it had bled, as if, perhaps, pellets had been removed from it, not unskilfully. 'Someone take a pot shot at you, did they old boy?' Rachel murmured to Mick. She was not supposed to know of Abel's night-time trade as poacher, not officially; but she suspected that he knew that she knew. She found in her case a small bottle of antiseptic lotion. 'Have this on the house, Abel. It's probably quite good for sprains.' He took it, without comment.

'You tell your Tom I've got those piston rings he wanted,' he instructed her.

Abel provided for the creatures he loved not only piped nourishment but spare parts as well, which he rescued from a great boneyard of wrecked vehicles which he kept behind the shack. To these his attitude was that of the surgeon: let the dead give up their organs to the living; and many an ailing car knew the benefits of Abel's restoration work.

With Jessica replete Rachel headed for her farm visits; routine stuff this morning, but she was content with that. She was still not quite accustomed to the fact that her living was earned doing the job she had always wanted to do; hard work, dirty, sweaty and unglamorous for the most part, yet she scarcely regretted a moment of it. Come to think of it though, one or two of the less pleasant moments had been caused by her first customer that morning, John Hamden, who had been so reluctant to allow her to treat his beasts at all, and whose uncooperative attitude had often made her work difficult, to say the least. Now, however, he did accept her, albeit dourly, but whether the cause was her proved ability, or the fact that all the other local vets fought shy of his short temper and financial amnesia, she could not judge.

He came stumping across from the cowhouse, where Rachel could hear her patients bellowing in protest at being kept confined for longer than they were used to.

'Oh,' he said. 'It's you.'

Whom did you expect, thought Rachel. Albert Schweitzer? 'Good morning, Mr Hamden,' she said crisply. 'Let's get straight on then, shall we?'

Her course that morning was a long half circle, bringing her gradually down from the high plateau into the smaller, steeper valleys at the escarpment's edge. The landscape could alter totally within half an hour's driving, and that was part of its fascination for Rachel. She began to know it quite well now, unlike her early days when she could lose herself easily in a maze of lanes, or find there was no road across from one ridge of land to another, so that she must drive miles to the valley head and turn back upon herself again to reach some farm which she could see, tantalizingly near on the hillside. Now she knew, on most of these roads, what scene would unfold round the next corner, yet it all varied, constantly, from season to season, from crop to crop, from grey days to golden, so that it was never truly the same, never totally as expected.

She knew, and was known in, most of the villages whose surrounding farms she visited on her rounds; and each of these, too, was subtly different from every other, and not just in the different arrangements of its houses and lanes.

Each village kept its own peculiar flavour, even now when large towns all seemed in competition to look exactly the same – same facades, same plate-glass precincts, same wares for sale, same food to eat, same expressions on the faces of the hurrying passers-by. Milchester, in Rachel's opinion, was one of the few that had resisted. The villages though, isolated by progress, drew into themselves and remained obstinately unique. Upper Coldhill, clinging to the shoulders of the plateau, its one steep street staggering down towards Lower Coldhill from which a sudden winter snow could cut it off within minutes, had no contact now with Milchester, or anywhere else, except for those with cars. The bus was no longer economic, and those who did not or could not drive seldom stirred out of the village. Television made them familiar with people and towns at the ends of the earth, yet they remained isolated from their own, except when neighbours remembered to be kind. Rachel would sometimes bring small items with her, if she had reason to call in the area, for some of the old dears who could now travel no further than they could walk, which often was not far.

These villages of the high plateau were secret places, often publess, usually shopless, not quite cosy enough to attract the summer visitors. The gusting Cotswold winds blew sneakily among their stone walls, and the same stone littered the surrounding fields so thickly it was hard to imagine how the crops grew.

Further down the scarp slope and into the little valleys communities were more sheltered, softer perhaps, nearer to the towns and fed in and out of them by main roads and frequent buses.

These drew to themselves the families who wanted country living without isolation, who needed to hold hands with the town like a child keeping hold of its nursemaid, and their coming altered the nature of the villages. It was beginning to alter the nature of the veterinary work, too, as these new countrymen tried their hand at goat-keeping, or poultry, or having a pony for the children: 'Seems a shame to have all that grass and not make use of it.' These places were at the furthest limit of Tom and Rachel's practice, but even so they seemed to spend a good deal of time rescuing these innocents from the results of their undertakings. Perhaps the most ill-advised of all these was the purchase as a pet for the children of a dear little goat kid, impish and appealing, that grew with immense speed and vigour into the randiest and most malodorous billy that the mind could imagine. He threw himself with gusto upon any creature who approached him, and none stopped to enquire whether his motive was lust or malice.

Appealed to for help Rachel had made enquiries, and with Mrs Holder's help had found a breeder willing to take him on; and Rachel and Tom had helped to load him into his new owner's trailer, waved off with enormous relief by his previous ones who had decided to buy a donkey instead – a female donkey.

Ilcombe was one of these valley villages, and it was last on Rachel's list for the day. Ilcombe straggled out along several lanes from its central green. It was neat and well tended, gardened and groomed by the retired and the prosperous, its houses, whenever they chanced to come on the market, snapped up with glee at prices that their original owners would have found impossible to believe. Ilcombe was all very tidy, and contended strongly each year for the Parsloe Cup for the best-kept village, which it had won once or twice and had plaques to prove it. Because of this any necessary agriculture – by which few of its inhabitants now earned their living – was kept discreetly out of sight. Rachel, having treated some scouring calves at Capmill Farm on the slope above the village, was very conscious of Jessica's mud-splattered paint-work and the dirt in her tyres as she drove down into the village to visit the shop. She often called in there when she was near Ilcombe because Mrs Bird, who owned and ran it, made toffee that Tom had particularly liked since the days when, as a boy, his Aunt Margaret had taken him to spend his pocket money on it. Mrs Bird had been in service as a young girl in the house where Aunt Margaret lived, and the two had become, and remained, great friends, despite the tart disapproval of a class-conscious society. Mrs Bird's native accent had been smoothed over in those days by her employer's wish that she should speak correctly. She had not the broad speech of Vi Partridge but the soft country burr still made her voice a pleasure to listen to, and Rachel tried always to leave time for a 'proper chat'.

It would not have been courteous to enquire into Mrs Bird's age, but she looked like an amiable prune, shrunk up into her wrinkled skin. Yet she had all her wits about her: knew where everything was, and the price of it, and she could add up with dead-on accuracy faster than you could press the buttons of a calculator.

Mrs Bird was a leftover from Ilcombe's working days, when almost every cottage sent its breadwinners into the fields, or to the clothmill, or to work at the big house. She spoke often to Rachel of the changes she had seen in the village, and how it was on her visits home as a girl: the silver band in which her father had played the tuba, and later, when she was a young woman, the drama group in which she and her cronies had got up to such larks.

She gave short shrift to the village's present activities and to most of her present custom, though they provided her living so she supposed she mustn't grumble. She broke up toffee for Rachel that morning with her little hammer, told her all the local news, and gave her a glass of lemonade on the house.

Rachel, sitting at the counter, drinking and listening, looked up to see what was the latest picture on Mrs Bird's calendar. This calendar was an annual gift from the cash-and-carry from which Mrs Bird's son Alfred brought all the goods for his mother to sell in the little shop, and this year it was 'Country Scenes' in glorious and sometimes scarcely credible colour. Rachel had watched this calendar's progress through the year on her visits to Ilcombe, and she saw that the present picture was of a thatched forge, with the smith outside it, bending his muscular back to the shoeing of a glossy chestnut horse while two extremely clean and tidy children stood by to watch. 'Pretty, that,' Mrs Bird commented, noticing Rachel regarding the scene. 'I've had no end of people say how pretty that is.' There was a pause, and then Mrs Bird continued, consideringly, and with a suspicion of malice: 'I'll tell you something though. If my grandson Fred – him who's a farrier over by Stroud – if he was to set up a forge here and now in Ilcombe, this lot'd be complaining within the week about the noise, and the smell, and the horse-droppings on the road. I can just imagine.' She cackled loudly, the wrinkles of her face stretching sideways from eyes and mouth as she pictured to herself the discomfiture of her patrons, brought face to face with such a reality where they had seen only a vanished charm.

Chapter Three

✎

Over these last months, living and working with Tom, Rachel had been amazed at how much at one they were, as if each had entered the other in every aspect of their lives. It frightened her, sometimes, to know that to lose him now would kill part of herself. The prospect of her own death had never alarmed her, yet even the thought of the possibility of Tom's death desolated her. How ridiculous, that something that filled her with so much pleasure, so much happiness, should bring with it this capacity for being hurt, this nakedness; delicious but so open to wounding.

Tom himself seldom hurt her. When they were working he was often brusque and preoccupied, but then so he had always been; and she had been accustomed, as with Malcolm, to having the highest standards demanded of her, and indeed expected them of herself. She and Tom were often apart for the job demanded it. This too she had understood, and had expected right from the start. Of course they argued, of course they disagreed, and shouted, and were childish, and the sparks flew. Yet that was the stress and thrust in the fabric that made the building secure. They rowed like two good barristers Tom had remarked once, after one good battle.

'Let's settle out of court then,' she had replied.

The time since their marriage seemed so short. Rachel, scrubbing down after surgery one morning, and watching the new and brilliant green of the horse-chestnut trees on the roadside beyond the wall, was looking back and remembering.

Their honeymoon had been three days at a riverside pub on the banks of the Severn; there was little time to spare with the new practice to be built up, and neither of them wanted to waste the precious hours travelling. Rachel would always remember those days, not only for their discovering in her passions in which she had sometimes half wondered whether she might be lacking – and in which she most assuredly was not – but for other quieter and lovely intimacies; their walking hand in hand for miles along the towpath by the gleaming silver water and pewter mud of the tidal river, watching the sun hang red in the sky over the long arch of the road-bridge, with his reflection dancing beneath it and splashing flame from bank to bank.

They had sat on a stile, just talking, telling each other of events in that now improbable time when they did not know each other. They watched a family of goldfinches squabbling over the last remaining seedheads in a clump of despondent thistles growing right at the edge of the mud. They watched boats drift downstream, black against the thin light of a winter's afternoon. They went to see Joe Barge. Tom had stayed with Joe Barge when he had come down to paint the Severn levels on a holiday the previous year. Joe had an ancient farmhouse of silvery-pink brick; a well-proportioned, workaday place with no nonsense about it. He earned his money grazing cattle, but his love was his horses: shire horses, which he bred for show and for work, and supposedly to sell, though he did this only when money was hard to come by. When he did decide to sell though the rumour would go round, and offers would come as thick as Milton's leaves so that the eventual purchase price would keep Joe nicely, thank you, for some time afterwards.

Tom introduced Rachel to Joe: a stoutish old man, beer-bellied, short-legged, and not much given to conversation except on the subject of horses. He showed Rachel around the house and the outbuildings, as if, in his opinion, this was what a woman would expect of you, but he said very little to her. Only when his mares bent their great heads down to her and she spoke softly to them, and when Hector, the stallion, came trumpeting across his enclosure to challenge her and she stood her ground and stretched up to pat his neck, did Joe decide she would do for Tom Adams. 'Got yourself a good 'un there,' he told Tom. 'Not much of 'er, but what there is, I likes.' They all three spent a long afternoon talking horses, looking at photographs, genealogies, cups and trophies as well as admiring the great beasts themselves, ambling placidly in Joe's flat meadows sheltered from the river breezes by the humped-up bank along which the towpath ran. At high tide the water would lap these banks, and without them those flat meadows would be waterlogged and useless. As it was they were green and in good heart even this late in the year, fenced in with trim blackthorn hedges, and gated stoutly with oak.

'Don't like metal gates,' Joe Barge said. ' 'Ad some once. Old Princess there, she just leaned on 'em. No good after that.'

Having been given a demonstration earlier on of the amount of deadweight Princess could pull without apparent effort, Rachel was not surprised. She had seen few creatures so gentle and biddable, yet with such size and weight and power. She was reluctant to leave them when it was time to go, but Joe Barge had invited them to come back whenever they had a mind to.

The last night of their three nights, as they lay together in the big bed in the guestroom of the little pub, Tom looked down at Rachel's upturned face and smiled at her, his expression quizzical. 'What did I know about women before I knew you?' he said. 'Fancies. Half truths. And, my heaven's, the Awful Anthea.'

'Do you think she's happy with her Peter?' Rachel asked.

'Deliriously, I expect. Money gave her pleasure all the time. One of life's great experiences, was Anthea.'

He laughed out loud and she could feel the laughter all through her. 'Oh, I've walked among the women all right, Rachel my love, and they've roused me up like old Mrs Holder's goat, but you . . . Just listen to the classic line. With you, it's different.'

She seized him by his beard and kissed him. 'Fool,' she said.

'Listen though,' he said, serious now. 'When I paint: when I paint I know where the centre of my passion lies. Not the brain, nor the heart, the loins, the bowels or whatever, but right at some centre of myself, as if I were drawn inwards like the horns of a snail. And there I am, at the centre of myself, while I paint; and my hands and arms and eyes and brain do what they must but it's from that centre that it all springs. I felt like that when I first saw you, and I thought "Good Lord, I must love her." A conclusion and a resolution all at once, you see. And now – oh now my dearest Rachel, you have drawn me to the very centre of that centre and made the whole of creation spin round us.'

Rachel explored his face in the half-dark, feeling the lines of it, reading his expression, learning it by heart.

'I love you,' she said. 'You say what I feel, but can't explain. You know what I feel without me telling you.' Then later she laughed and said, 'It's spinning again – all of it out there. And we're letting it gyrate away, with all its ailing creatures and no need to do anything about any of them.'

'Until tomorrow,' said Tom.

'All those divers diseases,' chuckled Rachel.

'Mallenders and sallenders.'

'Farcy and Gleet.'

'Strangles and Staggers.'

'Braxy and Blane.'

'And no-one's going to telephone and ask us to cure 'em.'

'You know,' Rachel admitted, 'I suppose before you bullied me into marrying you I was a bit of a prig.'

'A beautiful prig. Obstinately a prig,' Tom cheerfully agreed.

'Not much candlepower in me,' said Rachel, her voice quiet now, her tone more serious, as if she were afraid that she might in some way have been less than he might have wished her. 'Couldn't see your way to Babylon by the light of it.'

But Tom only drew her closer and held her hard against him. ' "There dwelt a man in Babylon, lady," ' he said. ' "And he lived in the light of the sun." '

Rachel came back from her dreaming, back to the reality of the present.

Everything was clean and set to rights. Rachel took off her surgery coat and hung it up. Tom would be back soon, and for once, just for precious once, they might manage to have lunch together. They ate at midday, when they were able to, in a grab-as-grab-can, hasty, peripatetic way which would have been the despair of any good dietician, but Vi Partridge saw to their evening meal and that always more than made up for the day's shortcomings.

Rachel had become used to this routine at Stapleton House, and as she admitted to being only a basic cook she was glad to continue it; yet she enjoyed the occasional chance to make a meal for herself and Tom, however swift and scrappy. She had become a skilled toasted-sandwich maker, concocting together all kinds of unlikely ingredients which nevertheless frequently tasted far better than she had expected they would.

She went into the kitchen and began ferreting about for likely substances to put between slices of bread.

Tom came in.

'You see,' he said, as he gave her a great crushing hug. 'You're a frustrated housewife really. Under that stern professional exterior lurks a concealed passion for the duster and the doyley.'

'Get off my foot,' Rachel said. 'Sardine and peanut butter, or cheese and pineapple?'

'Both,' he said. 'Injecting pigs gives one an appetite.'

'Rather you than me. You don't smell piggy.' She sniffed him. 'In fact you smell very clean.'

Tom laughed. 'That stupid old boar of theirs sent me flying. Mrs Maybridge gave me a bath. Not personally, you understand,' he leered. 'Lavender bathsalts and all. Well, it's better than pig-muck.'

They were halfway through their second sandwich when the telephone rang.

'Say it's the Chinese Laundry,' Rachel suggested.

Tom went to answer it. Rachel, eavesdropping, indulged in that most intriguing of pastimes, trying to deduce the whole of a conversation by listening to one half of it. However, as Tom's habit on the telephone was to be as brief as possible, and to confine his replies in the main to 'yes' and 'no' and 'I see', she learned very

31

little for her effort, and less from his enigmatic expression when he returned. One of his eyebrows was, however, fractionally higher than the other which might mean he was amused, or puzzled.

'Sexual discrimination, I call it,' he said. 'I won't do at all, it seems. It has to be you.'

'What does? Who is it?'

'Richard Bevan. Got someone he wants you to visit.'

Richard Bevan was the R.S.P.C.A. inspector. When he asked a vet to step in it was often in the most appalling circumstances.

'Oh dear,' said Rachel. 'What's happened?'

'It doesn't sound too awful. Just rather odd,' said Tom. 'Apparently some woman rang him up and said she wished to inform him that she had beaten her dog, and what would he like to do about it. She was most insistent that he ought to do something.'

'Sounds pretty unlikely,' said Rachel.

'I know it does. She's a bit loony, I expect. Richard said she sounded quite sensible though. The trouble is, he has to appear in court this afternoon – those boys over at Claybridge who hanged those cats, do you remember? Well, he feels someone ought to go and have a chat with her, and he thought perhaps another woman . . .'

'If she's some frustrated old dear wanting someone to take notice of her she'd probably rather have you,' said Rachel, acidly. 'And I was enjoying my sandwich, too.'

She felt decidedly cross as she set out. Tom hadn't helped either, making dramatic remarks about 'Strange goings-on in Milchester outskirts. Young vet savaged by dog-beater.'

'I hope you choke on your cheese and pineapple,' she had snarled, as she shrugged herself into her coat and left the house.

According to the directions she had been given it was not far. There was no point in getting the car out. After a sharp walk she might arrive feeling more professional and less disgruntled about her truncated lunch hour.

She stepped smartly along, wondering to herself what strange sort of person she was about to encounter and how best to deal with her. It sounded to Rachel as if the old dear might need a psychiatrist rather than a vet, though of course, if she had really hurt the dog that was a different matter.

It was hardly as much as what Rachel's father would have called 'a good breathing walk' before she was within sight of the house. It was about half a mile out of Milchester, in a place where several houses stood well back from the road, each in its own grounds, high-walled and tree-shaded. The houses were not old as Cotswold houses go, but had stood there long enough to blend mellowly into their landscape. The warmth of early summer washed pleasantly over them, and so did an aura of affluent ownership. Such houses as these the local estate agents would laugh with glee to have on their books, certain that customers would do profitable battle to own one.

'Well, she can't plead poverty, that's for sure,' Rachel said to herself.

Yet as she approached the particular house to which she had been directed – Knapp Hill, Margaret Sherwood – she began to notice a difference in atmosphere from its neighbours. There was not that same air of easy prosperity that the others exhaled. Here the drive was weedy and mossed, and the lawns to each side had run to riotous grass; this season's green pushed up through the tawny mat of last year's growth. The house, though solid and handsome, seemed to peer out through its unpruned roses from windowframes whose wood was starved from lack of paint. There was no sign here of the jobbing gardener, or the daily help, or the D.I.Y. enthusiast. Yet it was a gentle neglect, Rachel felt as she came closer. It was still trimmed here and there; muddle, but not dirt; a quiet and pleasant decay with nothing sinister about it: leaf-decay, not flesh-decay. There was a peaceful quality about the place that began to smooth down Rachel's hackles, and she began to feel less apprehensive about what she might find. Some dotty, harmless old recluse, perhaps. Maybe she did not even own a dog. Maybe, as she now suspected, it was the ruse of some lonely old soul to gain a little company for a while.

Rachel knocked at the door and stood waiting, still wondering what lay in store for her.

The door opened and revealed a pleasant, blameless-looking, late-middle-aged woman in skirt and blouse, woolly cardigan and stockings, and carpet slippers. At first glance she looked like everybody's aunt. Maiden aunt, unmarried sister, unmarriageable widow: the kind that fades comfortably into the wallpaper of other people's lives, baby-sitting, looking after the canary at holiday times, knitting sweaters and baby-boots and reading endlessly to measled children. She could indeed have been called on to do every one of these things, Rachel considered, yet there was far more to her than that. Bracing the cardiganed bosom was a spine of steel, and there was a hawk's glance in the eyes that welcomed her from the round, lined face. Rachel felt a need to mind her manners.

'Are you Margaret Sherwood?' Rachel asked. It sounded a little abrupt, but Richard had not given the woman a title.

'Indeed I am.' The voice was cool, educated, neither welcoming nor distant.

Rachel gave her name and stated her reason for coming, and a brown, stained hand grasped and shook hers, firm and dry. What looked like relief illuminated Margaret Sherwood's face.

'I am so glad you came, though I suspect you think I'm barmy. Do you?'

Rachel stammered a denial, of which the woman took no notice at all but drew her into the house, saying, 'Bound to, I suppose, but I had to tell someone, didn't I? I just had to. Can't talk to friends: all dead or gone, mostly. Can't talk to neighbours. They move in and out at a rate of knots these days, and I'm too busy for getting to know new people. Well, better come and see the victim, hadn't you?'

She led the way down the central hall of the house, opened the door of what turned out to be the kitchen, and there bounded towards Rachel a large, curly-coated, cream-coloured dog of vast size and unfamiliar breed. The dog greeted Rachel by placing his paws on her shoulders and applying his tongue to her face, neck and ears with wet, ecstatic enthusiasm.

'Oh do get down, Sago,' said his owner, and after a moment or so Sago obliged. It would have taken a navvy with a bargepole to inflict any noticeable punishment on Sago, but all the same Rachel examined him for any marks, bruises or cuts consistent with a beating.

'Have I hurt him?' Margaret Sherwood asked, anxiously.

Rachel suppressed a longing to laugh out loud, and assured her the dog was quite unharmed and in splendid condition, which indeed he was: firm-fleshed and muscular under his amazing woolly coat.

'He really is a splendid dog. What is he?' she enquired.

'Lord knows,' Margaret Sherwood said. 'And He has not vouchsafed the information. If it were not so unlikely, I would hazard Great Dane crossed with a Standard Poodle. I was given him when Mother died. The children thought I would be lonely. I have had him for six months now, and have grown quite accustomed to him.'

The cool phrase was belied by the affection with which she stroked the big dog's head. 'Apart from his exuberance, he has never been a tiresome dog. I seldom raise my voice to him.' The woman hesitated, as if trying to guess how well Rachel would understand the thing that had roused her anger.

'Then he ate my manuscript,' she said.

Rachel's brain put up images of this crime. Musical or literary? Her own or someone else's? Original or a copy? Valuable or sentimental? Form, content, size?

'Please,' she said. 'Tell me all about it.'

'Come with me. I'll show you. I think perhaps you will understand what I did, though I have no intention of asking you to approve it. I am totally culpable.'

They left Sago in the kitchen and walked along the hallway to another door, through which was a room containing more books – or so it seemed to Rachel – than the whole of Milchester Public Library. Every wall was lined with shelves of them, every table space was piled high with them, and there were, in addition, two large revolving bookcases, beautiful period pieces of satinwood and inlaid mother-of-pearl. There was a huge antique desk

35

covered in papers; some hand-written, some typed, some scrumpled up ready to be hurled towards a wicker wastepaper basket which already overflowed with them.

'Oh, you're a writer,' Rachel said, and felt instantly hot at the obviousness of the remark. She half expected some cutting rejoinder but Margaret Sherwood only said, 'As you see. But not a published one. David and I were going to write a book together. David was my husband. Then he died, and I always said I'd finish it on my own. But there were the children, and then David's mother became ill and came to live here. She never got over his dying before she did. Well, the children grew up and went abroad. Mark's in New Zealand, Sarah's in Canada. I began writing again while I was nursing Mother, and have gone great guns since I've been here on my own. Ten years in all I've been working seriously on it. It's taking a great deal longer than I imagined, and now, thanks to Sago, it will take considerably longer.'

Margaret Sherwood paused and sighed, and looked at the door of the library as if it might provide her with an answer when she said she had no idea how the dog had got in, but he had chewed up chapters eight to twelve so thoroughly that they could no longer be read.

'Thank God I had put away the first seven chapters, manuscript and typescript, but I had not typed the rest. I am very slow at it, you see.'

She shook her head and sighed again.

'If he had chewed up a baby I could not have been angrier,' she said. 'I set about him with my walking stick. I am not like that, Mrs Adams. I was brought up to have control of my emotions. I was so sick and ashamed that I had to tell someone.'

She looked at Rachel, and her hands were trembling. 'You must think me ridiculous,' she said. 'But I felt that for a moment I had been insane. Not merely angry, you understand, but totally insane. I could have killed him.'

Rachel was not sure whether this meant 'I might have' or 'I wanted to'. The first was totally unlikely, and the second, though she would not appear to condone it, was entirely understandable.

'I expect a great many people would have reacted as you did,' she said reassuringly. 'I am sure I would. All that hard work, all those ideas, and now you have to start again and hope you remember everything you wanted to say. And truly, Sago is quite unharmed.'

'Ah, but you have not heard the real irony of it yet,' Margaret Sherwood said, and a wry smile was beginning to lift some of the worry from her face. 'The book I am writing is a study of the history of cruelty and persecution, and how it affects both those who inflict and those who suffer. Perhaps it surprises you, that we should choose such a subject. Well, my husband's name was not always Sherwood. He was Jewish, and in the war was interned with his parents, his brothers, and many other relations. There is no need to tell you details. You will know what those places were like. But David's father was a good man, and a resourceful one, and somehow he managed to arrange a way for David and his mother to escape.'

Margaret Sherwood's voice faltered. She was silent for a while, and Rachel sat very still. This woman was recalling times more terrible than Rachel had ever known. She was the expert here, not Rachel.

The voice continued. 'Yes, he managed to get David and his mother out, but he himself died there, with David's two older brothers and most of the rest of the family. There had been a whole street of them: all close relatives. All gassed.'

'I am sorry,' Rachel said. 'I am so sorry.'

'People were,' said Margaret Sherwood. 'You would even hear remarks like "Of course I can't stand the Jews myself, but you shouldn't do that sort of thing, should you?" But you see, when we began to work on the book and to look into history, we discovered that people could, and did.

'I had been keen to visit the place where David's family died and I, too, could not understand how such things can take place; but the more I read and the more I learned, the more I discovered this was no new thing. Hitler was only the latest ogre. A large-scale, well-publicised ogre, the latest in a long and terrible line which still exists, still spawns. It is the dark side of humanity, and it is in

37

every one of us. We were fascinated, horrified, David and I, by what we discovered.

'He knew how the Jews had been persecuted throughout history, of course, for all kinds of motives from the killing of Christ onward, conveniently forgetting, of course, the Jewishness of Christ himself. And people have, for the sake of a religion that preached love from the beginning, burned and racked and tortured anyone whose interpretation differed by a split hair from their own. In our time we've burned heretics, chained the insane like bears in a pit, enslaved the coloured, decimated native populations in our greed for territory, and then had the effrontery to preach a religion of love and forgiveness to those we left alive. Genocide isn't new, you know. Hitler didn't invent it. Our good queen Bess had a somewhat similar attitude where the Irish were concerned. She would gladly have had them all dead, and certainly made no political moves to keep them alive. And it's not gone out of fashion yet, has it: this hatred of whole creeds, whole nations, where the only good one is a dead one?'

The voice, quiet and intense, carried Rachel along with it into the mind of the speaker, whose face was alight now with passionate enthusiasm for her subject. She had come prepared to meet a lonely loony, and had found someone so breathtakingly different that she sat entranced, listening to the flow of words and ideas. There was power behind the words, but no sentiment. Statements were proved, facts documented, in a swingeing case for the prosecution against mankind. In her ten years' work on the theme Mrs Sherwood had become well versed in the action and motive of cruelty. She had discovered vast seas of it, washing under humanity, fathoms deep, its waters polluting everything they touched.

'We float about on it,' she said, 'we who like to call ourselves "civilisation" – in our little, shallow boats, in constant danger of swamping. And monsters lurk in it, too: greed, self-interest, bigotry, ignorance, uninformed sentimentality. We need more arks on the flood, Mrs Adams.'

She stopped and gazed at Rachel, and the bright fire of her enthusiasm seemed to die. Her face once more became wretched.

'And what do I do?' she asked, angered against herself. 'I add another bucketful to all that great ocean. Oh, I know I didn't hurt the dear old chap, but that isn't what matters. That old schoolboy chestnut about hurting the beater more than the beaten is true you know. Cruelty damages the perpetrator every bit as much as the victim. And deliberate cruelty has a further weapon still, for it arouses in us a desire for an equally cruel revenge. Christ knew that. So he preached that impossible command to love one's enemies that so few of us can manage to obey. Though Sago seems to have managed it.'

'Yes, he has,' said Rachel, 'and you were instantly sorry for beating him.'

Margaret Sherwood smiled. 'You're right, of course you are, but I was horrified at such a violent reaction in myself, so unthinking. It staggered me almost as much as my discovery, long after the war, after all those years of "we're right, they're wrong", that "our side" was not always as true to its heroic image as we had been taught, and that Saint George can easily turn out to be every bit as bloody as the dragon.'

'And what is the answer?' Rachel asked. 'How do we stop it?'

Mrs Sherwood shook her head. 'I suppose that Man's impossible gospel might do it. But so few of us have come anywhere near that sort of perfection in two thousand years.'

'It's back to your arks on the flood, then,' said Rachel. 'We all have to be Noah, or Deucalion, if you prefer, saving what we can and trying to keep seaworthy.'

Mrs Sherwood nodded. 'I have often wondered,' she said, 'if Noah grieved to know that all the other poor creatures were drowning.'

Chapter Four

Richard Bevan was proving elusive on the 'phone, and as Rachel wished to report to him her interview with Margaret Sherwood she decided to track him down at the market.

She had learned more about Mrs Sherwood, as she had hoped she might, from Vi Partridge who, had she had the urge to do so, could have written a detailed study of a large number of the inhabitants of Milchester and its surrounding villages with no research and no reference other than her long years and capacious memory. It was as well she was totally without malice, and not given to gossip except with those whom she felt would let her words go no further. From her Rachel had gained a great fund of useful information, and an insight into the character, circumstances and idiosyncracies of many of her customers, the owners of the creatures she treated day by day.

'Nice woman, that,' was the verdict on Margaret Sherwood. 'Nursed old Mrs Sherwood for years and years she did, and 'er weren't no blood of 'ers neither. Partridge used to do odds and ends of jobs for 'em in them days, and sometimes if 'e was working of an evening I'd go with 'im, and I'd 'ave a chat with the old lady. Kept 'er beautiful, young Mrs Sherwood did.'

Rachel smiled to herself at the naming of 'young' Mrs Sherwood; but she could imagine the devotion she would give to the job, and the love, too, not just the washing of an elderly body, the providing of clean sheets and meals on a tray. Certainly, Rachel had come away from their interview filled with a pleasant elation that her own job fitted her to battle in however small a way against the enemy Margaret Sherwood had named. She felt as some plodding Christian may feel who is suddenly shaken by a zealous evangelist.

However, market day brought her sharply back to reality. The noise and the clatter, the bellowing beasts and the fruity language of the stockmen, were as old as herding itself. It seemed to Rachel that the relationship here was a practical one, neither sentimental nor deliberately harsh, and if cruelty did show itself Richard Bevan would rap its knuckles soon enough. She set off to find him.

She tracked him down in the market office talking to a young woman, who even in market coat, baggy trousers and wellies was very pleasant to look at.

'Hello, Jan,' Rachel said, and the girl looked up and smiled. Jan Kingsley was the new Animal Health Inspector, still finding her feet in the job and glad to have met Rachel, whom she regarded as a staunch ally, a lighthouse in a sea that was given to storm and squall.

'Morning, Mrs Adams.'

'Oh, hello Rachel,' said Richard Bevan. 'How did you get on the other day?'

She gave him a brief account of her interview at Knapp House, ending with an assurance that there would be no need for him to visit the dog, unless he wished to.

Jan, who had been listening, rivetted, to Rachel's reportage, complained that some people had all the luck, that she never met anyone interesting like that, and that all she had done all morning was issue one pig licence.

'You be glad it's quiet,' Richard Bevan chided her. 'You'll learn soon enough to prefer boredom to high drama, I can tell you. Now, as you aren't busy for a moment, just nip across for some milk, will you, and we'll all have a cup of tea.'

'O.K. It'll be a change of scene, anyway.' When Jan had disappeared in search of milk, Rachel enquired how she was getting on in the job.

'She's very good,' Richard said. 'Does her best to overcome the

42

handicap of looking so dishy. Do you know she nearly didn't get the job because of her looks. That grouchy old chauvinist Peterson – you know the one, face like a rat, and taps his teeth with his ballpoint all the time – said the usual tired old thing: no good employing her, she'll only get married. I pointed out that no-one had overruled his first appointment because he was engaged to Mrs Peterson at the time. He laughed. He thought I was joking.'

'And she copes all right?' Rachel asked.

'Yes, fine. She was a bit lacking in confidence at first, but most of the farmers round here seem to have taken to her. Some of the chaps in the market gave her a hard time to start with, but she's got the measure of most of 'em now.

'Old Bill Farrell quite fancies her, I think. He came in last week for a pig movement licence and took ages and ages to fill it out, and looking all daft at Jan the whole time he was in here. Then I saw him in the pub, dinner time, and I said to him I didn't know he was going in for pigs again. I'd heard him say over and over that there was no profit in 'em. Then his mate, Tom Prentiss, gave him a funny look and told me Bill hadn't had pigs for years, and what was I talking about. Then old Bill went quite red and said, "It may be against the law to move a pig without a licence, but it's no crime to ask for a licence if you haven't got a pig, is it?"

'You can imagine how Tom Prentiss laughed, but as Bill said, he doesn't see anything much all week but his cows, his missus, and Katy down at the Mason's Arms who's as plain at fifty as she was at fifteen, so what's wrong with him having a good look at a pretty face if he gets the chance.'

Rachel laughed. 'Poor old Bill,' she said. 'Look Richard, I don't think I'd better wait for tea, I've got one or two things to do. Thanks anyway.'

She walked out into the hubbub of the market and began to thread her way through the pens, glancing at the sheep and cattle as she went with an eye long-practised by her upbringing, as well as made more expert by her profession. She had been coming to markets for as long as she could remember. Even now she felt that if she turned suddenly enough, she might see her father striding along, catch a glimpse of his long back, the unmistakable angle of shoulder and head. He must exist, somewhere, that essential part of him. A man like that could not be extinguished, surely, all his bright fires burnt out? She felt tears prickle the backs of her eyes. Then a loud voice dragged her thoughts from the past, and she saw at a distance Jan Kingsley in conversation with Bert Reeves – if you could call it conversation, when the bulk of the talk seemed to come from Reeves, fortissimo. It was an angry voice, and unpleasant in its tone.

When at last there was a small loophole of silence, Rachel could hear Jan speak up for herself, however, apparently not the least bit awed by the farmer's shouting and cursing.

'You can say what you like, Mr Reeves,' Rachel heard Jan tell him. 'But this lorry is not in a fit state, and you must clean it.'

'I ain't got time,' Reeves replied, looking thoroughly put out. 'I'll do it when I gets home.'

'You may think you haven't enough time, Mr Reeves, but you'll have even less if you don't clean your lorry. You know the regulations quite well, Mr Reeves. I can't let you leave with a vehicle in this state.'

The farmer was by now hopping with rage and his expression was murderous. He told Jan, amid a welter of expletives, to try and stop him.

'Certainly, Mr Reeves.' Rachel was amazed at the young woman's self control. If she had begun her job lacking in confidence, she had certainly found it now. Rachel had half thought to step in and champion Jan's cause, provide her with moral support, but she could clearly see she was not needed.

'If you set foot in that lorry before I am satisfied with it, Mr Reeves, I shall have every exit from this market locked, and I shall inform all the other farmers here of my reason. I don't think they'll be very pleased with you, and I expect they'll make their feelings quite clear to you, Mr Reeves. Don't you agree?'

Furious, frustrated, Reeves glared at Jan as if he wished her dead, but he was beaten and he knew it.

'She's a cracker, that one,' someone remarked from behind

Rachel. Rachel turned, and there was Bill Farrell, his face all moonstruck by the sight of Jan Kingsley.

'Oh, hello Mr Farrell,' said Rachel, wickedly. 'Come to buy a pig?'

She walked on swiftly, leaving him with his mouth half open as if searching for an adequate reply, for she had seen in the distance another familiar figure, this time not one from the shadows of the past but the quick, thin shape of George Baker homing in on some creature, hidden from Rachel by the crowd, but which had evidently caught George's eye.

She walked towards him, thinking to try to engage him in conversation. She felt she was progressing a little in her attempts to make friends with George, but it was slow work.

Rachel had felt during her life at Milchester a growing and particular affection for old men like Harry Ellis and Joe Barge, and now, at Painters, George Baker, for whom the land had provided for so many years a harsh and sometimes bitter living: long hours and short commons. Men like these, and there were still many like them, would work all day and then come home to tend their own patch and their own pig. They looked at the complexities of modern scientific farming and were not particularly impressed; suspicious of the youngsters who looked at the land in terms of years, and not decades or centuries. Still, perhaps the young 'uns were scarcely to be blamed. How can you farm as if you meant to live a hundred years when you might get blown to Kingdom Come tomorrow?

She looked at George. He had come to a halt now and stood surveying the market scene, his hands so folded and rootlike across the top of his stick that you could scarcely tell hand from wood. There was a lean horse ambling by, head drooping at its rope's end, and George's small eyes under their tufted brows were keen with long-held knowledge of horseflesh. So this, of course, was what had seized the old man's attention from among all the other beasts of the market place. Not many horses were seen at the run-of-the-mill market days, though there were special horse-sales from time to time at which George, of course, was always to be found. As

Rachel continued to watch, George, one hand unclasped from the stick, rubbed a crooked forefinger reflectively along the side of his beaky nose – a sure sign, as Rachel had learned, that the horse interested him. It didn't look much, but evidently George must have thought he could make something of it, at the right price.

'Oy!' George called, and the man leading the horse stopped.

'Well?'

'Let's 'ave a look at 'im.'

The man hesitated, considered, and decided George's interest might be genuine and not just a waste of time.

'All right then, but don't be long. We're due in the auction ring.'

Rachel, still unobserved, watched with admiration George's swift, thorough appraisal of the horse. Within a minute he seemed to have examined the teeth, felt the legs, squinted into eyes and ears and under the tail, regarded the creature from every angle, and seen it walk and trot along the asphalt.

'Hum,' said George. 'What's your price?'

'I can't sell him to you here,' the man said. 'He has to go under the hammer. You know that.'

'What's your reserve?' said George, scornfully.

The man told him.

'I'll see you after,' said George. 'You won't get it.'

Rachel walked on towards the nearest gateway of the market, hurrying now to make up for lost time, anxious not to be late back and keep Tom waiting. She would be on to easy money, she felt, if she were to lay a bet that there would be a horse-lorry outside George's yard later that day, and that the animal she had just seen would come clattering out to take up residence with George.

She wondered if she would be invited to see the new purchase. Perhaps. George could scarcely be called neighbourly, but then Rachel had learned something of the causes of his rooted suspicion of anyone who showed an interest in his life and the place in which he chose to live it.

The yard, with its stout stone buildings and the small acreage of well-fenced land behind it, made up the sort of property which whispers in a great many ears the words 'conversion' or 'development'. Over the years there had been attempts to bribe, cajole or in other ways dislodge George from his roost in the stable loft, to leave the way clear for those who could see in the place the means of making either a pleasant residence or a quick financial killing.

George's presence, however, continued to foil all plans to convert, demolish or in any other way put to profitable use what was to him his home and his business. Indeed, only a few days previously Rachel had seen a pale man in a grey suit walking up and down outside George's closed gate as if expecting it to open and admit him of its own accord; or maybe he was hoping to stumble across some computer-clearance-code or some other Sesame word that might open it for him. Certainly, George was not at home to do so, and Rachel told the man as much. She found herself regarding him with a suspicion akin to George's. Officialdom marked him as unmistakably as if it were branded upon his forehead with a rubber stamp.

'Mr Baker is out, then?'

'Yes,' Rachel reiterated.

'I'll be back. Be so kind as to tell him. Marchant's the name. From the Planning Office.'

It was in discussing the visit of Mr Marchant that George began to show signs of seeing Rachel and Tom as allies, if not yet as friends.

'It's them Buckles sent 'im, you can be sure o' that,' George told them when they saw him later that day. Frank Buckle and his sons were among those with the greediest eyes on George's home. 'That chap come and said 'ad I got planning permission, 'cos I'd changed the use of the buildings by keeping 'orses in 'em,' George explained. 'I laughed. I don't think that pleased 'im much.'

Rachel could imagine Mr Marchant's reaction to George's laughter. One did not laugh at council officials. Not that they were all like Marchant, Rachel considered, and she murmured as much to George.

'One of 'im's enough,' said George. 'They wouldn't need no more.'

'What did you say to him?' asked Tom.

'I said there'd been 'orses in these stables since long before 'is Dad was a gleam in 'is Grandad's eyes. 'E didn't like that much, neither.'

'What happened then?'

''E went off,' said George. Like a bomb, probably, Rachel thought.

'What will you do, George?' she asked.

'Don't see I need do anything,' George said. 'I've got photographs of these stables, and the old missus looking at the 'orses, and some of me stood with 'em, all 'arnessed up ready for work. Even a daft fool like that can't fight proof, now can 'e?'

It seemed George was right, for Mr Marchant did not appear again. But a woman from Environmental Health came, and a man to inspect his drains, and someone from the Social Services asking if he felt able to cope on his own and would he care to join the Senior Citizens' Club. If the law had not forbidden it George would have sent the last one to join his ancestors, judging by his furious words as he slammed his gate on the unwelcome visitor.

He averred again that it was the Buckles who were stirring up trouble for him, hoping one way or another to drive him out and leave their way clear to purchasing the house. Mrs Painter had left it to him for as long as he needed it, but as George said, 'If them Buckles thought they could get away with it, they'd 'ave me certified and put in the mad 'ouse. "Doesn't need it now, does 'e," they'd say, and they'd be in 'ere like a shot, just you mark me.'

Chapter Five

✳✳✳

'Stow on Thursday,' Tom said at breakfast, his mouth full of. hastily chewed toast.

'What?' Rachel's attention was on the visiting list for the day.

'Stow Fair. D'you want to go?'

He knew how horses drew her like a magnet, and she needed a day off. Sometimes he felt she tried too hard to prove she could cope with everything the practice threw at her. There was no need of proof; she could do it all right – no-one better, in his experience – but she needed to learn to switch off, to be off-duty, to be herself.

She had protested a little at his insistence, but only half-heartedly. It would be a real treat: time out to do as she pleased and to be caught up once more in the magic of the horse-fair, with its unforgettable sights and smells, its amazing cornucopia stalls, selling harness and tools, bedding and crockery, wicker baskets, barbed wire, socks and shovels, frilly petticoats and fudge, and fish and chips, and marvellous implements to ease your life in kitchen or farm or workshop. And all this profusion of commerce was secondary to the Fair's main enterprise. The selling of horses.

Rachel drove away from Painters on the Thursday morning with all the tingling pleasure of a child sneaking a day off school, and not even a grey sky and a most un-Maylike chill to the air could spoil it.

Jessica took a steady pull at the upward gradient, and sang cheerfully along the undulating high wold roads where the landscape, though greened over with early summer, still had that spare, sparse quality that Rachel loved. It lay open to view, unclothed, unwooded, and in some places almost treeless, so that you could see each swell, each undulation, stretching to the skyline. The rare clumps of beeches, scarcely yet into their summer clothing, still showed sky through their branches which were patterned into shapes as round and exact as if they had been trimmed with shears. Young beeches might have a carelessness about their heads, but these big old elephant-skinned giants were precise in their outlines against the sky, their shapes reflecting the swell of the hillsides to which they clung.

Despite the cool greyness of the morning the drive was pleasant, the road swooping and curving ahead of her between the high-walled fields of the wold, and Rachel drove perhaps a little faster than she should, tempted by the beckoning tarmac and the irresponsibilities of a day off and precious time to spend. Corn sprang green to either side of her, and rich silage grass; and grazing stock pulled eagerly at the best eating of the year. Burly, beefy lambs nudged and bullied their mothers; a suckler herd of Friesian cattle seemed arranged against the green like a child's toy farm, the young calves playing prettily, or asleep with long legs folded under them. It was a chilly enough day for young creatures, but they seemed not to care.

Rachel sang, silly little snatches of song with half their words forgotten, and grinned at the drivers coming towards her in the other direction; and some returned her smile or waved, and others looked at her with that amazed curiosity with which the English tend to regard the cheerful.

In general, though, she met little traffic until they drew towards Stow itself, when one by one and little by little the yellow car was joined by other cars, and Landrovers and horse-boxes and trailers, until the whole line slowed, and queued and crawled into the little town.

Policemen in day-glow yellow tabards moved the traffic through. Long-distance lorry drivers bound for Moreton-in-Marsh and points north leaned from their cabs and swore at the delay, in every degree from cheerful 'gawd-'elp-us' to red-faced fury. A once-in-a-blue moon trailer driver forgot his load and took the left-hand turn too sharp, scraping the tyres against the curb. A lad on a motor-bike weaved among the traffic, revving impatiently.

Already, down the narrow street, people were walking, jostling, inspecting the stalls. Already, from her wound-down window, Rachel could hear the amazing patter of the auctioneer.

Driving down, Rachel felt like a steamer coming into harbour among a flotilla of rowing boats. Forgetful of the lethal nature of the motor car, or convinced perhaps that just for today the pedestrian was king, people ambled in cheerful clusters about and in front of Jessica's wheels.

The driver of the car in front seemed quite heedless of his *entourage*, yet amazingly seemed to inflict no damage on the crowd as he nudged on through them. Rachel put on a little speed until she was tucked in behind and followed close in his wake, using the space his progress created, until at the bottom of the hill both vehicles could turn into the huge green field which was car park for the day.

Rachel found a space, put on her anorak against the chill air, and having locked up the car made her way at once towards the sale ring, which was in fact more a sale corridor, with the auctioneer's box at one end and tiers of seats along the side from which hopeful buyers could survey their possible purchases. There were also places where you could stand and look, if you could elbow your way in.

A girl was riding a big chestnut hunter up and down, encouraged by someone in the crowd who obviously knew her. Amiable banter flew between the rider and the onlooker, punctuated by enormous bucks from the chestnut horse. 'Quiet to ride,' quoted the auctioneer from his catalogue, and the crowd cheered and laughed.

The chestnut left, short of his reserve price, and a little fat grey pony entered. He trundled up and down, sold not too badly after a rapid volley of bidding, and gave place to a yearling pony, still in his woolly underwear and looking at the crowds with startled amazement. Bidding began again.

Rachel dodged from out the press of the crowd, and walked on among the ponies and horses awaiting the sale. A more heterogeneous collection of horseflesh you could reckon to see nowhere else, except perhaps at Appleby, where the gypsies stand and wash their ponies in the stream. There were ancient cobs, unbroken youngsters, thoroughbred stock with fine heads and fine bones, coloured ponies, heavyweights with feathered fetlocks and behinds like the Cook in Alice. Rachel wondered about their histories – how and why they came there – and about their destinies from today – for some, for just a few, rosettes and applause and the hero-worship of horsy little girls; for others, the short journey to the slaughterhouse.

Mostly, though, they were just changing from one owner to another owner, no better nor worse than the last, and whose attentions they would endure with patient tolerance, as most equines do. Rachel was certainly not in the market to buy one. Childhood dreams of rescuing great herds of horses from neglect or cruelty had had their interpretation, in part at least, in the job she had set her heart on and worked so hard to achieve. Yet still she could taste the flavour of these dreams.

She walked now between the grassy amphitheatre in which great rows of second-hand tack and general horse-furniture was being sold at a fast rate to an enthusiastic crowd, and a splendid collection of horse-drawn vehicles, which were due to come under the hammer later on. She had seen the mouldered skeletons of vehicles like these on farms she had visited as a child. Now they sold for good money, even in poor condition; and, renovated, would sparkle around the showing ring later in the year, drawn by some flash pony with a spanking action and driven by one of the many formidable whips who took all the local prizes.

She was back on the narrow road down which she had driven, and free now of the necessity of concentrating on her progress could look about her at all the amazing variety of the scene, which seemed to glow like high summer even under a leaden sky. Now she herself was one of the proud walkers, heedless of the hemmed-in, impotent traffic, nudging and tooting its way through the press of people.

Among the stalls were horse-boxes and barrel-topped vans around which the gypsies clustered. The vans were opened to view so that you could see inside the gleam of highly patterned china, the sparkle of crystal – all the magpie-collection of bright objects, like a treasure horde.

Under the vans dogs sprawled and slept, oblivious to all the noise and clatter, tied to the wheels by chain or rope among the buckets and metal jugs and piled-up horse harness. Under one van Rachel noticed a bunch of rabbits, dead but unskinned, and under another a crate of chickens, very much alive and cackling.

Behind one of the horse-boxes was penned a gang of wild-eyed ponies brought in from the hills, not to go under the hammer but to be sold to anyone passing who might care to buy one. They would not cost you much in money, but later the cost in time and temper would reveal itself as the new owners tried to get their purchases through the crowd, with a rope halter to control the front end and a firm hold on a woolly tail to steer the rear.

Among these unkempt youngsters, their winter coats clinging still in great knots and daggles, stood one pony of a different kind: a dark bay with a thin, fine coat and quality head who stood in the angle of the horse-box and the wall, gazing out into the distance while the others jostled and pushed around it. It was thin and its bones showed, but you could see how it might look, given care.

'Want to buy 'im, lady?' a man asked her, seeing her interest, hopeful of a sale. Rachel said no, but it was a lie. The ghost of her childhood self, vehement against injustice to any four-legged creature, full of an incandescent but totally impractical idealism, longed to reach out to thrust money into the gypsy hand, to seize the gaunt pony and lead him off in triumph through the crowd. Rachel turned her back, both on this phantom and on the gaggle of woolly horseflesh in the pen.

Stupid, the feeling of betrayal. Ridiculous. As a child she had felt that being grown-up would bring omniscience in its train: that all life's puzzles and injustices would be resolved by the magic of adulthood. Now she felt, like some creature in a fairytale, that 'the more she grew the less she knew'.

Rachel was drawn out of herself then by seeing familiar faces in the crowd. It was impossible to walk through the Fair without meeting someone you knew. These faces were girls from the Riding Centre: trainee instructors, young and enthusiastic, drinking in like wine the heady horsiness of the day.

She joined them, and drifted back in their company towards the horse-lines, where they gazed and commented and exclaimed, dreaming of ownership, of success under the lights, of riding alone into the acclaim of the crowd. She saw in them something akin to her own single-mindedness at their age, and smiled, and felt cheered again.

She discovered they had brought no food with them, and knowing they had probably frittered all their funds on horsey goodies she offered them a share of her picnic, which Vi Partridge had put together the previous evening and which would have kept Mafeking going for several days. So they sat in a wintry huddle, wrapped in rugs, and ate and drank and watched the world go by. Why it should be such a pleasure, when people and horses were jostling past and there was a mean wind sneaking between the folds of the rug and the sandwiches tasted of grass and the coffee of car oil, Rachel really did not know; but it was.

Replete and grateful, the girls took off again, having promised to meet their employer at the market area where she was stocking up on sheets and towels for the students' rooms. You could furnish house, stable, garage and toolshed from the market if you had a mind to.

Rachel set out to walk the perimeter of the Fair to make sure she had not missed anything. Coloured ponies grazed on chain-tethers at every fence-post, looking glossy and well on purloined pickings and overnight stops on roadside grass. Around the hind legs of one skewbald mare a foal kicked up its heels, enjoying its freedom, until the gelding at the next door post came towards it with lowered head and teeth displayed in threat. In a second there was the mare, at the end of her tether, hindquarters bunched under her, muscled and menacing, and out flashed her great hind feet, pile-driving into the astonished gelding's shoulder. Her stolid placidity evaporated on the instant: she screamed, savage and vengeful. The gelding retired, sulky, surprised; and the mare, having sniffed her foal meticulously and found no damage, began to graze again as peaceful as before.

Such were the creatures on which Rachel was so often called on to practise her skills, who submitted themselves, for the most part anyway, with such amazing tolerance to her prodding and poking and application of needles and rasps; yet with a kick like that they could smash her to the ground.

Horses were beginning to be loaded now, for the auction was half over and it was wise to get your lorry on the road before the day broke up in a confusion of homebound traffic. From one such vehicle came the sound of loaded horses shifting and fidgetting, but the tailgate was still down and a small girl was leading a chestnut pony towards it under the eye of a little fat man in tweeds. From the child's tearful expression she had been at this exercise for some time. A small crowd had gathered to watch and advise, and the little man was obviously beginning to play to his audience, shouting alternately at child and pony and swishing a long stick to encourage the latter.

The pony had both forefeet on the ramp when the stick hit home, and it swerved sideways off the ramp in surprise and nearly fell. Rachel heard the crack of the stick on the creature's hip-bone; saw the weary desolation on the child's face as she turned to trudge yet again towards the lorry, awaiting the next blow of the stick.

'Too blasted soft, these kids,' announced the fat man to the crowd. 'Got to show 'em who's boss, that's what I say.'

Rachel swallowed down all the remarks she wished to make, and asked instead if she could help. The man's treatment had not yet amounted to what officialdom would call cruelty, and if she antagonised him, he would send her packing and carry on in his own far-from-sweet way.

'You think you can do it, you just try,' he said, inviting the crowd to join him in his air of disbelief that anyone could hope to achieve what had so far eluded him. The child gave Rachel the rope with an air of resignation.

'What's his name?' asked Rachel.

'Toby.'

'Have you had him long?'

'Just bought him.'

'Did it say in the catalogue if he was good to box?'

'Dunno.'

'Have you got any pony nuts, or anything?'

'No.'

Rachel sighed. She began to wish she had walked on and minded her own business. The pony looked at her sideways and suspicious.

The first try, it took root at the foot of the ramp. The crowd tittered. Rachel turned the pony, spoke quietly, scratched its neck and felt some relaxation of the tension in its body.

Again, the walk towards the ramp and the lorry's dark and waiting interior. Rachel heard, scarcely able to believe it, the clunk of the pony's leading forefoot on the ramp and saw, almost simultaneously, out of the back corner of her eye, the stick begin its upward arc in the fat man's hand. She dared not raise her voice for fear of frightening the pony. She dared not remain silent for fear the stick should come down on it again.

'Stand back,' she said, in a voice like a razor's edge. 'You hit this pony again and I'll have your hide.' He stood there with his mouth open for just long enough. The pony went up the ramp as if it had never considered doing anything else. Rachel tethered it, closed the gates and came down the ramp, almost into the upraised fist of the fat man, bristling, purple, incoherently asserting that 'No bloody woman's going to speak to me like that.'

'That's no ordinary woman,' said a voice Rachel knew. 'That's Mrs Adams, the vet over to Milchester, and you keep a civil tongue in your 'ead or I'll finish the job for 'er.'

It was Abel Cash, obviously having a day off from his petrol pumps. It appeared he had been on the lookout for spares for his beloved cars, for a clanging bunch of miscellaneous bits of metal was slung over his shoulder and a length of exhaust pipe dangled casually from his right hand. At his heels, Mick the lurcher was airing his teeth.

Without a word more, the fat man slammed up the tailgate and pushed the girl up into the passenger seat of the cab, into which he too presently disappeared and drove off with a cacophony of grinding gears. The little crowd melted like summer snow.

'All right then, Mrs Tom?'

'Thanks, Abel,' Rachel said. 'I shouldn't take on what I can't handle, should I?'

'Go on with you,' he said. 'You'd put the fear of God in 'im already. I was only putting my oar in. Tell your Tom I'll expect him Tuesday. O.K.?'

'O.K., then.'

He vanished into the crowd, carrying his metallic burden. Tuesday evening he and Tom would spend playing around with the acetyline torch: Abel ministering to sick cars, Tom finishing a metal sculpture that he was trying as an experiment.

The afternoon was drawing on. To be fair to Tom she should at least present herself in time for evening surgery. He would probably insist on doing it himself. 'Make it a real day off,' he would probably say; but she felt uneasy, taking it for granted.

She was pleasantly tired from walking among the stalls. Her mind was full of the familiar sights and sounds of the day that never seemed to change, however often she came to the Fair, and she imagined had not changed over longer years than that. Models of cars and fashions of dress and hair might change, and some of the bright tat on the stalls, but the essential ingredients were unchanging.

The whole day had been a pleasure, even though not everything in it was pleasurable. Still, she would enjoy, in retrospect, telling Tom about the fat man in the tweed suit. As for the bay pony. For him she could only hope . . . But then as she walked towards her car she saw him. At the edge of the car park, its occupants obviously packing up to leave, was an ancient short-bodied Landrover with a trailer behind it.

The ramp was down, and sitting upon it was a child, a boy of about eleven, in faded jeans and a T-shirt which had been patterned with bleach. His hair was dark, the same colour as the pony he held – the bay pony. The boy sat quiet and still, his arms around his knees, watching it as it grazed along the edge of the ramp, pulling at the bruised and trodden grass with relish.

Rachel stood at a distance, looking at the two of them. She was full of questions, full of the need to speak, to advise, to say, 'Make haste slowly with him, he's only young.' She wanted to say, 'Worm him, feed him, build him up before you ask anything of him.' She wanted to say, 'I'd have bought him, if only . . .'

She knew she must not. Then as she watched she sensed that already there was a bond between the two: fine threads of trust, of affection between the boy and his horse.

A man climbed out of the Landrover. 'Ready then, Dave?' he asked, and the boy nodded and unfolded himself onto his feet, slowly, as if it were bred in him to move without causing alarm. Even so, as the man went to the end of the ramp and waited for the pony to move, Rachel tensed, dreading a repetition of that incident so short a time ago. She stood, willing the pony to be unafraid, to step quietly, not to resist.

The boy walked up the ramp, nonchalant; the rope dangled between his hands and the pony's lowered head.

'Go on. Go on,' Rachel said inside herself. Her hands were clenched, the nails dug into the palms.

But the pony was not listening to her inner voice. He was listening to the quiet talk that came to him down the slack of the rope. He smelled the smell of friendship and walked quietly towards it, not afraid of the darkness of the trailer and the echoing clatter of his hoofs.

Chapter Six

✻✻✻

Until the end of April, the year's weather had been exemplary. January's snow had been brief, and had melted into a sunlit February that sparkled with occasional frost but brought no real hardship. March was lamblike, April smiling. But May had come in sulky, and gloomed and wept until it seemed the sun had gone for ever. Prospects for the hay season looked bad, and there were many hasty changes of plan to make more silage instead. Lambs were old enough and stout enough now to resist the constant downpourings from a grey sky, but the foals at the Ashton Stud were shut in their boxes and grew fretful, wanting to stretch and run in the fields. Harry Ellis, the stud groom, was as careful of them as an old nanny though, and would not risk their fine thoroughbred limbs pounding hell-for-leather on the slippery, treacherous going.

Any outside work was wet and uncomfortable. The choice was to soak, or to be so cluttered up with waterproof clothing as to feel like the Michelin man. Every going out and every coming in meant a lengthy session of vesting and divesting oneself of supposedly impermeable garments.

So it had continued, with scarcely a glimpse of blue sky for the whole of May and June. Rachel recalled the chill wind across the Stow on the day of the fair. She could remember brief blue days if she put her mind to it, but rutted tracks, muddy yards and disheartened seedlings in the village gardens were witnesses to the appalling wet. There was a fruitful harvest of grumbling, of course, and blame was laid at many doors from the weather-men to the Russians. It made no difference; but a scapegoat is a comforting creature and eased, at least to some extent, the frustration and heartache that weather can bring to livelihoods still so much at its mercy.

Then one morning, as if on a sudden whim, the clouds departed, the pressure rose, the sun streamed down and proclaimed the advent of July with glorious warmth.

It was just in time for the R.S.P.C.A. coffee morning, which was planned as a Garden Occasion Unless Wet. Mrs Stratton-Davies, in whose garden it was to be held, must have thanked heaven for the change for now the hurly-burly would not have to be invited indoors onto her Aubusson carpets and parquet flooring, and there would be no careless fingerprints on the fabric and paintwork, no coffee droplets and biscuit crumbs, no lingering air of too many people escaping from a wet world in dripping macs and soggy headscarves.

Rachel had some weeks ago been pressed to accept an invitation to come and open the proceedings, as Richard Bevan, who usually officiated, was unable to come. Fiona Stratton-Davies did hope that Rachel would not feel in any sense that she had been chosen as a substitute; they had, of course, fully intended to ask her anyway. Indeed Mr Bevan had made it quite clear that he himself would be delighted for Rachel to be asked to speak, whether or not he was able to attend. The invitation had been made soon after Rachel's talk with Margaret Sherwood; and still fired with Mrs Sherwood's zeal she had agreed. It would be a chance, wouldn't it, to spread a worthwhile message?

Now, with so much to do, with so few hours to spare, she had been regretting it and would have seized on any excuse not to go.

As it turned out she had every excuse. The night before the coffee morning she was involved in one of the worst incidents of her life. She and Tom had been called out to attend a road accident, in which a motor-coach had been in collision with a horse lorry. The coach had been heading for Cheltenham, bringing back an excursion to the South Coast. The horse lorry had been taking competitors to the three-day event at Hillbank. It had been a nightmare so appalling that while they were working, doing what they could, which was horribly little, there had been a numbing, blessed sense of unreality, of total removal from the normal world. Now in daylight, however, scenes came flashing back into Rachel's mind that she would much rather forget, and she felt sick and shaken. The temptation to cry off the morning's activities was strong. Tom insisted, though.

'You must go,' he said. 'Keep your mind on that. O.K., it's only a trivial thing, and it probably won't make much difference to the profits if you don't turn up, but it's better than dwelling on what we saw in the night. Go and give them a nice little speech. Make them feel they're doing their bit to make an awful world a bit less awful. Concentrate on making them feel important, and make yourself forget last night. It's over. Understand?'

Rachel nodded, miserable, her ears still hearing the screams of people, of horses, in the smashed, wrecked vehicles. Her eyes still hurt from the glare of searching lights and she could still taste the smell of hot and oily metal and burnt hair. And flesh, dear God; and flesh. She felt the crawling horror in her stomach.

'Stop it,' Tom ordered. 'Rachel. Stop it.'

So she dressed herself carefully and got herself under control. If she looked pale they would assume she was nervous of making a speech. The bright sunshine mocked her mood as she walked into Milchester towards Burton Court and Fiona Stratton-Davies.

Soon Rachel was looking around her at an acre or so of striped lawn that basked in that amazing, sudden, picture-book sunshine. It was a total contrast to the day when she had first been asked to attend this function, for then it had been raining coldly out of a Stygian sky and a coffee-morning alfresco had seemed a most unlikely event. Rachel had been told firmly, however, that Mrs Stratton-Davies always had good weather for her coffee mornings, and it seemed that she had been given special dispensation once again.

At the very centre of the brilliance of the sunny lawn, a great blue cedar made a cool umbrella of deep shadow. At the edges of that cossetted and pampered turf, broad borders of well-kempt flowers swept up to the outer walls of the garden, beyond which Milchester traffic mutedly rumbled. The sun, reflected off the soft grey Cotswold stone, splashed back onto blue delphiniums, red-mouthed peonies and tall, thistly artichokes, military and silver-grey, with every spine and spike at attention.

'Major and Mrs Stratton-Davies, without whose kind etcetera,' murmured Rachel to herself, rehearsing those few well-chosen words which she would be expected, at any moment now, to deliver. The Major, she knew, had very little to do with the proceedings, and was probably at this moment in the stables talking to his horse, but courtesy demanded the mention of his name.

It seemed to Rachel that the owners of such a magnificent place as Burton Court could quite easily and painlessly have handed over to the R.S.P.C.A. at least as much as the morning's affair would bring in, and without all the bustling effort it was obviously calling forth. 'But it's such fun, my dear,' she could imagine Mrs Stratton-Davies cooing in defence of her event, 'and it's so good for people to be involved with this sort of effort, don't you think?'

Well, she was probably right at that, Rachel admonished herself, trying to draw out from within a proper charitable enthusiasm. She would have preferred to go home and go to bed. She felt dog-tired. She closed her eyes, just for a second, and those scenes came back, superimposing their ghastliness on the garden's peaceful activity.

'Are you all right, Mrs Adams?' One of the committee, hurrying past, had seen her pale, beginning to sway.

'Oh, yes,' Rachel said. 'It's the sudden heat, I expect. I'll just sit down for a moment.' But she shivered as she sat, even with the full warmth of the July sun on her back.

Slowly the shivering stopped, and Rachel got up and made herself look about her to where, at the entrance to the garden, brightly dressed women were beginning to intrude upon its shades of green, their voices humming and undulating like the sound of bees as they busied themselves setting out tables, covering them with white sheets and coloured paper, and arranging upon them the contents of innumerable cardboard boxes.

All these gaudy treasures they hoped to sell during the course of the morning. None of it would bear too much looking at, Rachel guessed. Seen from a distance, all this piled-up stuff had an odd kind of magic, an illusion of being just what everyone wanted. It was only if you got too close that you saw the cracks in the glass, the missing handles, the eyeless plastic dolls, the calendars with half their months already in the past.

She drifted around like an onlooker in a dream, a smile available to anyone who needed a smile returned, but everyone was far too busy getting ready for the influx when the gates would open at ten-thirty, fifty pence entry fee to cover coffee and biscuits.

When the time came an amazing number of people flowed in and around the tables, clustered themselves round the produce and the cakes and the bric-a-brac, and here they picked up the gaudy stuff and examined it and turned things over, as excited as if this were some merchant caravan arrived across a desert. They began to ask prices, to haggle already, despite the organisers' pleas of 'No sales until the official opening'. They need not have worried, though. The stallholders were unmoved by waving hands and proffered coins and stood, arms folded, awaiting the proper time, like Cerberus without his supernumerary heads. The splendid ordinariness of all this activity gradually brought back to Rachel a sense of normality. She felt less nightmarish, though no less nervous of the wretched speech that must be made. She glanced around her and saw that she was now the dam, the sluice-gate, the log-jam that held back a flood of potential commerce. There was a growing feeling of frustrated energy moving like ripples along a shore.

She saw Fiona Stratton-Davies moving towards her.

'Shall I begin?' Rachel asked, anxiously.

'Oh dear. Oh, yes dear by all means. I'll hush them, shall I?' Rachel nodded, her smile in place, and wiped her hands nervously on the cloth of her skirt.

Mrs Stratton-Davies led her to a microphone, switched it on

and tapped sharply on it with her fingers, making a noise like a robot coughing, and in a voice suddenly amplified from its normal tone to a huge and far-reaching one said, 'Ladies and Gentlemen!' There were just sufficient of the latter to justify their being categorised.

A reluctant, fidgetty silence descended. Rachel was introduced to her audience, for the most part unnecessarily as nearly everyone knew perfectly well who she was, and then there was a crackle of applause as she gathered her wits to address them.

'I am sure you don't want me to speak for long,' Rachel said. She had seldom been so sure of anything. 'I'll just say how glad the organisers must be to see so many of you here to support this very good cause; how grateful we are to Major and Mrs Stratton-Davies for allowing us the use of their beautiful garden, and how fortunate we are in the weather.' There was more applause here, as if the weather were in some way Rachel's doing.

She took a breath and prepared herself for the meat of her speech. 'Cruelty in all its forms needs fighting at every turn,' she told them.

'Hear hear,' said a large woman in a feather hat.

'And by your presence here and your support,' Rachel continued, 'you are helping the long battle against suffering among animals.' She heard her voice continue, and supposed the words were making sense, but her mind had returned to the blackness of the night, and the smell of terror and the sounds of intolerable pain.

'I shall never get used to it,' she said inside herself. 'We must not let ourselves get used to it,' she told them. 'Unnecessary and deliberate infliction of pain is always cruel and is not acceptable. But it has become so widespread that it is tempting to accept it as normal: a part of life that we may regret but that we cannot change. We cannot change or prevent it all, but that is no excuse not to fight it where we can.'

Rachel was tempted to go on, to give them instances, without of course naming names, from her own experience; but she was aware that they had heard enough. They were doing their bit, weren't they, coming to spend their money, giving up their time? Now they were impatient to browse, to buy, to drink their coffee under the shade of the cedar tree, and perhaps if the Major wasn't about, to filch a snippet of this and that from the herbaceous borders in the hopes that they might take root in their own gardens. 'I now declare this coffee morning open,' she said. More clapping, but briefly, and the crowd made off, arms outstretched, money at the ready, before the astonished Fiona Stratton-Davies could open her mouth for a vote of thanks.

'A good speech, Mrs Adams. I do agree with you. The world seems such an uncomfortable place these days. There are not the same values as there once were, wouldn't you agree?'

'Perhaps,' said Rachel. She remembered a story that Harry Ellis had told her about John Sheffield, the redoubtable Fiona's father, who had beaten to the point of death a gelding which had stumbled at a ditch and tipped him headlong when he was out hunting with the Cotswold; and when Harry, who was coming up with his employer's second horse at the time, had caught his arm and tried to stop him, Sheffield had set about him too, until at last some other members of the field saw what was happening and pulled him away.

'Come along then, my dear, and have some coffee. It's the least you deserve.'

'Thank you,' said Rachel, and they made their way through the press of people, who apart from the occasional smile or word of greeting seemed totally to have forgotten she was there at all.

She wondered what Margaret Sherwood would think of this gathering; what sort of speech she might have made. Perhaps I should have suggested her, Rachel considered. I certainly ought to have invited her. Stupid not to have thought of it. Then she looked again at the darting, jostling women, and heard the chattering gossip and the shrill laughter, and considered that she had perhaps been wise in her forgetfulness.

When she got home there was a note from Tom to say he'd gone to the police station to give them what information he could about the accident, and to report on the condition in which they had found the two horses left alive and the reasons for putting both of them down. He had saved her from that, then, by packing her off to Burton House.

'You're a lovely man, Tom Adams,' she said. She wished he were at home. She missed him. The house felt empty without him, and indeed was empty for Vi Partridge had gone to Gloucester to see one of her complex network of peripheral relations, but she would soon be back. However, Rachel had only been home a short while when the phone rang.

'It's Abel. Abel Cash.' The voice sounded hoarse: unlike him.

'Did you want Tom? He's just gone . . .'

'Look, can you come? I've got the p'lice here,' Abel interrupted, urgent, as if the least delay could mean disaster. Surely they hadn't caught him poaching at last? Or maybe a stolen car had ended up in the scrapyard. That wasn't like Abel though. He was no thief. Poaching, of course, didn't count, but Abel would have nothing to do with knocking off vehicles.

'Come over, will you. Have a look at Mick for me. That old faggot says she's seen 'im chasing sheep over at . . .'

'That old faggot,' Rachel knew, was Amy Gunter, the bane of all that was enjoyable in life: a fat, lonely old killjoy across whose path Rachel had stumbled more than once.

'She's always had it in for my Mick, ever since he was a pup,' Abel went on. 'He wouldn't harm sheep, Mrs Tom. I knows that, and so do you.'

Lurcher or not, game-killer or not, Rachel would not easily believe that of Mick either. He never stirred anywhere without Abel, and when he chased and killed it was stealthily and on command, not out on his own in the light of day.

Rachel left a note for Vi Partridge to explain where she was going, and why. She knew what her reaction would be. Mrs Partridge never swore, even under the greatest strain, but the contempt in her voice for Amy Gunter and all her works outdid expletive. 'Any emergencies, ring me at the petrol station,' Rachel wrote, and hurried out to Jessica and drove speedily away, dodging through the outskirts of Milchester, around the industrial estate,

66

and striking north from the roundabout.

When she arrived at Abel's a police car sat blinking its light in the forecourt. Inside the shack two policemen were drinking tea, while Abel himself crouched over his pot stove holding Mick by the collar. It was as well, Rachel thought, that Abel's larder door was not transparent. There would be no pheasants hung up to age into juicy succulence – Abel was a great respecter of the close season – but she knew for a fact there were more rabbits in there than any man could reasonably claim to have run over by accident.

One of the policemen was a young constable, and the other was Mark Boswell, an old acquaintance of Rachel's, and he rose from the table and took her hand.

'I heard at the station about last night,' he said. 'Proper mess, wasn't it?'

'Yes,' said Rachel. 'Tom's at the station now.'

'Thought I saw him in the interview room. Nasty business. Nasty business. Took the injured to Cheltenham, I hear. They'll look after 'em all right.' Then he smiled at Rachel, and said, 'First time I've seen you since you got married. To your liking, is it?'

'Very much,' said Rachel cheerfully, trying to lighten the strained atmosphere of the little room where Abel sat exuding misery like a cloud.

'Let's have a look at you, Mick,' she said. She looked him over carefully.

'How long ago did she say this happened?' Rachel asked.

'About an hour ago.'

'You were pretty quick off the mark then,' she said to the policemen.

'We were in the car, coming back from Nether Leybourne. They radioed from the station,' the constable replied.

'And was Mick at home then?'

'Well, yes.'

'He must have come back sharpish then,' Rachel commented.

'He'd have had time,' the other policeman said.

The lurcher was certainly not in the excited state that Rachel would expect from a dog who had been seriously after sheep, but she knew she must make every possible test, and not be influenced by her affection for the dog or her friendship with his master. Even the gentlest and most respectable pet dog could turn sheep-killer under the right circumstances, and Mick was of a breed that could catch and kill a hare, perhaps even bring down a deer. He had both skill and weaponry.

Rachel could find no traces of blood on him, nor any sign of any having been washed off. She examined his teeth particularly and minutely and found neither blood nor wool; nor was there any trace of the oily, sour-sweet smell of panicky sheep anywhere on Mick's body.

'I'm satisfied so far,' Rachel said at last. 'But I'd like to make an experiment.'

'You carry on,' said Sergeant Boswell. 'Will it take long?'

'Can you spare half an hour?' asked Rachel.

'Just about.'

'Come on then.' She beckoned them all out: the two policemen, Abel and Mick.

'We'll take him to the sheep,' Rachel explained. 'And see what he does.'

'That's a bit of a risk, isn't it?'

'I don't believe it is,' Rachel said. 'And I want to prove Mrs Gunter wrong.'

They set off in the police car, to Abel's embarrassment, and drove to the farm near which the sheep were grazing. The farmer, understandably, was not enthusiastic about the experiment, and said as much.

'You got a gun?' Abel asked, as they all stood about wondering whether to press the idea.

'Course,' the farmer said.

'Licenced I hope,' said the young constable.

'Don't be so silly,' said the farmer snappishly. 'Yes. I've got a gun, and I'm bringing it with me.'

'Good,' said Abel. 'If my dog so much as breathes on one of your stupid sheep you can shoot him. And that's in front of witnesses.'

'Deal,' said the farmer.

The four men, Rachel and the dog walked across a field to the wide meadow where the sheep were grazing. If they were still panicky from their encounter with the dog – and there had been a dog, for the farmer verified that though he had been too far away to see it clearly – they might easily run and tempt Mick severely. It occurred to Rachel that it was surprising that Amy had been close enough for a clear view too: she was short sighted, though it never seemed to interfere with her spying activities.

Despite her belief in Mick, Rachel's heart began to bump as they drew towards the sheep. There would be no chance now for the dog if he made any wrong move, even if he had been totally innocent before. She looked sideways at Abel, but his face gave away nothing of what he was feeling. Mick trotted along head down, tail down, not close to Abel at all but somehow in contact with him. Suddenly, the dog's head came up, the ears at the alert, the breeze blowing the hair back from his lean body, and streaming his tail out behind him. He gazed out to the horizon with his beautiful topaz eyes: a hound the Pharaoh himself could have taken pride in. He stood, rocklike, and some signal passed between Abel and the dog. Rachel saw and heard nothing, but she knew it. Then she saw the hare running just below the skyline and was aware that this was what had held the dog's interest, and not the clumsy sheep.

The party walked on across the meadow. The sheep milled and turned and stood at a distance, ears up, suspicious and fearful. Mick, with his old hangdog look, trotted on past.

'Stop here,' said the farmer. 'See what he'll do.'

They stood in a knot in the middle of a dozen or so acres of grass, and watched. Mick trotted about a bit. Sniffed at a tussock of grass here, a pile of rabbit droppings there. He scratched, without much enthusiasm, at the centre of a molehill. One or two sheep, emboldened, ambled a little closer. Mick lay down, couched on his elbows like an heraldic device, his hips and haunches in a pleasant symmetry about the curve of his spine. He arched his neck a little, stretched his jaws in a delicate, brief yawn that showed his tongue and his sharp white teeth. Then he laid his head and neck down along his outstretched forelegs and closed his eyes.

"Well I'll be,' said the farmer, when they had all watched the dog for a while. 'The bugger's gone to sleep!'

Across Abel's face there stretched a smile of great width and beauty.

'Satisfied?' he asked.

Chapter Seven

꒰꒰꒰

Dentistry was not one of Rachel's favourite occupations, and when there appeared on her morning list the extraction of a tooth from the pet donkey at the Albury Children's Home she was not overjoyed. It was Tom's case really – he had taken the preparatory X-rays – but he had been delayed at a foaling, so there was nothing for it but to pick up her chisel and go.

She took the Gloucester road for a mile or two and turned off towards Albury. The road ran through fields that had once been parkland, carefully landscaped and planted but run somewhat to seed now, the old trees untended and dropping their branches, docks and nettles creeping into the pasture. Iron railings fenced the drive down which Rachel swung the car, though at times they too were made invisible by high-grown weeds.

The children were housed in a square, solid Victorian mansion which had once been the home of a gentleman farmer, and its dark panelling, encaustic tiled floors and ubiquitous stained glass seemed better suited to tweeds and whisky and tobacco than to T-shirts and jeans; but the atmosphere of the place, which oppressed Rachel the moment she arrived, seemed to have not the least effect on its present inhabitants. They came clattering and whooping down the echoing stairs, slithered along the red and blue and purple tiles of the entrance hall, and put to flight with their high chatter the disapproving ghosts of the departed squires.

A woman appeared from behind the horde of children who were now pressed about Rachel and introduced herself as Jenny Philips, the Assistant Housemother.

'I'll take you to see the patient,' she said.

They walked through what had once been a splendid garden to a small paddock fenced with iron park railings like those on the drive, now all bent and twisted but still capable of keeping a small donkey in his place. There he stood: brown, hairy and decidedly miserable.

Even at his best, Sunny Jim's name belied his temperament. His long years of being poked and prodded by inexpert fingers and having his back sat upon and his ribs drummed by unskilled but enthusiastic riders had given him a melancholy air, and the offering of far too many titbits had made him snappish with his teeth, as well as been the main cause of his present problem. Now his gloom was profound, and he and Rachel viewed each other across the paddock fence, neither liking what they saw.

Mrs Philips had had some difficulty in prising Rachel away from the house, away from the insistent tuggings and questionings of the children, all of whom begged to be allowed to watch and who were gleefully comparing Jim's ordeal with their own experiences at the dentist. Jenny Philips had been quite firm and had insisted that Rachel must examine the patient in peace.

'I knew there was something wrong when he wouldn't eat,' Mrs Philips explained, 'and then I saw this lump on his face. I thought he'd been hiding stuff up there. He does sometimes: great wodges of grass and chewed-up carrot. But when I touched the lump he bit me. Look.' She showed Rachel two purple arcs of toothmarks on her forearm.

'Ow,' said Rachel. 'That must have hurt.'

'It did,' Mrs Philips agreed, with feeling. 'And I was just going to belt him for doing it when I realised he was really in pain. His fur was all wet down his neck where he was sweating, and his eyes had that look, you know: not evil, like he can look when he's in a mood, but really agonised. Poor old Jim. I was so glad when your husband came and discovered what the trouble was. He did say he'd be back to take the tooth out.'

'He's still out on a case,' said Rachel. 'Don't worry. I'll soon have the job done. Now, where do you suggest I operate?'

'This way please,' said Mrs Philips.

She put a headcollar on Jim, and leading him gently, showed Rachel to a little shed, well strawed down, and very clean.

'Will this do?'

'Perfect,' said Rachel,

She had decided to use chloral hydrate in a drip. She wanted plenty of time to work. The tooth looked pretty nasty. The X-rays showed, and the unpleasant smell confirmed, that Jim would be a good deal better off without it.

A little later, anaesthetised and prostrate on the floor, the little moke looked like a hairy rug thrown out to air, and innocent in his sleep of all his waking ill-temper. The tooth was rotten, and stood in its mound of inflamed gum like a crumbling fortification. It took Rachel all her skill to remove it, making a flat incision, positioning the chisel, and, with a fervent prayer to the gods of dentistry, knocking the tooth from the jawbone. She was relieved to see that she had made a fair job of it, and that despite the angry swelling there was little suppuration. She cleaned and plugged the hole and gave an anti-tetanus injection. Then she sat back and waited for Sunny Jim to return to the world again.

It was peaceful in the little shed. Sun crept in through a little slatted window and dropped tiger-stripes of light across Jim's recumbent form, and splashed the pale yellow straw with gold. All the textures of the place, stone, and straw and timber and donkey-fur, were pleasing, satisfying. It was rather like being part of one of those stable-scenes that Victorian painters loved so much: 'The Cart-Shed', or 'Shoeing the Bay Mare'. Even the cobwebs hanging down in grey drapery from the ceiling caught the light and were gilded by it.

Rachel sat back on her heels and contemplated her surroundings, and was able to forgive her occupation its more traumatic moments when it allowed her to be in such a place on such a beautiful day when other people were penned in office, or factory, or school, or even on the jolting seat of a tractor, removed from the outer world of sweet earth and birdsong by the roar and stink of the diesel engine and the stuffy safety of the cab.

She felt cheerful and content, and could afford to be. A job she loathed was over and successful. She watched with pleasure as consciousness crept back into the shaggy hide and the long ears began to stir. Once she was satisfied all was well with the donkey she carried the tooth out in triumph to show Jenny Philips, who had retired outside the door once the donkey had slumped down asleep.

'He'll be glad to get rid of that,' she commented.

'He mustn't wear a bit for at least a week,' Rachel advised. 'And no more toffees and sugar lumps. That'll do his temper good, as well as his teeth.'

As they walked back towards the house to show the gruesome relic to the waiting children, Rachel saw some sheep in the corner of the paddock. Her attention had been concentrated on Jim, before, and she had not noticed them. One was rubbing against the railings, wriggling herself desperately as if to be rid of a maddening itch.

'I didn't know you kept sheep,' she remarked.

'Oh, we don't,' Jenny Philips laughed. 'It's just that a local farmer gave the children some orphan lambs a couple of years ago and somehow they were never sent to market, so we've still got them.'

'Have they been dipped?' Rachel asked.

The question seemed to surprise Mrs Philips. 'I don't know. I shouldn't think so. They're only pets, you know.'

'I'd like to have a look at that one if you don't mind,' Rachel said.

'Of course. I'll call her. They're all quite tame.'

Even if she hadn't been, Rachel doubted if the ewe would have run off. She was too absorbed in her itching. Dags of wool hung down from her fleece. Her back was raw and smelly.

Fly-strike had been Rachel's immediate thought, but on looking closer and parting the fleece there were no maggots heaving against the flesh. That would have been bad enough, but what she now diagnosed was worse. A notifiable disease, no less, and one Jan Kingsley would not be pleased to hear about.

'Oh dear,' said Rachel. 'I'm afraid you've got trouble here. It's sheep scab.'

74

'Is that serious?'

Give me strength, Rachel thought. She could hardly be angry with Mrs Philips: she was a housemother, not a farmer. Still, the chap who gave them the lambs in the first place ought to have told them.

'Didn't the farmer explain that you'd have to dip them?' she asked.

'Well, no. He said we must send them to the butcher when they were old enough, and we didn't like to tell him we hadn't. We sheared them though. My friend who's a hairdresser came and did it. They looked very nice. She said she'd come again this year and do it. We found a pair of those old-fashioned hand shears in one of the sheds down in the farm yard. She managed very well with those. The children all stood round and watched. It made quite a picture. I wished I'd had my camera.'

'I'm sure,' Rachel said, checking her exasperation once again. 'But look, anyone who keeps sheep must dip them. It's the ministry rule. And even if it weren't, sheep need doing, to keep them clear of all sorts of pests, as well as from this.'

Mrs Philips seemed at last to take in the sorry state of the sheep Rachel had examined. 'It's awful, isn't it. I'm ashamed I hadn't noticed.'

'If I had a magnifying glass I'd show you the mites that make the poor creature itch like this. Now, you can't take these sheep near anyone else's, so I'll tell the Animal Health Inspector, and she'll come over with some scab-dip and sort you out. Have you got anything to put them in? A big water-tank would do.'

'Yes,' said Jenny Philips when she had considered for a while. 'Yes, there's the old header tank out of the house roof. It's going home, but it still holds water. Will that do?'

'Yes, I should think so,' Rachel said, and Mrs Philips looked relieved to set this one idea in the balance against so much inadvertent carelessness. 'I hope she won't be too angry, this Inspector. We didn't mean to neglect them, you know. It's just that we're short staffed, and we're always so busy, and the children need . . .'

75

By now she looked so anxious and so guilty that Rachel's exasperation melted away. Of course it was serious. Of course they must keep these sheep isolated and get rid of the scab as quickly as possible, but being angry with Mrs Philips would not cure them one whit sooner. And at least Jim's toothache had brought the problem to light.

'Stop worrying,' she said. 'Don't let *anyone* near the sheep until Miss Kingsley arrives, and we'll both go and have a good wash now. At least they haven't been in contact with any others.'

She saw the look on Mrs Philips' face then and felt an awful chill in the pit of her stomach.

'Well I'm afraid they have,' Mrs Philips said, her expression woebegone. 'There were sheep in a field just down the lane a few days ago, and one of the children left our paddock gate open. Our sheep come when they're called usually, but they were so excited to be with the others that it was quite a while before we got them back.'

'And did you tell the owner of the sheep?'

'Well, no, we didn't like to. We thought he'd be angry.'

Not as angry as he's going to be, Rachel thought. What a mess, and all so innocently caused. She took a deep breath, to control her thoughts, and began to order in her mind the things she must do, the people she must notify. It had been going to be a quiet day.

When she discovered who was the owner of the contact sheep, Rachel was appalled. It was Colonel Sutherland of Wick House, long retired from the military but still a blimpish little man, who lived in the world as if it were the officers' mess and who had authoritative words to speak on every subject, whether he knew anything about it or not. His attitudes were without flexibility, his beliefs not so much rock-like as cement. He was the sort of man who would wish to bring in the death penalty for attempted suicide. Tom always referred to him as 'that old harrumphing hippopotamus'.

Rachel was unhappy at the prospect of the interview, and when it was over her unhappiness had been entirely justified. Colonel Sutherland had made her feel, totally without justification, that she was to blame in that the incident had occurred because of the stupidity of a woman, and that she, Rachel, as a woman was therefore culpable along with all her sex.

Usually she was more than a match for the likes of Colonel Sutherland, even though in prospect such men made her nervous, but she had shrunk into herself at the onset of his empurpled rage and his bully's technique of giving no space in his oratory that might allow a reply. She had done her best, but she still felt as though she had been stood on. Now she would have to send young Jan Kingsley to oversee the necessary dipping of the sheep.

However, having watched her vis-à-vis Bert Reeves Rachel felt she might be less worried by Colonel Sutherland than Rachel herself had been. Still, you could scarcely blame the man for his anger: he kept a closed and well-shepherded flock of Dorset Horns; was scrupulous in every necessary, as well as every legal, attention to them. Now, as scab-contacts, they would all have to go through the time-consuming process of being dipped again; and scab-dip, like time, cost money. She sighed, wishing life did not have to make itself quite so difficult, and hoped that the authorities could be persuaded not to fine the Children's Home for their sins against the Ministry of Agriculture.

She tried to talk to Tom about it when she got home; but he had that gloom on him that seemed to draw him down when he was very tired, so bone-weary that even the urge to paint could not stir him but, if anything, frustrated him further, for it was an impotence worse than sexual to see the forms and colours there and not be able to rouse up the skill in his hands. She understood this, and was usually able to let the cross mood that accompanied it wash past her.

Now, for some reason, this common or garden attack of the grumps, in a man who she knew would soon shake it off and be himself again, reduced her to misery and near to tears. When he came to himself and saw it, he was amazed.

'Hey, what have I done?' he enquired, contrite. 'This isn't like you. Dear old thing, you look as though I've beaten you half to death.' He came close and put his arms around her.

'Lord knows,' Rachel said. 'I'm sorry Tom. I suddenly felt . . . I can't tell you. I've never felt like it before. When you came in, and I heard you stumping about, I just wanted to hide, to wait until you'd stopped being angry about whatever it was. It wasn't you I couldn't face. Just your anger. How stupid. I'm fine now, really I am.'

After supper they sat and talked, Tom commiserating with her about the scabby sheep and the furious Colonel Sutherland. He himself had spent an exhausting afternoon operating on a gelding at a farm high up on the plateau, remote, still with well-water, and only the sketchiest electricity supply. He had chosen to operate outside as the stables were filthy, and the gelding's chances of infection from them remarkably high.

'It's like asking doctors to do modern surgery on the kitchen table,' Tom said. 'I wish we could offer something better. If only we had a surgery big enough to make a theatre for the larger animals.'

'That would be marvellous,' Rachel said.

'But impossible,' sighed Tom, and stretched to ease his aching back.

Early next morning, just as Rachel was putting the kettle on for tea, there was a knock on the door. Outside, cap in hand, stood George, hesitating on the doorstep, hunched up with some matter of concern that made him look more like an ugly gnome than ever.

'You got a minute?' he asked.

'What's up?' Rachel enquired. The little man was rubbing the boot on his left leg up and down the boot on his right leg until it seemed quite likely that he would fall over, and on his face was an expression that could equally well indicate worry or bad temper. The two showed remarkably similar symptoms in George.

'It's that cob of mine,' he said, in explanation. 'The one you saw me after in the market' – so he had noticed her watching him, the sly fellow – ''e's in a bad way.'

'Any idea what's wrong?' Rachel asked. It would need to be serious for George to come asking for help where horses were concerned.

'Every thing,' George said. 'Looks wretched, sounds worse, won't eat. 'Ead down like it 'ad weights on. Snotty nose. Strangles, I reckon. Ain't seen 'orse with strangles, not for years, but I reckon that's what 'e's got.'

'I'll come at once,' Rachel said. She was half surprised that he had not insisted on Tom being woken to help him, but then George so seldom reacted as one would expect. He was as full of unlikeliness as a hedgehog of fleas.

As Rachel began to walk with him in the direction of the stables, he made it clear to her that her visit was on business terms, that he would pay cash on the nail, and that she was not to imagine he was asking any favours. Rachel gravely assured him that this was quite understood, and he trotted off ahead of her, angled forward in his anxiety as if he were breasting a force nine gale rather than the mild air of a summer morning.

Rachel followed him through the gate in the wall into his yard, and from there into the first loose box, where the horse from the market stood, a picture of abject misery and discomfort. Everything had been done to keep him warm – deep straw bed, rugs and bandages – but still he stood huddled as if cold, with hanging head and clamped-down tail. A particularly unpleasant discharge streamed down from his nose, and it did not need a thermometer to tell Rachel that his temperature was high.

'You're right, George,' she said. 'Streptococcus equi, strangles it is.'

George held the cob while she examined him further.

'No abscesses yet, George. We might catch him now, with penicillin, and with luck that will fix him. The danger with strangles is the infection moving elsewhere, perhaps to the lungs.'

She glanced up at him, aware that she was teaching him to suck eggs. He'd been dealing with horses since long before Rachel was born, and even if he didn't know the scientific reasons for the cure or the worsening of the disease, he would have seen and experienced over the years what worked and what did not. Much of the time he would have worked in the dark, hoping for a cure, but so did the vets of his generation.

After all, it was hardly any time ago that firing was the remedy for almost any disease that blood-letting would not cure. Most of the humane medicine that Rachel was able to practise was still new and unfamiliar to old men like George; and yet men of his generation had cared for and cured creatures by skill and knowledge and experience. He must know the possible pattern of strangles every bit as well as she did, yet he only nodded his agreement and fetched out of his memory an instance of his own where just such a thing had happened.

'And then another time, years ago,' George said gloomily, 'we had one poor plough 'orse die on us.' He shook his head at the memory. 'A great abscess in 'is gut. Boss treated 'im with turpentine, with camphor and laudanum mixed in. Didn't do no good though. Bastard strangles they called that.'

'That's what they call "atypical", now,' Rachel explained. 'Abscesses form in out of the way places. Your cob has classic strangles, no doubt about it, and this crystalline penicillin should do the trick. There's still a chance he may produce abscesses though, in spite of the treatment. If so, let me know at once. Meanwhile, nurse him as you have been doing, and obviously keep him isolated. Did you keep the address of the man you bought him from?'

'Did I just then,' said George. 'I'll tell 'im, don't you worry. I'll tell 'im.'

The cob, his treatment over, slouched into a miserable doze. He would soon begin to feel more comfortable, but there was no way in which Rachel could assure him of that. He snorted despondently, shaking his head and streaking Rachel and George with yellow mucous.

'Best get cleaned up, 'adn't we,' said George. 'And after that you'll take tea,' he added as they left the stable. It did not sound quite like an order, but it carried the same weight. Rachel followed the old man up the wooden stairs to the stable loft where he lived. The room was dark, furnished mostly with tea-chests and an iron bed, and the curtains at the window looked more as if they had grown there than been hung. Rachel was shown where she might wash, and George in the meantime had cleaned himself and put on the kettle. Despite the room's shortcomings everything was orderly, and the cups in which George poured the tea were clean and shining. From an ancient tin proclaiming the coronation of King George V he produced a packet of Fine Fare digestive biscuits.

They sat, drinking and eating, not saying much, except to discuss the treatment of the horse. George was not one for small talk.

Then abruptly he announced: 'It's Fire Regulations now.'

'Oh?' said Rachel, hoping he would clarify this remark, but half aware that he was probably about to tell her of further visits from officialdom.

'Them Buckles. Sent the Fire Prevention man.'

'What did he say?' Rachel asked.

'Said I'd fry if me stairs caught fire. I said I wouldn't.'

There was silence, except for the gentle slurping of George's lips against his cup.

'What happened then?'

'Showed 'im three ways out of 'ere, quick as light. Took him downstairs then: showed 'im me fire-buckets, water and sand, and me fire blanket. Says to 'im, 'orses and fire don't mix, I says. 'Oo do you think got the beasts away safe when next door went up with a bang in the war, I says. I did, I says, while you was in your Mickey Mouse gas-mask. You won't find no fire-risk in my yard. Then 'e asked me if I smoked. I told 'im I saw no sense burning money, and even the smallest 'prentice-lad knows you don't smoke in a yard. I asked 'im if the Buckles sent 'im. "Not at liberty to divulge that," 'e says. Huh!'

Exasperation lent George an infrequent aspirate. It was the sound of a trumpet against officialdom and the persistent Buckles. Rachel felt a strong urge to join in George's battle. It was not fair, this long drawn-out siege of his rightful home.

When she got back to her own kitchen, where Tom was buttering toast, she said as much.

'I wish we could do something to help.'

'I suppose if we were a good deal richer than we are, we could buy the place and let him stay there as our tenant,' Tom said. 'Outbid the beastly Buckles and send them packing.'

'If only we could,' Rachel sighed.

Tom was very thoughtful all through breakfast. All day he seemed to have something on his mind, a mental sharp tooth, constantly catching his attention. When Rachel demanded to know what the problem was, he just shook his head and said, 'Motive. Motive, my dearest Rachel, mocks every action we take. D'you know, you could stand every pure motive on a pin's head with all those angels, and there'd still be room to spare.' And he would not go further than that. Rachel felt like kicking his shins, but he would say no more.

All day Rachel felt needled and niggled by the sheer short-sightedness of the Buckles. What hope for world peace, she thought, if just one world leader is a Buckle at heart? And that was scarcely unlikely, when Milchester itself had its fair share of the crankier side of human nature, and where situations existed which were really very funny, if you were not involved in them. There was Hollow Lane Farm, for instance, sold to a newcomer from Kent who did not pause to wonder, as he struck his bargain for it, why the locals had not snapped it up at the price. One field of straggling weeds lay between the farm and the main road. Common sense and a fair price, and there's your access; save going a mile and a half round Hollow Lane to join the road further down. No-one had mentioned that the owner of the field, John Lackidge, had been pressed to sell for decades, and would not sell, and would have no trespass over his land, for he 'knew his rights,' and enjoyed them.

If the farmhouse had been a raging inferno no fire-engine would have dared set wheel on Lackidge's field, and the new owner's children had been sent packing more than once for trying to take the short cut after school. You wouldn't believe it, Rachel felt, if you didn't live with it.

Chapter Eight

Surgery had been full of familiar faces, and the inevitable pleasant talk that went with seeing again old friends, both human and animal, had made the session a long one. Miss Pringle, who was Mrs Frobisher now, had come with her terrier, Simba, clawed above the eye by the ginger cat with whom he now shared a hearth, and whose patience he sometimes tried beyond its already narrow limits.

'It's as well the Major and I don't fight like that,' Mrs Frobisher said, smiling. The marriage of the two elderly people was a delight to Rachel. They were so uncomplicatedly happy together and both still seemed amazed to be so, as if some prize usually only conferred upon the young had out of the blue been handed to them.

Mrs Adler from the Golden Pheasant had brought her Pomeranian, Pickles, for a check-up. He had had such a shaky start in life, weaned far too young by an unscrupulous breeder, and was a half-dead scrap of fluff by the time Rachel had first set eyes on him. Now his little foxy face was perky and alert, and his fluffy tail curled over his back like a happy pig's. His only problem now was a tendency to portliness through his owner's indulgence, and the unending supply of delicious scraps the hotel could provide. Rachel had handed out yet another diet sheet, sighed, and shaken her head.

'More exercise, less food,' she grumbled. 'He looks like an entry for the fat-stock show.' She made a mental note to telephone Mr

Adler and ask him to try to control his wife's passion for feeding Pickles to excess. It would be more to the point if she fed herself a little more. Pickles had been excellent therapy for her, as her husband had intended. She seemed far less tense and neurotic, but she was still thin as a blade-bone.

Now Rachel was driving to see yet another patient from the Stapleton House days. This was the foal, now nine months old, that had come almost as near to death as the Adler's Pomeranian, and whose cure had helped Rachel to the realisation of her feelings for Tom Adams. Tom had diagnosed the foal's trouble where she had floundered, yet had not belittled or questioned her skill for all that: had, as it were, lent her his greater experience. He could so easily have allowed her to feel inadequate and taken the credit for his diagnostic skill, but he did not, and that had shone such a light on Rachel's half-awareness of her growing affection for him that she could no longer deny it.

Rachel took particular interest in this foal, not only because of the high drama that attended the filly's birth but equally because it had been Rachel's idea that Anne and Bill Fowler should take on the care of the pregnant mare in the first place. Chaos and mismanagement were the only words to describe the Fowlers' agricultural enterprises, and it had been something of a gamble on Rachel's part to arrange for them to have the Connemara, Belmont Honeydew, to take the place of Anne Fowler's Arab gelding who had died, horrifyingly, from tetanus. Rachel had had terrible doubts herself, yet she felt that beneath the bitterness of the marriage and the devastation of redundancy and shattered finances, there might be something saveable.

She had waved no magic wand. The two still squabbled and fought and made mistakes, but Anne's job as the new chef at the Golden Pheasant bolstered their resources, and Bill was learning: haltingly and often reluctantly but still learning, and doing much better as a result. In one concern they did work together, however, with total devotion, and that was in their care of the dun filly, Belmont Golden Girl, who had been given to them, to their great delight, by Honeydew's owner when she returned from abroad.

Rachel was on her way now to give the filly her second anti-tetanus injection. If they had done as much for Hassan, their Arab gelding, she would never have had to shoot the poor fellow, Rachel considered. Still, that was all in the past. Mistakes were best learned from, and then buried and forgotten. 'If only' was never anything other than a waste of time.

The long growth at the road's verge rattled against Jessica's side as Rachel pulled the little car close in to let another pass from the other direction. In these narrow lanes it was pure luck if two vehicles met near one of the infrequent passing places, and the psychology of 'who-backs-down' was a subtle art that Rachel had rapidly learned to be mistress of, but today it was not necessary. The two cars passed with no delay to either, and Abel Cash's cheerful face and waving hand greeted her.

'Fine morning,' he shouted.

Rachel smiled, agreeing. 'How's Mick?' she asked. Abel jerked his thumb towards the rear seat, and there was the lurcher enjoying the luxury of a ride.

'Takin' 'im to the sheepdog trials,' bellowed Abel through the window glass, his face alight with pleasurable malice as he accelerated away.

Rachel drove on through the woods towards the Fowler's house. The trees were heavy with summer now, the leaves nearest the roadside dusty from the passing of traffic, and there were shreds of hay caught in the lower twigs where a late load had been carted from Waites' Farm fields. Jim Waites would do better, having waited and cut late, than his neighbours who had cut in May and watched the hay go black on the fields. He had an instinct for weather, did Jim Waites, and was right far more often than the telly man about the sort of local weather conditions Milchester and its surrounding countryside could expect. Not that he was prepared to act as official weather forecaster: he would never commit himself at the time. To the question, 'Will it be wet tomorrow?' you could only expect, 'Maybe,' or 'I daresay,' or 'Maybe not,' but if you were clever you would take example from him and cut and turn and bale, or cart and carry when he did, and nine and a half times out of ten the weather would be kind to you.

Anyway, it was straws snatched from his tractor, passing and repassing, that hung on the beech-twigs now, and drifted down from time to time as the light wind wafted them. Rachel loved these beech woods. She thought of the picture Tom had painted for her, as a reminder of one of their first outings together: grey beech-trunks rising from a bluebell-bed – an evocation of late spring. He had left it for her the day of the foal's birth, and she had been so caught up with that event and all its subsequent happenings that it had been days before she had remembered the parcel waiting to be opened, and had sat, entranced, in her room, examining every detail of the picture which she had first seen when she had visited his flat one day in his absence; had marvelled at the skill and originality of the man, had seen her own self portrayed half-hidden in the amazing detail of tree and flower, and had interpreted the message it spelled out to her.

There were no bluebells now of course: it was too late for them. Now this year's bells and leaves were rotted to mulch on the beechwood floor, and the bulbs underground were already working on next year's design. Rachel felt that there was nothing so soothing, so healing to the mind, as this never-changing pattern, this underlying rhythm of existence which went quietly about its business, regardless of the meddlings and insanities of man. Even on the bloodiest of battlefields grass eventually grew again; or at least, so far. Perhaps, in a hundred years or so, even over the final one. It was a gloomy enough thought to have come uninvited into her mind on such a bright day. She shook it away from her and concentrated on the road ahead. She was passing the orchard now, where once the sight of a Jersey cow in obvious distress had led her to her acquaintanceship with the Fowlers. Now here was the driveway, and the handsome little house, still tatty and neglected, but not quite the dispirited place it was when she first encountered it.

'Hello stranger,' Bill Fowler called as she pulled up in the yard.

Rachel smiled to herself. It was no small victory that Bill now actually invited the presence of a vet to his premises, rather than regarding them as some kind of avoidable luxury.

'She's here!' Bill called to the open back door of the house. 'You'd better bring it.'

'What's all this "stranger" business?' Rachel demanded. 'I was here only a month ago for Girl's first injection.'

Anne Fowler appeared then. She looked so much better, Rachel thought. More relaxed, more human, more in control of her life. One great credit that could be marked up to Bill was that he seemed totally without jealousy of her success in getting the job at the Golden Pheasant. Mind you, in a roundabout way he had been a cause of her finding it, so perhaps that helped.

'What Bill means is that you haven't been here since we made history,' Anne said. The Fowlers stood looking at her, each bursting with an undeniable but still unexplained exultation.

'For heaven's sake, tell me,' said Rachel, beginning to feel exasperated.

'You know I wanted to take Girl to Three Counties,' Anne said. Rachel nodded.

'And I said we couldn't afford it,' Bill added.

Rachel nodded again.

'Well, Mr Adler said he'd pay the entry fee, because of her name and his hotel both having "Golden" in them. Said it might bring us all luck.'

Anne brought out from behind her back a blaze of bright blue colour, a beribboned rosette, long-tailed and luxurious. Her expression was understandably smug.

'It did,' she said. 'Look. Look what Girl won.'

Rachel was so pleased for them. It was exactly the kind of reward they needed. It was a ridiculous enough pleasure, this pursuit of coloured ribbons; but Rachel remembered what they had meant to her father, had stood with him often enough on that same showground where the Fowlers had triumphed, that broad stretch of green under the shadow of the whale-backed Malvern Hills, waiting to see which number the judges would call in to victory.

'It'll be a red one next year, just you see,' said Bill.

'For heaven's sake,' Rachel laughed. 'Haven't you done well

enough already? Three Counties is pretty fierce competition, you know, and the filly's young: not truly a yearling till August. Congratulations, anyway, and when am I going to be shown this paragon of yours?'

'I'll bring her,' said Anne.

Rachel fetched the ampoule of vaccine and the disposable syringe from the car. There was the yearling waiting for her. Even in the month since Rachel had last seen her Girl had grown and blossomed. She had become that marvel that is so often hoped for and so seldom achieved: the perfect genetic marriage between the native sturdiness of her mother and her sire's classic, thoroughbred bone and quality. Perhaps Rachel had known her too well to see her true beauty before; perhaps she had only just this moment attained it, like a child putting on womanhood. Her body shone deep gold in the sunlight. Her head was small and fine-boned, and her eyes shone out of it, dark, and fringed with dark lashes. Her legs were black to knee and hock, the bones as all load-bearing pillars should be, seeming slender and yet immensely strong. She stood four-square over the ground as if she owned it, and her whole aspect called out to the world to look at her.

'Well?' Anne said, awaiting Rachel's judgement far more nervously than she had awaited the show-judge's decision.

'She couldn't be better,' Rachel said. 'Well done, the pair of you.' They both smiled at her with delight, as if she were entirely responsible for their success. Her approval was important to them.

This was an aspect of veterinary work that had not occurred to Rachel while she was training. In her view of what her work would entail she had envisaged only herself and the creatures she hoped to treat. Colin Ross, the vet with whom she had seen practice, had soon made it clear to her that the owners of her patients would be every bit as demanding of her skill as the patients themselves: that even the simplest treatment might fail without the cooperation of the owners, while, with their help and their own skills, even the most doubtful case might pick up and thrive. Experience had taught, and was still teaching her, when to bring out from her armoury of psychological skills, tact, firmness or charm, to recognise genuine interest and desire to help, and to put no reliance on those whose apparent involvement with her treatment was nothing more than politeness.

She had not realised how many of her customers would draw her so much into their own lives. She would be introduced as 'Rachel Adams, our vet,' as though she were to each of them a personal minister, which indeed she was; and remembering Malcolm Halliday's advice it was her hope to make each one feel that while she was with them their particular animal was the most important of the practice. There were some, of course, for whom such an attitude was a waste of time: those who felt that her visit was a waste of time, and money too, and to be avoided at all costs.

Bill Fowler had been among the worst of these. Was that the challenge that had drawn Rachel into such involvement with them, or was it pity for Anne Fowler's loneliness and misery? She could not stand far enough back from herself to see clearly; but whatever her motive, involved she had been, almost to meddle-someness, and had had far more success than anyone deserves who projects their nose so far into a private predicament.

All day Rachel kept before her the vision of the little golden horse. She was a victory for Rachel as well as the Fowlers, and such victories were worth treasuring.

The rest of her day's work was routine stuff: cattle testing for the most part – never boring, for cows are sufficiently unpredictable never to be that, but certainly not the dramatic errand-of-mercy stuff which some of her less realistic friends imagined her pro-fessional life must consist of. By the end of the day she felt extremely tired and more than a little smelly. Cows have little overt sense of humour, yet they defecate as though the whole thing were one huge practical joke, with an apparent carelessness concealing deadly accuracy.

Rachel's overalls and – in spite of their protection – her whole person was redolent of cow; and inside Jessica this odour put up a strong fight against the equally pervasive stink of sheep-dip from the ewes at Hollow Lane, who had pressed close about her while she was examining the feet of one of them who had stood on a tin can someone had disposed of in their field, almost shearing off one of the cleats of a forehoof. They had been dipped only a day or so previously. Rachel had cast off that overall, feeling that its blatantly insecticidal smell might offend the cattle, and it had lain in a heap on the back seat. It had certainly kept the car free from flies, and any germs Jessica might have been harbouring must have fled by now to the four corners of Gloucestershire.

Vi Partridge was cleaning up the kitchen when Rachel got back to Painters. Her nose quivered a little as Rachel came in, but she did not comment.

''E's in a funny mood,' she announced as Rachel came into the kitchen where the contents of cupboards were stacked up precariously on the table while the insides of the cupboards themselves were being scrubbed out and relined with shelf-paper. With any other man this might have been the cause of the 'funny mood', but domestic upheaval never normally put Tom out of countenance.

'I says to 'im, you looks as if you've lost a bob 'n found a tanner,' Mrs Partridge announced. ''E says, "You're right, you old beson," and stumps off upstairs.'

'I'm sorry,' Rachel said. 'That was rude of him.'

Vi Partridge snorted with sudden laughter. 'I've 'eard worse than that from that man of yours, all the years I've known 'im. Leave 'im be. 'E'll come to 'isself soon enough.'

Before long, Tom came down to join them as they sat sharing a pot of tea. His face looked bleak.

'It's gone,' he said. 'Sold. I was too late.' The two women waited for him to explain himself. 'Next door,' he said. 'George. The Buckles. I started off thinking, how can we help George? Then I started thinking what a marvellous hospital that yard would make. I told you motives are the devil, didn't I? I went to the bank to see if we could possibly raise a mortgage, and said what I wanted it for: that George could stay, we could develop proper operating facilities and all would be merry as a marriage bell. The manager gave me a funny sort of look and said had I contacted the Painters' executors, and I said no, not until I'd worked out the money side.

Then he said the executor's solicitor was a friend of his, and he thought it would be in order if he told me that the yard's been sold.'

Rachel, having had such a marvellous idea as Tom's suddenly thrust under her nose and snatched away again, said 'Who to?' in a rising tone that was almost a cry. Half-ideas, half-dreams had occurred to Rachel too about the possibility of an animal hospital so close at hand, but she had not allowed them to take on any substance. Tom had thought them through to reality, and tried to bring the reality to practical terms, and now it was all snatched away.

It would have been so good, too, not just to have that precious space they needed but to know that crabby, cranky old George was safe. It was bound to be the Buckles, of course. One of their sneaky plans must at last have worked, and some loophole been found in George's supposedly unquestionable right to the yard for his lifetime.

'Who's bought it?' Vi Partridge asked. 'Them Buckles, I suppose.'

'He didn't know,' Tom said, 'or else he wasn't saying. But I can't think who else it would be.'

They sat gloomily drinking tea, the two women infected now by Tom's mood and by the news he had brought.

'Oh well,' said Tom, at last. 'It was all a dream anyway. Finding that sort of money would have stretched us to the limit. We'd have had to go out touting for custom: stood on street corners waiting to pounce on poorly pets.'

Rachel sighed. Mrs Partridge tipped the teapot to its utmost into her cup, set the pot down, lifted the lid and surveyed its depleted contents glumly. There was silence again.

After a while Tom roused himself, with an effort, to ask, 'How's that horse of George's then? Any improvement?'

'A lot better,' Rachel said. 'Though I'm not sure it might not still develop an abscess. Mind you, you can imagine the nursing it's had. It's lost a lot of weight, but George'll build it up again.'

'What's 'e going to do when they throws 'im out then?' demanded Mrs Partridge. 'Old man Baker without 'is 'arses. I can't imagine it.'

'We could try to help him find somewhere where he could keep a horse or so,' Rachel suggested.

'And where's that likely to be?' asked Tom, crossly. 'Places where you can "keep a horse or so" are worth a fortune round here. And no-one's going to employ him in horse work. Not at his age and with his temper.'

They all subsided into silence again, until Mrs Partridge, anxious to change the subject, announced that her niece's daughter Mandy was thinking of buying a pony.

'Bin savin' up for years,' Vi Partridge said. 'Got 'er eye on one at Smailes Barn.'

'What!' Rachel exclaimed. Janet Andrews, who kept ponies at Smailes Barn, was not renowned for the quality of her horseflesh.

'I told her you'd say she was daft,' Mrs Partridge commented. 'Still it looked all right to me when she took me up to see it. Fat little pony it is, and she can just afford the price.'

'Well, I'm glad she's getting a pony, anyway,' Rachel said. 'She's worked hard for it, and she's learned a lot at the Riding Centre.'

It was to be hoped it would be enough to counteract any effect on the pony that its sojourn in Janet Andrews' slapdash care might have had.

Tom looked at his watch. 'Time for surgery,' he said. 'By the look of all the cars that have been coming in it's going to be a busy one. And Mrs Holder's just arrived with a van full of goats. Both of us this evening, I think, partner.'

'Done,' said Rachel.

'Yer clean overalls are in the 'all,' Vi Partridge announced. 'Though clean ain't what they'll be by the time you've seen to them goats.'

She picked up the day's discarded overalls from the corner where Rachel had left them, and walked with them at arm's length in the direction of the washing machine. A small sigh depressed her shoulders for a moment, and told the whole story of this particular battle waged here, and at Stapleton House before that, for over a decade now.

'A bath wouldn't do you no harm neither,' she said to Rachel. 'Wouldn't take a minute.'

'Oh, so it's you, is it,' Tom said, sniffing hugely. 'I thought the drains had gone wrong again.'

Chapter Nine

Any wicked Fairy Godmother worth her salt should be aware that the most terrible gift of all to give any human being must be that of second sight, the ability to know the outcome of events before they happen. It was fortunate for Rachel that she had no such ability, and that the day to which she awoke next morning seemed no different from any other. She had no premonitions, smelt no disasters, only felt faintly unwell and reluctant to tackle her breakfast.

Tom had gone out early to fit in before surgery a visit to some cattle belonging to an old man at Upper Cold Hill. He had farmed all his life, and now kept just one or two store cattle to keep himself occupied. Being an old chap, he slept little and started his day early, and liked his veterinary work done betimes, as well. Tom always allowed himself time for a talk, too, for the old boy had little company and obviously craved it.

When Tom had arrived at the yard, there had been no sign of man nor cattle: only a broken gate dangling drunkenly from its hinges, and in the distance the sound of agitated beasts. He had walked towards the sound, and found the old man lying unconscious in the mud.

'I got help at once,' Tom reported to Rachel on his return. 'I could see it was a stroke. Lord knows how long the poor old sod had lain there. I suppose the cattle must have broken out and he'd chased after them. When they'd taken him off in the ambulance I rang down to his daughter in the village. "No idea he was ill," she told me. "Don't see much of him these days. He's quite happy by himself, with the telly for company."

'What's it coming to, Rachel, when people think a lot of little lines on a screen is company? To think that is as much an illusion as the pictures themselves. What's happened to people when they can't recognise loneliness when they see it? He would never *ask* her to come. He's far too independent. But that's not the same as wanting to be isolated.'

Rachel could feel the anger in him as she laid her hand on his arm: frustration, exasperation, pulsing in him like an electric charge.

'Will he be all right, do you think?' she asked.

'With luck,' said Tom. 'But what then? He'll be taken into a home, I suppose, and she'll sell his cottage and live high on the proceeds.'

Tom's anger on the old man's behalf stirred Rachel's conscience. She remembered that she had not called in on Mrs Kyle for a few weeks. She would pay her a visit on her way home from Claybridge. There were some pigs on a farm near there with suspected Aujeszky's disease, and from the symptoms she had had described to her the suspicion seemed pretty well founded, though she was amazed to hear it. Mrs Winterton kept a disease-free herd. Her attention to the regulations was pernickity in the extreme, her hygiene precautions stringent and well enforced.

Usually, of course, it would be a ministry vet who would be called to suspected Aujeszky's, but there was an anthrax panic the other side of Gloucester and they were all involved with that, running about – as one of them had informed Rachel when she had phoned them about the pigs – 'like hens in a high wind'.

When Rachel arrived at the piggery she drew Jessica up in the reception bay, where everyone was required to stop, park, and disinfect their boots before proceeding any further into Mrs Winterton's porcine premises.

Everything was concrete and metal; all was angular planes, hard smooth surfaces; all gleamed, all was scrubbed. Not one green thing had dared to intrude within the walls.

The whole place was surrounded by notices indicating that visitors, representatives and animals other than the resident pigs were not welcome. As Rachel, in her clean boots, walked through the inner gateway, a bell rang to proclaim her presence, and Mrs Winterton, in gleaming overalls and equally spotless wellies, came trotting towards her. Rachel was glad her face was a known and requested one, as Mrs Winterton was not to be crossed lightly.

She was a small, plump woman, with a square, unsmiling face and short wiry hair which stuck out from under her canvas hat like steel wool. Only the tip of her mind seemed to register Rachel's presence; the rest of it was obviously concentrating on the probable disaster that she was about to have to face.

'Will you show me the sick pigs, please?' asked Rachel, beginning to move towards the sow-housing. This concentrated Mrs Winterton's attention at once.

'Not that way, Mrs Adams,' she said, her voice sounding reproachful and surprised as if Rachel had been caught out in some stupidity. 'In the isolation block, if you please.'

She led the way through another gateway, through yet another footbath to a long building divided into miniature looseboxes, from some of which one might expect the sound of pigs, eating, grunting, snoring, scratching themselves. If there were pigs in there, they were ominously quiet.

'Twenty-one days they stay here, when I buy them in,' Mrs Winterton announced, changing her overall for another, which she produced from a cupboard full of similar ones ready to hand in a small room at the end of the block. She gave one to Rachel, who was about to say she had brought her own but changed her mind on seeing the steel in Mrs Winterton's eye.

'I usually only buy through the Scheme,' she informed Rachel, as they moved towards the third box along. 'But my husband saw these at market and thought they looked good sorts.' She snorted to herself. 'Men!' she said, witheringly. ' "Good enough they may look," I told him. "But heaven knows what they'll bring in with them." ' She opened the door and bustled Rachel in to see her prospective patients. Mrs Winterton continued to castigate, in his absence, the unfortunate Mr Winterton, who had introduced into her hygienic haven pigs which had brought disease with them.

'Offered to take them back,' she was hooting. '"Too late," I told him. Still, at least he had the sense to put them here. Lord help him if he'd taken them in with my girls. I never should have married a man who only knows about cattle.'

She spat out the last word as if it were distasteful, and then fell silent, so that Rachel was at last able to concentrate her attention on the pigs, each in its separate box.

There was no doubt at all. Dull, listless, they stared at their troughs with no enthusiasm. They were constipated. They had been vomiting. At least she could make a positive diagnosis and not have to get the ministry's decision.

Rachel confirmed Mrs Winterton's suspicions, and she looked down at the third of her husband's purchases with even greater distaste.

'I'll have them slaughtered at once,' she said.

'Very well,' said Rachel. 'But keep the carcases for the Ministry Inspector. He'll need to see them. Now, are there any others in the block?'

'None. Just the three he bought.'

'I'll let the ministry vets know,' Rachel said, 'and they'll put a movement ban on for a two kilometre radius. You won't be able to move any stock for a while, I'm sure you realise.'

Mrs Winterton sniffed.

'I fully understand the regulations,' she said, stiffly.

'And you had better keep a very close watch on all your other pigs,' Rachel warned, though it seemed highly unlikely that any infectious organism could bridge Mrs Winterton's highly efficient precautions – unless, of course, it was a wind-borne infection, as some vets were beginning to think.

She walked towards the central yard, peeling off the overall she had been given.

'Not that way,' Mrs Winterton snapped, and pointed to a small side entrance with a high gate that lay beyond the isolation unit. 'Use that exit, if you please. The gate opens only from the inside. It will lock itself behind you. There is disinfectant in a bucket, some soap and a towel, if you wish to use it before you go.'

Rachel, feeling like the Ishmaelite woman, said goodbye to Mrs Winterton's retreating back, washed her hands and also her boots with the disinfectant water provided, and left through the side gate. It clanged shut behind her, and she was out on a muddy path, right the other side of the piggery from where she had left her car. She set off on her muddy trudge, and took particular pleasure in it and in the soft green of the hedgerow trees.

Highly disinfected though she was, she called in at a friend's home the other side of Claybourne and had a further wash. She had a couple of dogs to visit, and to them Aujeszky's would be fatal. Joan Soper kept no pets or livestock, and had met Rachel as a concert-goer, not as a vet, so she was most amused at Rachel's request and offered a sumptuous, sweet-smelling bathroom in which Mrs Winterton's iodophorous compounds stank incongruously.

Later, clean, fortified by coffee and the promise of two tickets for a performance of Vivaldi's 'Seasons', Rachel felt fit to go on with her morning.

The prospect of the Glevum Ensemble playing alfresco, then in the Rococo summerhouse at Claybridge Manor on a summer's evening, was a civilised delight that removed from her mouth the last lingering flavour of disinfectant and Mrs Winterton.

At lunchtime she rang in to Tom to tell him about the pigs, and to see if she could safely stop for a sandwich at a pub. The Fox and Hounds was not far and she now felt peculiarly empty, having not managed more breakfast. There was no hurry, he told her. She could take her time. He would 'phone the ministry for her.

The Fox and Hounds was on the far side of Richard Harris's estate which stretched in a fan-shaped wedge of land from Milchester House itself: an elegant house, bowered neat and immaculate on the parkland that his enthusiasm and his finances had saved from neglect and restored to sweet order. From the car park of the pub a right of way led into the estate to a famous viewpoint over the escarpment's edge to the Severn Valley far below, with the river making its slow sinuous way across the flat land in a landscape where agriculture and industry met and mingled, and distance lent enchantment even to cooling towers and smoking chimneys.

Hungry though she was, Rachel decided to take a walk up to the viewpoint. Often, when the chance came to do so, she would choose to stand and look around her at the pattern of fields and woods and hills, not even consciously thinking them beautiful, but absorbing them, like some vital food. Today, with a flitting sun, great shadows of clouds rode over the vale, marbling the fields with bright and dark. She wished Tom were here to share it.

It was the best thing ever, she felt, about her life with him: that while both lived, neither would ever suffer that poor old man's isolation; that every pleasure, together or apart, was a shared one, and every anguish, too.

Romanticism? she quizzed herself. Sentimentality? No, nothing so superficial. It was in their bones, as the rock shapes underlay the landscape which lay below her now and whose changes could be measured in the rhythm of centuries, while the beauty of the seasons came and went.

As she stood looking at its present loveliness from the highest point, a buzzard planed even higher above her, seeming to enjoy the feel of the air currents on which it rode. It looked so effortless, so peaceful. Then, suddenly, out of nowhere, came a pair of black ragged crows which began to dive and swing about the buzzard in short, steep plunges and veerings, disturbing the bird's serenity so that he banked and climbed to avoid them. Rachel thought for a moment that he had shaken them off and that they would leave him alone now, but they followed, and mobbed him again, their wings beating rapid and threatening while he continued with dignity to spiral upward with scarcely a movement of his own broad sails. Rachel longed, quite ridiculously, to be up there with him, beating off those pestilential birds. They should leave him alone. Let him be.

'They're only defending their territory, you know.' Rachel had been so absorbed in watching that she had not heard the approach of the horseman over the soft turf. Richard Harris was sitting on his big grey hunter, watching her with amusement. He dismounted and came towards her, joining in her upward looking at the birds.

'I must admit,' he said, 'that looking at kingship from a distance like that, you're on its side at once. Real Prisoner of Zenda stuff. Majesty is so much more appealing than the masses.'

Rachel laughed.

'Ah, but if you were a crow, and the mother of crows,' he went on, 'you'd be up there driving him off with the best of them. There's no romance in Socialism, but there's a heck of a lot wrong with tyranny.'

'You're a fine one to talk,' Rachel said. 'A child of capitalism if ever I saw one.'

'And you make a living out of the suffering of creatures,' he replied cheerfully. 'Let's go and hide our heads in shame at the Fox and Hounds. You're looking cold and peaky. You need something to eat, and as much brandy as the law allows. Come on. They're quite used to Boyo here. I put him in the garden and he trims the grass. Prunes the roses a bit too, but they don't seem to mind.'

He led her down to the pub and parked Boyo in the pub garden, where the grey horse began to nibble about among the trestle tables with as much relish as if this were all the grass he ever ate, and his five-acre paddock of pampered turf a mere figment of equine imagination.

The pub itself was quiet, being a weekday. At weekends tourists invaded it and drove the regulars to the small snug at the back where they could sup and grumble undisturbed, but now there were only one or two figures propping up the bar and an old man eating pie and pickled onions in a corner.

Richard ordered food and drink and they sat down on the bench between the window and the hearth, which in winter ate its way through several tons of estate timber, releasing the wood's bright flame of energy, letting it die to the grey light ash that fed the pub's roses which now filled the copper jug standing in the summer hearth. Heavy-headed, old-fashioned blooms, they spilled scent and stray flame-coloured petals into the room.

The two of them had a pleasant, sociable meal that seemed too soon over, and outside again Rachel waved Richard Harris off into the distance as he cantered away across his own well-tended estate. She thought of the old man who had also owned a few acres, and would not in all probability tend them again.

'Money's a bugger,' her mother's old cowman Sam had often told her, 'whether you've got too much or too little.' Too much was more comfortable though, on the whole.

She drove quite fast towards Milchester, pleased that she would have plenty to talk about with Mrs Kyle, news to catch up on, scenes to describe, cases to comment on. All would feed an insatiable appetite for things outside the confines of Mrs Kyle's world. She would like to hear about the buzzard. Rachel would tell her about George Baker too, and that would bring the light of battle to her eyes. She had heard from the beginning the story of the machinations of the beastly Buckles. Perhaps she might devise some means of retribution that Rachel and Tom could carry out. Rachel chuckled maliciously at the prospect.

As she drove she recalled her last meeting with Mrs Kyle. It had been far too long since. The business of life should not get in the way of friendship, but it so easily did.

They had talked then about Peter Kyle, who had been dead a good many years now; but photographs of him stood everywhere about, showing a handsome man, relaxed, carelessly dressed for his generation, and accompanied in some of the photographs by a slim graceful girl, not pretty, but lively and intelligent-looking, and very obviously the centre of Peter Kyle's attention.

'The thing I thank God for most in this world,' Mrs Kyle had told Rachel, 'is that he died without knowing I should end up like this.' She made a gesture which encompassed all her disabilities. 'I'd been to a specialist. He'd told me where all these vague pains of mine were going to lead: and more than – yes, oddly more than – the dread of that, was the horror of having to tell Peter. He was such a physical man, athletic. He loved to move – running, swimming, climbing. He loved me – in part anyway – because we did all these things together, and he loved my body, as it was then. Age would have been acceptable, I expect, but not this warping of what he had always regarded as perfect. Only in his eyes, of course; only in his eyes. But who else's mattered?

'I tried so hard to tell him, but it's not the sort of thing that day to day conversation leads up to, and somehow I could not just out with it. It would have seemed so bald and nasty.' She cackled then. 'Not so nasty as the reality, however. Just look at me. I ask you.'

Then there had been a pause in their conversation and Rachel had wondered if the older women wished to close the subject, but suddenly Mrs Kyle said, 'He was killed, you see, before I could tell him. Run over by a bus. Ridiculous, isn't it? We set all the possibilities of real horror against such a chance: cancer, an air crash, The Bomb. Much more likely to be run over by a bus, we say. Peter was always one for a joke. He'd have laughed, you know, but he couldn't, being dead.

'When he was dead, and I began to be crippled, I hated myself and the world so much that I thought I had killed any pleasure there might be left in me. For a long time I might as well have been dead too.

'But somehow, things will grow, no matter what, and small pleasures began to grow in me like shoots out of an old dead tree. That's pretty much what I look like, I've no doubt. An old, dead tree. But now I delight in those small pleasures, and each is to be enjoyed for itself and not measured against the sum of possible pleasures, where it is bound in the nature of things to fall short. The movement of this hand' – she splayed the fingers of her left hand and curled them in again so that they met, precise as a crab's claw – 'is a pleasure to me because it can grasp, whereas the other cannot. That way the triumph of ability outweighs the frustration of disability.' She paused, shifting her lumped weight in the chair. 'But there are frustrations enough. Worse at the beginning, of course, but they continue. Immobility, celibacy.' Mrs Kyle looked up sharply, caught Rachel's surprise and said, 'Oh yes, my dear, it is not just Peter's mind I have missed all these years. Not only the beautiful are capable of passion, you know, and we had been such lovers in our young time, as I hope you are and will continue to be. The young find it so difficult to understand that passion exists still

103

in those who may no longer be able to attract it. Harnessed, we could light up the world, dear Rachel. Unused, we channel our energies into good works and committees. Well most of us. I only crochet. The left hand is a fair hand at crochet. I can't stand the stuff, but it sells well.'

She had then with some difficulty opened the lid of a large box that stood by the wheelchair, and showed Rachel a multicoloured profusion of crocheted wool: cushion covers, pram blankets, waistcoats, potholders.

'Dreadful, isn't it?' Mrs Kyle had commented cheerfully. 'Can't understand why anyone should want it, but it's the sum of my creative ability now, except for my prowess in annoying Mrs Teape. I'm an expert at that.'

Rachel laughed as she drove home, warmed by this remembrance of her old friend.

She had reached the outskirts of Milchester now, but it was not until she was passing the Cottage Hospital that she began to feel something was not as it should be. There was an ambulance leaving the gate at speed. In the distance a different siren was sounding. Over the rooftops Rachel suddenly saw smoke.

Concern for whoever might be involved in the fire made Rachel accelerate and drive towards it, yet still she had no sense of real foreboding. So when she turned the corner of Sheep Street and saw whose house was ablaze, she cried out as if she had been hit, thumped hard where it hurt by a totally unexpected blow.

She braked and, leaving Jessica askew at the pavement's edge, ran towards the engines and the onlookers standing agape.

'Mrs Kyle!' she shouted. 'Where's Mrs Kyle?'

A fireman on a ladder was bringing someone out from the upper floor, and in the smoke-filled entrance Rachel could see another figure. She pushed through a knot of people and ran inside, hidden by the smoke.

Why are you doing this, she cried out inside herself to some unknown force of fate. Why? They were only small pleasures: a buzzard flying, a meal shared with a friend. Why must this horror be waiting for me. Why have you done this to someone I love.

Anger kept her going forward into the heart of the burning house. A terrible resentment shielded her. She felt nothing.

Further on, she crouched low against the wall, calling out until she heard a voice say, 'Who the heck's there? Get out quick. I've got the old woman.'

But Rachel would not turn back until she had seen for herself the fireman who carried Mrs Kyle in his arms.

Something fell: a beam, a burning door . . . She could not be certain, but it crashed down behind her, and she went sprawling into blackness.

A long time later as she began to drift towards waking it occurred to Rachel that she felt like a dead whale, wallowing in the shallows, pulled and tugged and wafted at the whim of the tide. She must be dead, in her whale's form, because she felt so heavy and yet so empty.

Then there came a slow metamorphosis, gradually allowing her to become herself again, knowing who, though not yet where, she was.

'She's lost it, I'm afraid,' someone was saying. What had she lost? She could not remember losing anything. Then came a panic thought that broke through into words.

'Where's Mrs Kyle?' The words hammered in her head.

'Mrs Adams?' a voice enquired, carefully enunciating as if she might be deaf or daft. She heaved open her eyes into the brightness of artificial light and the gleaming white uncompromising clean-ness of a hospital room. A man was bending over her, and she tried very hard to focus on him. His outlines swam about disconcert-ingly before coming together to reveal an obviously medical identity: white coat, stethoscope, slightly weary air of concern. Why did doctors look at you as if you had undertaken your particular affliction on purpose to annoy them?

Then the figure spoke, and the voice was not irritable but compassionate.

'It's Dr Mason here. You're in the Cottage Hospital. Do you remember what happened?'

At his words the panic returned. Her mouth felt stiff, as if unwilling to work, the lips forming the words long after her brain had thought them. At last: 'Where's Mrs Kyle?' Rachel said, conscious and obstinate, and ignoring the hammer blows.

The doctor looked at the nurse who stood beside him.

'I want to know,' Rachel said, and knew already, and did not need to ask again.

'The other fireman got you out just before the top storey collapsed,' Dr Mason explained. 'He had got Mrs Kyle out too, but she had already been overcome by the smoke. It all happened so quickly.'

Rachel, to give herself time, to let her mind accept the fact of her old friend's death, to beat back the rising misery in her throat, looked down at her own body under the blankets; and Dr Mason interpreted this as a wish to know about her own injuries.

'You have one or two minor burns,' he said. 'Nothing else, no injuries we can find, though they'll want to make tests in case of concussion or anything like that, for you did knock yourself out, after all, and you have been unconscious for quite a time. But there is something else, I'm afraid.'

He took her hand, obviously expecting some emotional reaction, and said, 'I'm afraid you've lost the baby.'

Rachel stared at him. Stupid man: what was he talking about. She hadn't got a baby, so how the heck could she lose one?

'What baby?' she asked. The hard light shone off the pen-tops in his pocket and the metal stethoscope. She wished he would go away so that she could give way to the misery that filled her; choking her throat, flooding at the backs of her eyes.

'What baby?'

Dr Mason looked nonplussed, gazed at her long and hard, and said in amazement, 'Didn't you realise you were pregnant?'

Still she stared back at him. She must have looked like an idiot: vacant, slack-jawed. Then having taken in what he had said she felt as though she had fallen down a mineshaft. Stupid, wasn't it? Surrounded in all her waking hours – and some of her half-sleeping ones too – by the procreation of animals, she had been too busy, too occupied, to see that the rules had also been applied to her. She had not married Tom for babies. She had married him because she wanted his love and his company for the rest of her life, and knew he felt the same towards her. She wanted him; not some by-product of him. They had not even talked about children. Maybe that was wrong, but whether or not, they hadn't.

Dr Mason left, and the nurse fussed around and straightened the bed, and bustled off, promising tea. Rachel, alone on the high bed in the clinical room, sat looking at her hands, folded together in the white lap that the hospital blankets made between her knees.

Propped up on her pillows she sat, and as time passed a feeling, strange and yet familiar, seemed to follow the course of the blood through every part of her body. Tearless, she grieved for her friend Mrs Kyle, burned to death in a fire from which she could not escape. And on the horizon of feeling there was another grief too, a totally illogical grief that she had no business to feel, that she had no reason to feel: for an odd little jelly, a human-shaped beginning, an unsuspected something that might have been a child.

She found no tears until Tom came, and then at last she was able to cry. He held her, and did not mock her grief with meaningless comforting words but let her shake and weep and rage at the wayward cruelties of life. He could see that Mrs Kyle's death had shattered her; was half aware of the effect, both physical and mental, of that other death.

'You didn't suspect, either?' Dr Mason had asked. 'I despair of the medical profession. Can't recognise their own symptoms.'

'We hadn't thought in terms of babies yet,' Tom said.

Dr Mason snorted. 'Even people who put up umbrellas get wet sometimes,' he announced. 'Sterility's the only fail-safe way to stop nature asserting herself. Women ought to have babies you know. Designed for it.' Tom thought it best not to pass on this opinion to Rachel.

During the few days that she remained in hospital, unless he was visiting her or on his rounds or working in the surgery, Tom shut himself up with canvas and easel and painted like a demon. It was strange stuff. He would not exhibit it; but it released in him feelings, only half admitted, that were coin-close to Rachel's own.

She came home, and tried to be her old self again, but all her sensibilities were raw as if the skin were flayed off them. She was, in the true and painful sense, vulnerable, and no relieving numbness came as it had done in all her previous experience of grief. She imagined that Tom thought it was the death of Mrs Kyle alone that had overset her; but she did not comprehend that he understood, and in part shared, her other unhappiness, for somehow they could not speak of it; and that in itself added to her distress.

These overwhelming feelings she attributed to the physical state of her body, reacting as if it blamed her for its loss and would not let her forget it. It was the altering of her body's chemistry that made her weep when there was no real cause to weep, that made light brighter, pain sharper, sadness more overwhelming, all sensation so much more immediate. This must be so, for she could not, in all logic, feel grief for a life she had not even known existed. She had not particularly wanted children. She had never thought of any other course than continuing to work at the profession she had trained so hard for. One day, perhaps, maybe . . . But then this small, determined, intruding life had latched on to her body despite all science's defences, and had stirred up in her, out of her grief, a desire more unaccustomed and more subtle than the desires of sex. It had been such a little life: short, unnoticed except with its ending; but it had left Rachel with an emptiness which she could scarcely endure.

Even work could not fill it, although the moment she was able, she did her share with her usual skill and efficiency. She worried about things unprofitably, often needlessly, so that she could not sleep for the burrowing anxieties in her mind.

Among these anxieties the frustration that she shared with Tom about the fate of George's yard grew in her out of all proportion, and she could not even relieve it by commiserating with George for he had vanished again, taking the cob with him, and Vi Partridge's theory was that he'd gone to his cousin's in Somerset, where there was grazing enough to bring a sick horse back from the dead.

Tom explained that he'd looked at the cob while Rachel was in the hospital because an abscess had developed as Rachel had feared it might, and needed treatment. 'I lanced it,' Tom said. 'Ripe and beautiful it was; just like striking oil.'

'Charming,' said Rachel. 'Then what?'

'Then I looked the cob over again and said he was fine now but would need building up and cossetting a bit. Next thing I knew George had upped and taken it off in a lorry.'

'He shouldn't have gone,' Rachel despaired. 'They're bound to throw him out as soon as they can anyway, and if they find the place is empty they may move in and not let him come back.'

'We aren't even sure he knows, yet,' said Tom. 'About the place being sold, I mean. I couldn't mention it, because the solicitor said he couldn't give me any information about the purchaser, and he'd only told me what he had in strict confidence. It's terrible. Poor old George.'

So the empty yard next door seemed to mock at so much they had hoped for, and at George, all unknowing, perhaps looking at horses in Somerset that he might have nowhere to house on his return.

Tom suggested that Rachel should go off to Parkwood for a week, to see her mother, to relax a little, for although her body was young and fit and soon quite capable of coping again even with the more strenuous side of the farming practice, he could still sense the strangeness in her and became anxious.

They had begun to quarrel, not in terms of fierce argument and discussion which was normal and acceptable between them, but snarling, unprofitable stuff that left them both exhausted and angry. Even this particular suggestion had annoyed her.

'I'm not going to be put out to grass like George's horse.'

But in the end she had agreed, and drove off one morning among fields beginning to take on their earliest harvest colours, and down at last into Parkwood's green valley.

For the first time since that new life had begun she felt Parkwood draw her back, as if all her adulthood, her independence, her achievements, had been stripped from her and she was ready to curl up into childhood again and be comforted. These thoughts, these feelings, were all kept well inside her, however, and her outward image was just as it always was. They could not see, all the people who met this bright, attractive, professional young woman who had come back to visit her old haunts, that she was only a cleverly disguised ghost of her own past.

Only her mother knew it, and sensing this strangeness began, after some days of allowing her absolute peace, to try to draw Rachel back to reality: spoke to her less and less as a beloved child, deliberately more as a woman and an equal; asking opinion, requiring judgement, brushing away the webs of self-pity that Rachel had let cling for too long.

In the late afternoon of the fourth day Rachel sat in the room that had always been hers at Parkwood and tried consciously to turn her mind to the memories it held for her: to recall scenes from beyond those many doors that had closed behind her. It should have been easy enough: the room was much as it had always been, carried its marks and scars of past years as the rest of the house did, the Bellamy budget being earmarked always for land and cattle rather than wallpaper and furnishing fabrics.

As she sat in the familiar place, however, her mind refused to divert itself with things past, and her thoughts remained stubbornly with present miseries. She regarded her face in the wardrobe mirror: pale, thin, and framed with dark hair which had been brushed some time earlier, but with little enthusiasm. Movement within the reflection caught her eye, and she saw that the side-panel of the triple looking-glass on the dressing table was swinging gently, as it always did, in a slight breeze, or even at the vibration of footsteps in the passageway outside the room. As it swung it brought into view a further reflection of herself. Two Rachels. Two aspects of Rachel. She had seen herself only as a reasonably able, pretty much dedicated, professional woman: married now, and happy to be so, but essentially the same person. But those incidents in her life that had caused her to be just here, just at this particular moment, had swung into view that other, that obliquer image. She was unsure of this aspect of herself: still felt uncomfortable with it, unsure of the truth of it, still half afraid that biology might be tricking her into something she might regret later. Was that strange awesome grief she had felt only a confidence-trick of nature? She could not make herself believe so.

She stretched out a hand, and the two reflected Rachels stretched out reciprocally, the mirror-image faces reflecting the perplexity she felt.

'Tell me,' she appealed to her reflected selves, but they only mouthed 'Tell me' in reply, and she got up and turned her back on them, moving instead to the open window to lean on the sill and look far out across the Parkwood valley at the uncomplicated green of the cow-pastures, shadowed at their edges by hedgerow trees, and dotted about with the caramel colours of the Jersey cattle that grazed placid and content with udders filling for the evening milking. How productive they were. Yet they were not just milk-factories: she knew them all, their breeding, their qualities, even now that she was not at Parkwood so often, for her mother kept her up to date and sent her photographs – much to Tom's amusement – of the latest calves. There was Bryony under the shade of the big ash tree, and Petal nearest the gate, the smallest cow with a ragged ear from an encounter with a stray dog when she was a down-calving heifer. Old Columbine stood nearest, rubbing her neck on the fence and crooning to herself with little soft noises, grunts of pleasure, as she found the itch and scratched it. Her sides were swelled out, the skin gleaming golden, like stretched silk over her roundness. She calved easily, did Columbine, never troubling anyone very much over the matter. Her daughters were among the best of the Parkwood herd.

'No-one ever asked you to make decisions, did they old girl,' Rachel said softly, but the cow was not listening. Having finished her massage she walked off through the rich grass, idly, unhur-riedly seeking out her companions and the friendly shade of a tree. What strange company Rachel felt urged to join: these heavy-bodied, ambling cattle, placid with approaching maternity; the mare at Stow, furious in defence of her young.

The act of creation was the same in all; the instincts, the urges, at root the same. Could she not undertake motherhood as simply, as instinctively as they did, instead of complicating her life with decisions? Ah, but humanity must be more rational, far-seeing, intelligent than these creatures, weighing up choices to the least scruple.

'Oh heck,' said Rachel, and the longing in her sent the scales flying. In the far-off days of her singleness when motherhood – for herself, that is – had seemed as unlikely as a walk on the moon, she had considered that for most people she knew, having a baby was either an accidental occurrence that might cause anything from inconvenience to real distress, or an intentional, cosy goal, a piece of pleasant self-indulgence. Yes, that was certainly how she had felt; that women who wanted to be pregnant, who wanted mother-hood, were engaged in a harmless enough kind of selfishness, the old childish cry of: 'I want, I want.'

Yet as she grew to understand the longing in herself she recognised that it was not the kind of wanting that desires some object, some particular thing. It was as if the life were there, already existing, waiting to be let in. It was an odd fancy, too ridiculous perhaps ever to be admitted to, but it was how she felt, and the thought of keeping the door closed on this child of hers and Tom's was unbearable.

She turned again towards the mirror, to her reflection which outwardly had changed so little over the past months. Apart from being a little thinner, she could have been the same self that had set out for her interview with Malcolm Halliday for the post at Stapleton House, hiding her terror under a brisk professional manner that she had laundered specially for the occasion, and which she knew now could never have fooled him for a moment.

So here she was now, as far as the world was concerned: skilled in her profession, dedicated to its whims and quirks and sometimes totally unreasonable demands. When it asked more of her than she thought she could possibly give, somehow the energy was there.

This was what she had wanted, always. This is what she desired to keep. Well, so she would, and undertake this other as well. She would. She turned to the window again and looked at the cows grazing, and she began to chuckle, and the chuckle grew to a laugh, and she laughed aloud until the tears rolled down her cheeks, and became real tears. She was on that high watershed between laughter and weeping, and even she could not have said into which valley she went down.

When the tears stopped, she dried her eyes and washed her face. She saw the cattle were now making for the milking shed and knew that the house below would be quiet and empty, but even so she crept softly downstairs feeling ridiculously as she used to feel as a child when she had been sent to her room for some misbehaviour, sensing that the time was right and she could expect all to have been forgotten, but even so she must tread gently, so that all would be well.

In the cool old kitchen she set to work peeling potatoes, and set the kettle on the Aga ready for when her mother should come back from milking.

The Parkwood therapy was at work in her; that and her growing realisation of how much she missed Tom. Desire for him returned, and the urge to be back at work, and one day she recognised that this was afternoon-land, that she had stayed there long enough and that gradually, inevitably, almost in spite of herself, she had healed.

On the morning she was due to return her mother said, 'Are you going to try again?'

Rachel looked up. 'Try what?'

'To have a baby, my dear. If you are, try soon. There's no reason on earth you should have the same problem again.'

'I never thought much about having children,' Rachel said. 'Not until this happened. I never imagined I'd feel like this. If Tom agrees, yes, I think we'll try again.'

'Well, think about it hard, my love. I come from a generation that accepted babies as an inevitable part of marriage. Nowadays they're mostly by deliberate choice, and that makes it far less easy. Sometimes choices made for us are the most acceptable in the long run. Anyway, if you do decide to make a grandmother of me, don't forget it isn't just a baby you'd be having but a whole person, with a whole long life, please God, and linked to yours for much longer than a brief childhood. Look at us, now. We can't undo our relationship, except by a deliberate withdrawal of our affection for each other. It's not just nappies and colic and breast-feeding, and how to get your figure back when you've stopped looking like a ripe pear. Being a mother is for life. You never stop being one, even when your children have grown up and flown and you feel redundant.'

'Well, you aren't redundant,' Rachel said. 'I needed you so much. Needed telling, just like I did when I was small.'

They were sitting in the farm kitchen at Parkwood, where a good deal of that telling had been done. It struck Rachel how amazingly lucky she was to have grown from such roots, to be able to come back to this sameness, this enduring place. Maybe it was better for people to be thrown headlong into their own lives, made forcibly independent, having to be self-reliant. Perhaps.

She thought of Tom, handed about as a child from one relation to another like an awkward parcel until his eccentric Aunt Bramwell had taken him on. She thought of Malcolm Halliday, stunted and stultified in childhood by a domineering father and a dominating mother, and saw that the very closeness she treasured in her own family can turn monstrous all too easily. How lucky she had been.

'What would I do without you?' she said, and the question was not a light one, although it was lightly asked.

Mrs Bellamy laughed. 'I can come out of retirement and give quite unnecessary and uncalled-for advice, like some old crusader wheeled out to give the recruits a pep-talk; but you can manage quite well without me, and would have thought out all I've said for yourself, given time, and that's just as it should be.

'All I'm saying really, all I'm warning you of, is that motherhood will change you. If I know you, you'll be determined it won't, but biology can be a slavemaker. It will alter your order of priorities. It will make demands on you that you have not yet experienced, and won't always be willing to share you with marriage, or profession, or anything else you now find important. You will have to

114

manage, and to balance, all these elements in yourself. It isn't easy. You'll have to tread gently with Tom, too. Men marry a woman, and then they find they've married a mother too: it can come as a bit of a shock, even though they were involved in the change.'

'Was that how Father felt?' Rachel asked. She had never envisaged anything but total content between them – never a placid, complacent content, for both were too different, too intelligent for that, but the roots were unshiftable, however much the branches might dance to the gale. Rachel had heard, as a child, plenty of good stiff breeze of argument, but she had never supposed for one moment that their disagreements might alter how things were between them.

'Was it how he felt?' her mother echoed. 'Perhaps at first,' she said laughing. 'He thought you'd break if he breathed on you. And I think he thought I'd gone fragile too. But then I brought you down to the cow-byre one day, even before you could walk, and sat with you, watching him work, and you chuckled and hicupped and waved your arms at the cows, even when they came right up close to you; and you've never seen a man more pleased. He saw you as a person then, you see, not just as a strange, miraculous object he and I had somehow produced between us.'

And the two women laughed, and if the immortal part of John Bellamy heard them he would have laughed too, remembering.

The journey home seemed to take too long. The roads seemed to stretch before her, tormenting her with the distance that lay between her and Milchester, but at last she drove in through the gateway of Painters and Tom came out to meet her, and dragged her out of the car into a great bear hug.

'That'll show 'em,' he said, grinning in the direction of the vehicles still disgorging customers for surgery. 'I can't stop. I've left a guinea-pig half bandaged,' he continued. 'It's got a scratch about half an inch long from a nail in its cage, but Tommy Farr says he always has a bandage when he cuts himself so we're putting one on his guinea pig, too.' Tommy Farr was six years old, and his bedroom housed more small creatures than an average zoo. He was a regular customer.

'Business before pleasure,' said Rachel.

'She smiled,' said Tom. 'The woman smiled.'

He began to caper about, deliberately ridiculous.

'You're mad, Tom Adams. Go and bandage your guinea pig,' she chided him.

'Welcome home,' he said. 'Welcome back.' He drew her against him, under his arm, and walked her towards the door. 'I'll tell you who else is back,' he said. 'George is.'

'He's in the flat?' asked Rachel. 'Living there?'

'Well only since yesterday. I'll have to go and see him. Find out what he knows.'

There was no need. They had scarcely sat down together after surgery when the door bell rang; and when Rachel answered it, there was George.

''Eard you'd been poorly,' he said.

'I'm all right now, George. Do come in. How's the cob?'

'Fair enough. Doctor Green was the curing of 'im. Four days good grass and 'e was right as rain. Found a buyer. Got a good price. Enough to pay your bill and give me a bit of profit too.'

'I'm glad,' Rachel said. She took George through into the kitchen and looked across at Tom, appealing to him, silently, to broach the subject of the sale of the next-door yard.

Tom invited George to sit, and hesitantly began to probe, to see if the little old man had any idea about what had happened.

'Oh yes,' said George. 'It's sold all right.'

'I'm so sorry, George,' said Rachel. 'We had hoped . . . well, Tom had tried . . .'

'I knows about that,' George said. 'Solicitors told me.'

There was a silence, in which Rachel stood, awkward, disappointed for them all and unsure what to say next, as George continued to sit.

'We're both so sorry,' she reiterated, stuck for anything more constructive.

'Sorry, are you,' he said, and it was more comment than question.

116

'What will you do?' Rachel asked.

'About what?' The query was accompanied by an odd grimace, which under other circumstances she might have considered had amounted to a smile.

'Well,' she said gently. 'I suppose the purchaser will want to take possession before long.'

'That's possible,' said George.

A feeling was beginning to germinate and grow in Rachel that the old man was up to something. Had he thought up some obstruction to the Buckles' plans? Some nice retribution on them for having robbed him of his home? Something was obviously giving him great satisfaction, and Rachel was now more than curious to discover what it was.

'When are they moving in?' It seemed callous to ask, but the words were out now.

' 'Oo?'

Was he being deliberately obtuse?

'The Buckles,' said Rachel, as patiently as she could.

'Not never, as far as I knows,' said George, and the expression widened across his face, stretching it like a comic rubber mask.

'They didn't buy it after all then? Someone else did?'

Tom, who had sat watching the two of them and listening to this conversation, could contain himself no longer.

'For heaven's sake, George, stop being so enigmatic and tell us who's bought it.' He rose to his feet, towering over the little old man; but he sat there quite undismayed and cackling now with laughter.

'I 'ave,' he said.

Tom sat down again. Tom and Rachel stared at George, completely flabbergasted, and unable to say a word.

'Well,' commented George. 'I might 'ave been looking enny whatever you said, but you two just looks poleaxed, like a bull at the butcher's.'

'Explain,' said Tom. 'If you want to, that is. It's really none of our business.'

'It might be,' said George. 'Or it might not. That depends. I got fed up with them Buckles so I bought it. Cash on the nail. Well, not cash but as good as.'

'But George,' Rachel said, finding her voice at last after a long and only half-believing pause. 'If you had the money to buy it why didn't you buy it before?'

'What sense would there 'ave been in that?' George looked at her as if she were daft. 'Old Mrs Painter thought she'd tied it up all proper with the law so I could 'ave it for as long as I'd need it. No point paying for what you can 'ave for free.

'I knew people'd 'ave an eye on this place and want to buy it, and they did, sure enough, but it wasn't till them Buckles started tryin' to prove I was too old, or off me 'ead, that I could see it was time to make a move. I'd never offered to buy it before 'cos there weren't no need to buy it, but I could see in the end they'd slide their way past the old girl's wishes, and I didn't want them 'aving it, even if they 'ad to wait till I was dead.'

The Adams continued to look wonderingly at George, and Tom began a question which he hastily swallowed. George cackled again.

'And you're sitting there thinking where did George Baker come upon that sort o' money, I've no doubt.'

Rachel began to speak, but he cut across her intended protest with: 'Well, this is 'ow. My pa taught me never to spend what I could save, and I've never been tempted much to spend anyway, 'cept on a bit of 'orseflesh now and again, and I reckon never to lose money more often than I gains it, when I comes to sell 'em. I used to keep me cash in an old brass kettle, till Mrs Painter found out and told me I wanted me 'ead examined.

' "Money's no good unless it's making money," she told me, and she said she'd put it somewhere where it'd do me a bit of good – some company she knew of. It wasn't much of a company then, but it's big enough now and it sends me more each year than I needs to spend.'

Rachel, listening to this little history of George's finances, considered the old man's frugal life: his old bed, his cardboard boxes, his threadbare carpet, and the curtains that hung limp with their weight of years. His food, as far as she had been made aware, was strong tea, bread and cheese, and various substances eaten directly from the tin. Apart from the occasional horse and the required fodder and bedding for it, he made no large outlay of money. Everything about the way he lived seemed to indicate that he was a poor man, and now it was made clearly apparent that he was not. Yet he was no miser, of that Rachel was sure. It seemed to her that he lived as he did not through meanness, but because it was how he wished to live: how it seemed best to him. Money was without real value to him, yet with inborn thrift he could not allow it to go to waste. There was a dignity to this philosophy that Rachel admired. It was as if someone whose life is such that he has no need to concern himself what time of day it is, should nevertheless take pride in keeping his clocks oiled and wound and accurate.

While this extraordinary conversation and revelation had been going on, Tom had been producing cups of good strong tea which he now handed round, and they sat and drank while George gave them the delicious details of his gazumping of the Buckles, and the fluttering this had caused in the solicitors' dovecote. It was marvellous stuff.

Rachel ached inside with suppressed delight. Too much laughter might have offended George by reducing the dignity of the transaction, but the scenes he described had such a gloriously Dickensian flavour, and were clearly visible and audible to the imaginative listener.

So that problem was over, at least. Their own possible plans would just have to be put away again and left to the future; but George would continue to be their neighbour, and that was as they had wished.

Chapter Ten

꙰꙰꙰

The next day after surgery Rachel walked out into Milchester, into
the usual bustle of the little town, and soon became absorbed in its
pleasant familiarity and the reassuring ordinariness of domestic
economy. Known faces greeted her in the supermarket: she
queued at the fish shop between a Mrs Ford (two alsatians and an
African grey parrot) and Major Plumtree (nice bay cob and a totally
undisciplined beagle puppy).

Outside John Porter's, the bookshop, she saw someone else she
knew. It was Margaret Sherwood in the company of a pleasant-
looking young woman who carried a large parcel of what must
obviously be books. Mrs Sherwood saw Rachel and called her
across to introduce her to the other woman, her daughter Sarah
Forbes, over from Canada for a fortnight to visit her. Sarah had
something of her mother's look, enough to make a strong resem-
blance, but the Jewishness of her father was evident too, in the
strength of the features and the darkness of the hair.

'Mother thinks she hasn't quite enough books,' Sarah Forbes
said, glancing amiably at Mrs Sherwood. 'We've come to
replenish her supply.'

'I shall get my revenge on the booksellers eventually,' Margaret
Sherwood countered. 'I'll make them fill their shelves with copies
of *my* book.'

'She will, too,' her daughter laughed.

'How's Sago?' Rachel asked, and was reassured that the dog was
fighting fit and kept strictly off a diet of precious papers.

As Rachel watched the two women walk away down the street with their parcel she never dreamed how soon, and under what strange circumstances, she would see them again.

When they had disappeared from sight Rachel continued her walk down the narrow, stone-walled street, past the pet shop and the hairdresser's to the bakery, whose old-fashioned frontage, freshly painted in a livery of chocolate brown and yellow, made it look for all the world like a railway carriage from the heyday of the old Great Western. She went in and bought some sticky buns, the shop's speciality, and exchanged a few words with Mrs Crabtree who worked behind the counter.

Mrs Crabtree was glad to see Rachel back: said she looked as though her little holiday had done her good and she hoped she wasn't working too hard too soon. Over the wrapping up of the sticky buns she regaled Rachel with some of the minor gossip of the little town. Sunlight from the street outside fell across the trays of bread and cakes and currant buns, the smell of which filled the little shop and perfumed every inch of Mrs Crabtree herself; and she was as plump as one of her doughnuts.

Standing there, on the customers' side of the counter, Rachel became suddenly, vividly aware of her own happiness. It was one of those surprising revelations of feeling that are like a present from the gods. In spite of all that had happened to her, in spite of the growing pressures of life, the serious commitment of her work, the inevitable tensions and adjustments of marriage, she felt now, just for a moment, the same upwelling, childish glee that had filled her when she danced on that spring morning into George's yard.

Afraid that Mrs Crabtree would think she had gone daft – for she could not suppress her pleasure – she hurried out of the shop, the bell jangling as she closed the door behind her. Then clutching among her other parcels a striped paper bag proclaiming 'A. J. Crabtree Master Bakers, Established 1895,' she wandered on, letting her elation take her, with no particular purpose now for that was the last of her shopping.

She turned into Sheep Street, and stopped, aware suddenly of where her legs had brought her. It took a great effort to overcome the sudden chilling of her bones and a powerful need to turn and go back. As suddenly as it had come, her exuberant mood left her; and she longed not to face the thing that had driven it away. But this was her home now, this little town, and she must live with all of it. There must be no corners whose existence she wished to deny. So she walked on, though she shook as she did so and was glad there was no-one in the quiet street to watch her.

The black bones of Mrs Kyle's house stood up against the sky. Rachel made herself look. She looked until her eyes ached and began to sting, but she held her gaze steady.

A building firm had already hung a notice on the burned-out door frame: 'Repairs and Restorations' it said.

There was no point waiting about. Rachel had done what she had come to do. 'Goodbye old friend,' she said quietly, and turned towards home.

The rest of the day passed uneventfully enough. Tom's visits had been routine stuff, surgery so thin on custom as to be quite extraordinary. They should have known, she and Tom, that fate was brewing up some mischance.

It was three o'clock in the morning when the telephone rang, and for once Rachel was down first to answer it. When the voice asked if that was Mrs Adams Rachel felt sure she recognised it, and yet could not place it.

'Mrs Forbes here.' Forbes. Forbes? The slight twang to the accent reminded her. Margaret Sherwood's daughter, of course. Something dreadfully wrong with Sago?

'It's a horse, Mrs Adams. A horse in the fields out back. Mother's sitting on its head.' The picture was ludicrous. The tone of voice was deadly serious.

'Can you come at once? And do you have some wire cutters? We can't rouse anyone round here.'

'We'll come immediately. Don't worry. We'll bring everything we'll need.'

Tom was half dressed already, sensing emergency. He always seemed to know without telling when a night call meant instant action.

'There's a horse caught up in wire in the field behind Mrs Sherwood's,' Rachel said. 'Can you find the wire-cutters while I get the kit ready?'

They were in the car within minutes for the short drive to Knapp House. Lights shone in the downstairs rooms and made a track of brightness down the back garden for the two vets. After that there was Sarah Forbes with a flashlight to augment Tom's own.

'The farmer's away,' Sarah explained. 'Mother says his son comes over to see to the stock, but he's not on the 'phone. Mother heard this noise, you see. She sleeps very lightly. She woke me and I heard it too; a horrible screaming, not the noise you'd expect from a horse. We came down, and found it in the wire. It's very bad: it must have thrashed about for some time.'

By now they were near enough to see the animal, a huddle of brown in the mud at the field's edge, its forelegs streaked with red where it was entangled in the barbed wire of the fence. At its head sat the hunched shape of Margaret Sherwood in a man's blue plaid dressing gown which was equally splashed and stained with red. She wore also a headscarf, woolly socks and galoshes.

'Thank God you're here,' she said. 'He's much quieter now, but I am not convinced that is a good sign. Was it all right to send for you? We could not think what else to do. It's Bill Parker's land and this is his horse, but I've no idea what vet he has.'

'It's all right,' Rachel soothed her. 'We'll cope. Mr Parker'll have to put up with it.'

'Let's get to work on this horse,' Tom said. 'I've sedated him.'

There seemed to be strands of wire embedded everywhere in the horse's forelegs. At each snip of the cutters the poor creature twitched and shuddered, in spite of the pain-killing drugs, but Margaret Sherwood continued valiantly to sit upon its neck, restraining and soothing it. Sarah had been despatched to the house for water, soap and towels.

'Are there any other animals in the field?' Rachel asked as they freed the last strands of wire and bent them back into the hedge. 'He won't be pleased if we let his stock out.'

'No,' Mrs Sherwood said. 'That was the cause of the accident, I think. The son moved all the cattle on to another field and left the horse on his own. He'd been cantering up and down and whinnying ever since.'

The deep gashes on the horse's legs gaped, welling with blood. In one place the whiteness of bone gleamed in the torchlight, but at least there was no gush of arterial blood and Rachel knew from experience that the gashes would look far less appalling once stitched. It was a cold, tedious and messy job. When it was finished, they were red to the elbows, stiff and shivering.

Sarah had brought down blankets, but those were for the horse, to help reduce shock.

It was beginning to grow light as they sat back on their heels, and gratefully drank coffee from a flask Sarah had brought down with her.

'Lord, what a mess we are,' commented Tom. 'Like refugees from a slaughterhouse.'

Rachel winced, remembering the Sherwoods' story, but Margaret only pulled a face in agreement and did not seem unduly perturbed by her gory state.

'We'll all go in for a wash,' she said. 'But what's to happen to the horse? He can't stay out here, surely.'

'We could put him in the tool shed, Mother, once he can walk that far. It's the nearest building there is.' Sarah pointed to a large timber structure at the bottom of Knapp House garden. It was a fair size for a toolshed, and might do at a pinch.

'There's not much in it,' Mrs Sherwood said. 'Come and see.'

Rachel went with her. The glittering morning cobwebs proved the building's long disuse. The doorway seemed to Rachel to be wide enough to get the horse in safely once he was able to make the short walk from the field.

'We'll have to cut more wire, to get him into the garden,' Mrs Sherwood said. 'Will it matter? It's Parker's fence.'

'I shan't charge Mr Parker for the demolition work,' Rachel laughed. 'Stop worrying. You've been marvellous. He'd have lost this horse if it weren't for you. We only just patched him up in time, I think. He'd have bled to death by morning, or died of shock.'

Sarah appeared in the doorway, looking pink and slightly guilty.

'I've been next door,' she said, 'and pinched a bale of straw. It was in that lean-to behind their kitchen. I just happened to notice it the other morning.'

'He keeps some for his strawberries,' Margaret Sherwood said.

'Will he mind?' Tom asked.

'They're away,' said Mrs Sherwood. 'I'll replace it.'

'I'll put it on Mr Parker's bill,' Rachel said.

When they had all washed themselves they returned to the horse, and waited for him to show signs of being able to move. Rachel had put on him a rope halter which she normally kept among the veterinary equipment. Some owners seemed unable to find one when one was most needed, so she had learned to provide her own.

'I'll stay here and watch this fellow,' said Tom. 'You'd better ring the house and see if Mrs P's arrived.'

It was Mrs Partridge's early start day, they had both just remembered, and they had left no note to say where they were.

When Rachel arrived back at the field, having given Vi Partridge an account of their night's adventures and assured her several times that all was well, and yes they had had a hot drink, and yes they would have time to have a good breakfast before surgery, she was delighted to see the horse up and swaying on its feet.

'Without busting a stitch,' Tom told her, proudly.

Slowly, slowly, with great patience, with many rests and much encouragement, they helped the horse to totter into its temporary hospital, where it sank down gratefully into the straw with a grunting groan of relief that its night's torment was over.

Tom gave its wounds a final inspection, and checked he had noted down all the drugs and vaccines they had used. He had written them in biro on the back of his arm as he normally did when working in such conditions, notebooks not being the most indestructible of items in a wet field. Then he announced the horse could be left to rest, and that he would tell Parker's son as

126

soon as he could be contacted.

'A good hot bath and plenty of breakfast for you two,' he instructed Margaret Sherwood and Sarah Forbes. 'And you'd better let that dog out before he batters your kitchen door down.' From inside the house a frenzied Sago was letting the world know that he was shut in and wished not to be.

At Painters Vi Partridge pounced upon Tom and Rachel as if they were delinquent children, bustling them out of their soaked and bloody clothing and castigating the whole world of animals for the trouble it insisted on causing in the small hours.

Rachel had to admit that it was bliss to be clean and dry, and the smell of breakfast was as welcome as spring water in the Sahara.

At their third cup of tea, Mrs Partridge ushered in a visitor to join them. It was George.

''Eard about last night,' he said. ''Er told me first thing.' He hooked his thumb in the direction of the back door through which Vi Partridge had just disappeared with the rubbish bin.

George sat, obviously expecting to be told the details, so Rachel described their night's adventure while George demolished the rest of the teapot's contents.

When she had told him all, including how they got the horse into the tool shed, George sat silent for a long while, considering.

'What'll you do with it?' he enquired then.

'When?' asked Tom.

'Can't stay in a tool shed, can it?' George commented. 'Bill Parker ain't got no buildings that end of 'is land. Better bring it next door 'ere, 'adn't you? Take care of it then, can't you? That son of 'is ain't no good. Wouldn't look after it proper, that one. It's as much as 'e can do to keep them cattle fed. I'll see to feedin' it. It'll be no bother.' Then, after a pause: 'I can get me expenses off Bill Parker, I daresay. Fetch it in me lorry later, if you like.'

It had to be admitted, it was a very sensible idea, and neither Tom nor Rachel could think of a better one. Rachel strongly suspected that if Bill Parker did not like the account he was eventually presented with, George might offer to take the horse in lieu.

They decided, then, that this was what should happen, and Tom agreed to telephone Margaret Sherwood after surgery to warn her of George's imminent arrival.

This having been decided, George noisily disposed of the last drops of his tea, set the mug down, and politely removed the moisture from his mouth with the back of his hand. Then composed himself as if about to make a speech. When the speech came it was, as always with George, brief and relevant.

'This 'ospital you was wanting,' George said. 'D'you still want it?'

'Well . . .' Tom said, hesitant.

'Yes or no,' snapped George.

'Yes,' Rachel said, firmly.

'All right, then,' said George.

They both looked at him.

'You can stop staring,' he said, 'as if you'd just pulled gold bricks out of a grain bin. If you wants to use me yard for a 'ospital, you can do it. I only needs a box or two at the most. You can 'ave the rest. Seems daft, now I come to think of it, not to do it. Tool shed indeed!' he said, shaking his head in weighty disapproval.

'Oh, George,' exclaimed Rachel. 'That would be marvellous. Thank you.' She felt like kissing him. He gave her another weighty look, as if to crush her enthusiasm. Perhaps kissing George was not the best idea she'd ever had.

'If you think,' said he, 'that I'm turning into a ruddy angel of light just because I says you can 'ave your 'ospital in my yard, you can think again. I'll want rent off you, and I'll want it regular. Business. That's what. Everything businesslike.'

Tom rose to his feet at this juncture. 'Of course,' he said, extending his hand to George with grave courtesy, and with all the solemnity of high finance. 'It's a deal, George.'

When George had left and was out of sight, Rachel and Tom danced about the kitchen with glee. Rachel felt happier than she had done for many weeks and it gladdened Tom to see it. Here was a plan going right for them: something that could develop their work and allow them to increase their skills. Tom hugged to himself the manifold advantages of having at least some of their larger patients more conveniently, comfortably and safely to hand.

'God bless George,' he said, and he took from a shelf beneath the table a pad of paper that he had hidden there, and looked at the swift sketches he had made in secret as the old man had talked, unaware. Tom was pleased. He had caught something of the essence of George Baker: enough to work on, anyway. All that luck, and a bonus too.

'Now all we need is the equipment,' Tom announced.

'A mere trifle,' Rachel giggled. 'Nothing your average million-aire couldn't nip down to the shops and buy. Think nothing of it.'

'You know what?' Tom enquired.

'What?'

'I'm darned glad you're back,' he said.

Chapter Eleven

Rachel too was glad to be back, to get to work again. She felt, without sin of pride, that she was working well; and the skill in her hands was satisfying. It was a pleasant upland plateau after a long pull out of the valley. She had time to examine her own land-scapes, to view her horizons, to wonder (with an explorer's curiosity) what lay beyond them. It was the fat time of year too in the real countryside that lay around her, crops and creatures growing and ripening and a mature sun washing the fields with its own colour. As if to compensate for its earlier misdemeanours, the weather was classic high summer and the harvesting began early, filling fields and lanes with the clatter and sudden surprising sight of huge combines in fiery red or yellow paintwork, gobbling up barley and bottling up traffic in the narrow roadways on their slow progress from one farm to another.

While Rachel was waiting for one of these monsters to manoeuvre a gateway so that she could drive on, she heard another vehicle tooting behind her and began to feel a little irritated, as it was quite obvious she could not get out of the way. Then in her mirror she saw the cheerful face and upraised thumb of Mike Barnsby, the blacksmith. He climbed out of his van and came towards her.

'Hoped I might see you,' he said. 'That pony of young Mandy Partridge's. Have you seen it?'

'No, I haven't,' Rachel said. 'Anything wrong?'

'Laminitis,' said Mike. 'Stood there like a rocking-horse when I saw it this morning. Feet so hot you could fry eggs on. Mind you, it's as fat as a pig so it's no wonder. I've cut the feet well back, of course, but the pony needs treatment.'

'Why on earth hasn't she called me?' asked Rachel. 'Or at least mentioned it to Mrs P?'

Mike grinned. 'I think she knows you don't approve of Janet Andrews,' he said. 'Maybe she thinks you'll say "I told you so" if you see there's something wrong. It wants looking at though, poor little devil. I've told her all the right things, I think, and got her to take it off that field she'd got it on. You could fatten Smithfield bullocks on it.'

'I'll call in,' said Rachel. 'Thanks Mike.'

'Any time,' he replied, and his rattly old van followed Jessica for a mile or so before he took a right hand turn towards the Ashton Stud.

Rachel drove on towards her morning's appointments, but as her road after that would bring her near the place where Mandy kept her pony she decided she would call in, on the off chance someone might be about.

After a morning of recalcitrant cattle, and some hefty Border Leicester sheep that had got into clover and blown themselves up like balloons with gas, Rachel was half inclined to leave the visit until later. However, if the pony was as bad as Mike said it would be in a great deal of pain, and the sooner dealt with, the better.

Rachel knew that the pony was being kept at Holcombe Barns because Mrs Partridge had mentioned it, saying how pleased Mandy had been to find somewhere so near home so that she could visit the pony before and after school. Rachel could see the barns now: a neat Cotswold quadrangle of grey stone and slate set down in a sea of green pasture, the grass blades rippling in the light wind. Ayrshire cattle ambled contentedly in the acres, stuffing themselves milk-rich with the lush stalks.

In the yard that the barns enclosed, a small figure sat hunched upon a staddle-stone as if petrified by enchantment into a personi-fication of gloom. Mandy sat so still as Rachel approached that Rachel wondered if she had moved at all since Mike's earlier visit.

'Hello, Mandy,' she called.

' 'lo,' the muffled voice replied, and a tear-blotched face raised itself reluctantly from the arms upon which it had been pillowed.

'Oh, it's you Mrs Adams,' said Mandy. 'I thought it was Mum come to fetch me home.'

'I've come to see Polo,' Rachel said. 'Mike Barnsby said he was worried about him. Would you like me to take a look?'

Mandy nodded, and led the way to the furthest barn where, in a railed-off corner, stood Polo, fat as a pig, sweating with pain, and shifting his great weight uneasily from one straddled foreleg to another.

Rachel went in and spoke softly to him, running a soothing hand down the hard crest of his neck, feeling the pads of fat on his shoulder, the heat in his forefeet. There was no need to lift and tap them for evidence of pain. He seemed to flinch even at the thought of it.

Mandy had trailed in behind her and stood looking on at the examination of the pony, but asked no questions, as if afraid to hear Rachel's prognosis. Instead she gazed at Polo as if she felt all his agonies in herself.

Rachel knew it would be important to Mandy to know exactly how she intended to improve the pony's condition. The child looked as if she expected to hear the death sentence pronounced at once.

'Don't look so worried,' Rachel began. 'He's very uncomfortable, but you've already started his treatment by bringing him in off the grass and Mr Barnsby's made a good job of his feet.

'Now look, Mandy, do you remember when you dropped a breeze-block on your toe and you got that big blood-blister under the nail?' Rachel asked.

'Yes I do. It didn't half hurt,' Mandy replied.

'Well, imagine how much more it would have hurt if you had had toenail all the way round, with nowhere for the swelling to escape. Poor old Polo's feet are inflamed inside, but his hoof holds all that swelling like a box. That's why laminitis is so very painful. That's why he's standing like this.'

Rachel had meant only to explain, not to criticise, but Mandy's face crumpled into tears. She did not sob or cry aloud, but the water spilled down her face, and welled up and spilled again, so that her misery, though from a different cause, was as evident and acute as the pony's.

'We'll get him right again,' Rachel assured her, hoping the assurance was justified, for Polo's feet showed strong evidence of earlier attacks of laminitis and his fatness was so gross that it could only exacerbate this present attack. The pony was a horse-butcher's dream of bliss, and Rachel could only suppose that Mandy had had to pay, from her hard-won pocket money, more for this now unrideable animal than the market price for meat.

'First, you must keep him stabled. He needs nothing but hay, and little enough of that. This rich lush grass is killing him. Are you allowed to use any of these buildings?'

'I can use this pen when I groom him. They might let me keep him in here.'

'We'll leave him here for now then, and I'll inject him with a painkiller to make him more comfortable. And you must exercise him. Short walks two or three times a day, even if he seems reluctant, and no nibbling at the verges. O.K.? And take him to the stream and stand him in the water for ten minutes twice a day, then bring him home and put hot wet cloths on his feet. Can you do that?'

'Right,' said Mandy, beginning to look a little more cheerful at having something positive to do to help her equine friend. 'There's an electric point in the big barn, and I'll borrow Mum's old electric kettle.'

'It'll mean a lot of work,' Rachel challenged.

'I'll do it,' Mandy said.

'I know you will. Then as he improves' – Mandy's face brightened further at this talk of improvement – 'he must go out onto a bare field where he can move about and exercise himself without being able to eat too much. I'll see what I can do.'

Rachel drove Mandy the short distance home, promising to find as soon as possible a suitable place for Polo.

Mandy lived in a straggle of newish roads of newish small houses that had been built in some of the last fields between Milchester and Street. Street had once been a village in its own right, but Milchester had reached out and drawn it into itself like a larger animalcule ingesting a smaller. Street nevertheless retained some of its own sense of community, and though denuded now of pub, school and village hall – all of which had been converted into expensive dwellings – it did retain its own church, and for the moment at least its own rector, though he would be the last when he retired.

The Milchester living would then be Milchester-with-Street, and the old pattern of services would have to be rearranged to suit the joint parishes.

Rachel knew the rector, Robert Ames, because of his labrador Sam, who suffered every canine ailment that obesity can cause but whose master's efforts to slim him were constantly foiled by the Sunday School children: they fed him sweets and titbits in order to see him beg, which he did with lugubrious and portly charm, balancing himself on the triangle of his fat black haunches and his thick, otterlike tail.

Mandy had been one of Sam's admirers for years, and although she had outgrown Sunday School and given up church in favour of the Riding Centre, she still spoke to the black dog whenever they met, and would smile, however abashed she may have felt about leaving his flock, at the rector himself.

Rachel saw Robert Ames in his garden as she drove through Street with Mandy and an idea suggested itself to her, which she did not propound to Mandy in case it did not work. However, when she had seen Mandy safely home, she reversed Jessica, turned, and drove back to the Rectory.

'Good afternoon, Mr Ames,' she called out, and the hunched form under the rose-bush straightened, peered, registered a known face, and returned the greeting.

They exchanged the usual pleasantries, the set dance-patterns that begin a rural conversation, until Rachel felt she could come to her horses – or at least, to the subject of Mandy's pony. Robert

Ames listened, nodded, and said he could see no difficulty at all about accommodating the pony. 'Of course she may use my little glebe field if she likes,' he said. 'It's had sheep on it all year and it's as close-cropped as a billiard table. That's why I asked for the sheep to be taken away. They'd got tired of it and kept hopping over the wall for better pickings. I would have offered it to her myself, but I had assumed that there was not enough keep there for a pony.'

'It sounds just right, if you wouldn't mind,' Rachel said. 'May I walk across with you and have a look?'

As they went, Rachel explained in more detail the problem that Mandy had encountered and the necessity of reducing the pony's weight if he was to be cured.

'Sounds like Sam all over again,' said the rector.

'Worse than Sam,' Rachel said. 'Being fat's bad for Sam, but it doesn't give him excruciating pain. You should try to get his weight down too though, Mr Ames. It's a strain on his heart, and you'll lose a good friend before you have to.'

'I know. I know. I wish I'd never taught the old fraud to beg. He always makes himself look so *hungry*. Honestly, the moment he gets some treat or other you could swear he was *thin*. He's a real con-man is Sam.'

They had reached the glebe now, a little bare field of about an acre which lay between the churchyard and the Rectory. The grass that grew on it had been nibbled down so hard that the brown earth below showed through.

'That'll diet him,' said Rachel, delightedly, when she saw it.

'Well then, perhaps you'd tell young Mandy she can bring her fat friend whenever she likes,' said Robert Ames. 'The fences are sound and the wall at the bottom there, where the sheep kept hopping over, would keep in a plump pony quite easily. She can padlock the gate if she likes, but I never bother.'

'I'll tell her. I know she'll be grateful.' Rachel glanced once more about the field, saw that none of the churchyard yews were within reach of an enquiring equine neck, and that the water trough by the gate was clean and full. It couldn't be better.

'Good afternoon, Rector.' High voices warbled from the church yard and there were two little old women tottering along the path from the vestry door, clutching bunches of wilting flowers.

'Good afternoon Miss Abby, Miss Daphne. Is it really your turn for church flowers again? It seems only a moment . . .'

'It's Mrs Williams, Vicar. She can't take her turn this week.' The smaller of the little old women came to the fence and murmured confidentially in Robert Ames's ear, but Rachel heard the word 'operation' spoken in holy dread. 'Of course, of course,' the rector replied, and Rachel could almost see the message racing to his brain: 'Remember visit Mrs Williams, hospital.'

The two women disposed of the wilted flowers on the compost heap in the corner and went on towards the lych gate and out onto the road.

'Can you spare a moment?' Robert Ames asked, and when Rachel smiled assent he led her out of the field and down the path to the church. She had one moment's horrified embarrassment that he might be about to lead her in a prayer of thanks for the use of his field. Rachel's convictions were clear, but her observances infrequent, for organised religion had never channelled her life into its regular courses.

However, all he did was to lead her along the centre aisle to the chancel steps, at which he made a genuflection in which he quite obviously did not expect her to join, then said: 'Just look.'

The whole chancel glowed with flowers. Every seasonal bloom and branch that a Cotswold garden could grow filled vase after vase and spilled their glorious colours against the rough stone of the chancel walls. They were not 'arranged' in the Constance Spry sense, but displayed with exuberance and enthusiasm that was akin to something in Tom's paintings. Rachel thought: as if it were done to some greater glory, which Tom had never named, but which the two old dears now trundling home to tea and toast had probably never doubted since their nursery days.

'Dear Miss Abby. Dear Miss Daphne,' murmured the rector. 'They strip their garden bare to beautify our little church.'

Rachel saw them again in her mind's eye: Miss Abby, her already small frame made smaller by the stoop of her shoulders which strained the fabric of her good grey coat, moving on thin wool-stockinged legs that strove to balance her curved spine and out-thrust head. She had been given a stick but scorned to use it, thinking that it made her look 'like an old woman'.

Miss Daphne, though her twin, had always been the taller, and having remained upright was now very much more so. However arthritis in her knees had made her progress equally unsteady, and the two tended to hold each other for support as they walked about the town. They kept no animals, so Rachel never saw them in the line of duty but had met them in Milchester, and at the district charitable functions one could always be sure of their presence. She recalled seeing them in the Stratton-Davies' garden on the day of the R.S.P.C.A. coffee morning, bringing stuff from their own garden for the produce stall.

'I have attended many debates on this vexed question of women in the ministry,' Robert Ames was saying. 'And all the old die-hards say no, yet again, and I sit and say little, and chuckle to myself.'

He chuckled now, recalling these occasions. 'You know, Mrs Adams,' he said, 'if all these unpaid and dedicated female servants of the church were to go on strike one day and withhold their labour, the Church of England would sink without trace. Not Christianity, of course; nothing can overwhelm that. Yet the bishops sit in their high places and let women like Miss Abby and Miss Daphne wash their feet. And which would Christ think the greater ministry? Tell me that Mrs Adams.'

It was a rhetorical question, but Rachel was struck by the fervour with which it was asked. 'Forgive me,' he said. 'It's an old hobby horse and I ride it too frequently. Thank you for listening, anyway. I have a great admiration for you, you know. Nothing anyone does in a rural area like this goes unnoticed, and I hear many good things of you.'

Now she was embarrassed; flushed like a schoolgirl abashed by praise, but he did not notice: he was already turning to leave the church, making his way into the sunshine again, assuming she was following. The light struck bright and warm after the coolness of the church. The graves stood proclaiming four centuries of memory, some recent and still painful, some forgotten long since, some remembered only by a continued name. Partridges lay there, and a Clissold or two, and some Holders, and a family of Shepherds. Miss Abby and Miss Daphne were Shepherds too and the plot under the tall cypress awaited their last sleep.

Chapter Twelve

✣

The picture that had haunted Rachel so long, of her last glimpse of Mrs Kyle looking like a dead bird in the fireman's arms, was at last beginning to fade. She could speak of her old friend now, think of her as she was, talk of her quirks and her wicked sense of humour and her high amazing courage, reminisce about her, with the inconsolable Mrs Teape whose other old ladies and gentlemen never gave her half the fun – though she would never have let them know it.

Rachel met Mrs Teape one morning outside the Black Cat, a tea and coffee shop which acted as an unofficial social centre for a great many of Milchester's elderly. It boasted no juke-box or piped music, it did not expect you to 'serve yourself' but sent you a nice waitress in a black dress and frilly apron who knew exactly which of today's cream cakes you were most likely to fancy, and remembered to ask not only 'black or white?' but 'strong or weak?' as well. It was worth the extra 5p slipped under the saucer as a 'thank you' to be assured that the good old days had not entirely faded.

Rachel remembered the place with affection from the time Tom had taken her there when distressed and distraught by one of her first encounters with the unpleasanter side of veterinary work: he had sat her down at a corner table and consoled her with tea and buns. So when she met Mrs Teape in the doorway and was invited in for elevenses, she accepted, and sniffed the homely, coffee-scented, chintzy atmosphere with pleasure.

'I've seen that Mrs Sherwood of yours,' Mrs Teape announced, as they sat before the gleaming crockery on its spotless cloth, awaiting the ministrations of one of the waitresses. Their particular table was served by Norah, whose badge on her plump bosom announced this fact just in case you were not already acquainted with her.

'They sent me because of her hips,' Mrs Teape continued. Rachel considered this mysterious remark for a moment, and in a moment interpreted it. 'They', where Mrs Teape was concerned, meant the Social Services, so it might be assumed that whatever was wrong with Mrs Sherwood's hips had given the Social Services cause to think she needed a home help. Rachel, recalling her visit, did seem to remember a certain stiffness in Margaret Sherwood's walk. It also occurred to Rachel to wonder what discomfort she must have suffered the night she had sat so uncomplainingly with the injured horse – which had gone back now, to George's disappointment, to its owner, whose ears George had bent considerably on the subject of barbed wire fences.

The coffee came, and as she began to sip at hers Rachel smiled, remembering the conversation between Mrs Kyle, Mrs Teape and herself on the subject of Margaret Sherwood. It all seemed so long ago now, yet it was in reality only a handful of months.

Rachel had put Margaret Sherwood to Mrs Kyle as a supposition, interested to know how someone so totally unsentimental would react to the whole business of Margaret Sherwood and her dog.

Supposing, Rachel had suggested, that someone had done such a thing and reacted in such a way. Was it ridiculous? A storm in a teacup? Totally eccentric? Or was the greater motive that underlay the apparently trivial evident to someone with wit enough to see it?

While they were discussing this Mrs Teape had kept popping in and out between the sitting room, which she was tidying, and the kitchen, where the churning of the washing machine was in competition with the radio, from which came the sound of raucous music interspersed with the voice of a D.J. whose intonation rose and fell with ersatz enthusiasm that strangled *bonhomie*, without which such men seem unable to ply their

trade. He had been extolling the virtues of a particularly
unmelodious tune that had been thumping out a doh-soh bass,
audible even when the washing machine thundered out its final
spin, and Mrs Teape came into the sitting room still gyrating to her
own hummed version of this. She continued to do so as she
straightened chairs and plumped up cushions.

'Oh do shut up, Teapot,' Mrs Kyle requested cheerfully. 'We're
talking.'

'I heard you,' said Mrs Teape. 'Person who'd behave like that
must be daft as a brush.' It was a pretty brisk conclusion, Rachel
felt, from someone who could scarcely have heard more than half
the discussion.

The radio was now occupying itself with news headlines. In
exactly the same happy-campers voice the announcer was quoting
from Amnesty International a list of tortures known to have been
inflicted on political prisoners during the past year. It was a
collection of horrifying and sickening inhumanities: pain
deliberately devised and excruciatingly applied by one human
being to another.

'Well,' Mrs Teape had announced, 'what's some silly woman
beating a dog, compared with all that?'

Rachel had felt inclined to agree, her head still full of those
descriptions of atrocity, but Mrs Kyle had blazed up into anger and
shouted: 'Can't you see, you stupid, stupid Teapot? Any cruelty
makes up the sum of cruelty, so it all matters: every grain of it.
That's the point Rachel's trying to make.'

Mrs Teape continued to dust, vigorously, seeming quite unof-
fended and unabashed by this sudden flash of fire.

'Seems to me none of it matters much,' she said. 'Can't see any
point in it, myself, getting all worked up about the awful things
people do when here we are stuck on a planet where you can get
squashed flat by earthquakes, fried alive by volcanoes, swallowed
up by crocodiles. It can happen to any of us, good bad or
indifferent. There's nothing to say these things can't happen to the
virtuous.'

'But not in Milchester, my dear,' said Mrs Kyle, with deceptive mildness. 'And anyway,' she added with a cackle, 'any crocodile that tried to swallow me in this' – patting the arm rest of her wheelchair – 'would get his come-uppance, I think.'

They all laughed then, and the tension that had crept in between them was eased.

Rachel had to admit that Mrs Teape had a point, however. There was in the natural world a heartlessness, underlying its undeniable and infinitely variable beauty: its only care for its own continuance; no room for compassion.

Perhaps then, that was man's unrecognised role. Because of that strange dichotomy that exists as evidently in human nature as in the two snug halves of a broad bean seed, humanity – which inflicts the most deliberate, the most savage hurt on itself and on the rest of creation – is, obversely, capable of the wisest and most sustained compassion, even in the face of totally indiscriminate forces.

Perhaps that's the best job we can do then, Rachel considered: to throw into the balance against nature's severe practicality of cause and effect a positive and constructive compassion. She felt quite pleased with this theory, and propounded it to Mrs Kyle. Mrs Kyle considered it, snorted, and said, 'Not making much of a job of it, are we?'

'Strong enough for you dear?' Norah's round face hung like a smiling moon above the coffeepot and milk jug from which she had swirled into Rachel's cup a second helping of brown, delicious liquid.

'Sorry,' said Rachel. 'I was far away. Yes, that's fine.'

'I thought it might be Mrs Sherwood, her you were talking about that day,' Mrs Teape was saying, as if she had read Rachel's thoughts. 'When I saw her with that dog I knew it. Then she told me all about the day you went to see her. When you meet her, when she explains things, you can't help but think she's right.'

Rachel nodded. It was entirely true. The things that people do must always be seen in the context of the sort of people they are, if there is to be understanding.

144

'Are you going to work there, then?' Rachel asked.

'Start Monday,' said Mrs Teape.

The day gathered momentum after that. Rachel arrived home a little later than she should have done to hear the telephone shrilling and the voice of Vi Partridge telling it to 'wait a minute for 'eavensake, I'm coming as quick as I can.' The instrument had been red-hot, it seemed, ever since Rachel had left the house. She felt guilt extinguish the small pleasures of her coffee with Mrs Teape. She sighed.

'No good you looking like that,' Mrs Partridge said, fiercely. 'You've got to have some time of your own. It's about time they realised that. Anyone'd think you'd been off to the South of France with a soldier for a fortnight, instead of slipped into Milchester to the shops. There's no-one on this list'll die for want of you for half an hour.'

Mrs Partridge showed her the calls that Tom had already taken on his itinerary, and left her with one mastitis, a constipated donkey, and some billy goat kids to be castrated. Most owners did their own with rubber rings and an elastrator, but these belonged to a woman who was new to breeding goats and did not feel competent for this particular job.

Rachel spent some time at this last call. The woman was new to their list and proud of her newly acquired animals, wanting to talk about them. She had two nice Anglo-Nubian females in milk, one of whom had produced nanny twins and the other, billies. When Rachel had finished altering their status they seemed totally unworried, prancing and playing as delightfully as before. Unlike most of their kind they were not destined for the freezer. They were to go to the Pets' Corner at a nearby Wildlife Park. Watching their pretty antics, Rachel was glad for them.

It had not been a hard day in comparison with some, yet she felt pleasantly weary as she turned towards home at the end of it into the long golden light of late afternoon, with the turning year colouring the undulating landscape through which she travelled.

She moved towards home like any tired creature towards a known haven. It was strange, she thought, that animals – who have in the main so little sense of past or future but live as small children do, for the instant – still have this strong pull towards home, towards the known, safe place.

She thought of old Toffer, the harmless eccentric who lived in Blackstock Wood, to whom death was this safe haven to which he travelled, and which held no terror for him.

She savoured the pleasure of her own homecoming now, and when Tom met her at the door she moved into his arms and held him.

'I love you,' she said.

He looked down at her.

'Of course you do,' he said grinning. 'I'm a lovable chap.' But she saw behind the grin, behind the reflection of herself in his eyes, and heard things that needed no saying, and knew she was home.

That night they both woke towards dawn and made love; and afterwards, when they were close and quiet as the two halves of an oyster shell, Rachel lay listening to Tom's quiet breathing. She thought of herself as she once had been: a child paddling about in the foam at the water's edge, watching the sea from the known enchantments of the beach, not quite afraid, not quite unafraid. Curious, making tentative forays into the shallows, but not at all convinced that here was something to be enjoyed.

And now? Now she rode the deep-water waves like a dolphin, as if it were her proper element. She made a picture in her mind of the two of them, and she laughed. That was one of the many delights: that love, which she had imagined was going to be such a serious business, was so amazingly funny. She chuckled again at the image she had made of herself and Tom, this sea-simile, the two of them sporting like dolphins. Yet what creatures were saner, more beautiful, more intelligent?

'Will you stop laughing, woman,' Tom said, stirring out of sleep and feeling the vibrations of her amusement right through his own body. 'Don't wear the old man out. He's got to last you a lifetime, remember?'

'Oh, I'll be serious then,' she said, but he read her face with his

146

fingers and felt the upward curve of her mouth.

'Are you happy, now?' he asked. 'Not just this minute, I mean, but happy?'

'Yes, I am.'

He hesitated, and she knew for a certainty what he was about to ask and that he was doubtful of asking it, but she could only wait.

'Would you like to try again?' he asked, at last. 'Would you make a father of me? I think I'd be not too bad at it.'

She raised herself on her elbows and looked down at his face, just visible in the pale light for the day was just beginning. Her dolphin image faded now and another took its place. It pleased her, this picture in her mind, and she smiled again.

'What are you thinking?' he asked.

'I'm thinking that you're right,' she said. 'And I'm thinking that you look like Noah, with that great beard of yours.'

Then she tucked her chin into the angle of his neck against the hairs of his beard, breathing in the warmth and the smell, and the loved presence of him.

'I was also just considering,' she said, 'that I might go down to the timber yard in the morning and order a few hundred cubits of gopher wood.'

'What on earth for, you madwoman?'

'To build us an Ark, of course.'

'Of course,' he said. 'What else. I should have known.'

Chapter Thirteen

✒✒✒

Watched by George between the seaweed curtains of his flat, Tom and Rachel walked about the next-door yard, half dreaming, half planning their hospital for larger animals. It was probable that most of their patients there would be equines. It was rare for cattle to be thought worth the expense of long-term treatment or complicated surgery: better to slaughter, claim compensation, and start again.

These plans, these dreams, pleased Rachel inordinately. She hugged them to her, reassured by the thought that if they all came to fruition then much of the work she most loved would be here, to hand. If she did have children she would not be tied by her lessened mobility to the small-animal work of the surgery. Heck, that sounded selfish. Was selfish? Perhaps. But she did not want to change too much in order to be a mother: wanted to remain herself, the woman Tom loved, the woman who knew her job. But perhaps biology would take over and make her cosy and cowlike, quite content with maternal domesticity.

'Good Lord,' groaned Tom when she spoke of it. 'Would *you* want a mother like that?'

She shook her head.

'You may get fat as a barrel and end up being the envy of the Milk Marketing Board, but it won't addle your mind and wipe your brain clean. If you think I'm going to let you vanish into the nursery for years you can think again. You're too good a vet to be wasted. I need you. And anyway, we'll both have to work like beavers if we're to make this hospital idea work. It's going to take money.

'I got the Bank to cost it all out for me. To do the job properly and have all the right equipment will take a frightening amount of cash. With luck I shall sell some paintings from that exhibition in Cheltenham, but even with the best possible luck that won't be enough. I hope we can do it, Rachel.'

'We'll do it,' she said.

The population of Milchester had for some weeks been doing its annual turnabout. Families were off on holiday, except for the farming community who would have to wait till after harvest. Many small shops were closed for a week or so while their owners took a break from commerce, and the publican at the local was away in Tenerife for a fortnight, leaving his father-in-law in charge. This meant a less elastic drinking-up time and a good deal of grumbling behind the tankards. Yet in spite of the departure of so many of its inhabitants the streets of Milchester were more crowded than usual: the shopping centre packed, and at every corner the flow of passers-by was held up by knots of people talking or looking about them, or consulting maps and guide-books – for the town was overflowing with tourists and foreign visitors of every colour and tongue. French and German conversations, voluble bursts of Spanish and Italian, even the high sing-song of Japanese could be heard in the streets and shops of Milchester. Cameras clicked and flashed, recording the quiet, understated loveliness of the little town and the delightful, small-scale landscape in which it stood. American voices exclaimed at the cuteness of the cottage gardens. Australia declared it had farms a hundred times the size of Gloucestershire.

French and German children on exchange holidays met up in the town's cafés to talk and take a break from the agonies of trying to understand and to speak a language so illogical and uninflected and often so incomprehensible.

One or two came to the surgery with their host families and Rachel tried to encourage conversation, helping out where she could with the stilted French and formal German she had learned at school and half forgotten. One small thin boy, Laurent, came several times with Mrs Bird from the shop in Ilcombe, whose cat had swallowed a large chunk of cod's backbone. Laurent watched intently, intelligently, at each stage of the cat's treatment and asked Rachel in slow, careful English about all the aspects of her job, about her own life as a child, about her travels, which were lamentably few. He was very interested in her stories about the Parkwood cattle, the Jersey herd that had been her father's pride and that her mother now bred and showed with skill and success.

'You must visit France, to my region,' Laurent said. 'You should see my father who lifts cattle.' Rachel regarded the slight, slender boy: tried to envisage a father of such strength. And for what purpose? A circus act perhaps? She smiled, polite but puzzled.

'Yes, as your father did, and as your mother too. He lifts cattle. The Charolais.'

Light dawned. 'I think you mean *raises* cattle,' Rachel smiled. She explained.

'That was a good English joke?' he asked.

'Very good.'

'I shall tell my teacher I made good English joke.'

But when he came again for the cat's final treatment, he was not smiling.

'I don't know what's wrong with him, Mrs Adams,' Mrs Bird announced, hiding her meaning from him by the rapidity of her chatter. 'Ever since he saw his friend Paul yesterday he's looked that worried, and I can't get him to say what's wrong except he wants to speak to you. He's been so bright and happy till now, and look at him. Looks as if the world's sat on his head, doesn't he?'

'Can you wait about ten minutes while I finish surgery?' Rachel asked. 'Then I can have a quiet word with him.'

Mrs Bird nodded, and took Laurent back to the waiting room. Rachel felt she had never seen a child look so agitated. She finished as quickly as she could and then went to recall him.

'*Madame*.' He sat looking very pale on the chair next to the surgery table. '*Madame*, what should I do?' Rachel could see he was almost in tears.

'Tell me,' she said, and in slow, halting English, with occasional recourse to French, he told her that he had been to visit his best friend Paul who was staying with a family at Nether Leybourne, in a house called Ladywell House, and the family was Margaret and Edward Parsons and their children Michael and Amanda. Rachel tried to recall if she had met them, and realised that she had not. She had seen the house, though: a huge, rambling place.

'He has this dog, *madame*. This little dog, Minou. She is very very small. The smallest.' He made measurements with his hands. There was a breed-chart on the wall. Encouraged by Rachel, he indicated that the dog was a Chihuahua.

'The family have given him the dog?'

'No, *madame*, no. It is his dog. His own. From France!'

Rachel froze, like a creature scenting appalling danger in a seemingly smiling landscape. She understood now the child's weight of anxiety. She felt the cold lead of it in her own bones.

'How on earth?'

'*Quoi?*'

'How did he bring the dog?'

'In a box. It looks like . . . like a thing for clothes.'

'A suitcase?'

'*Oui madame*. A suitcase. There are holes for air. Paul's father is a chemist. He took from his father medicine to make the dog sleep. He was afraid to be alone away from home. And also his father does not like the dog. So he brought Minou in the suitcase. He knew it would be a big house. Michael told him when he visited Paul's home. And also he saw a photograph. He thought he could keep her hidden, get food for her. He showed me yesterday. He showed me only because we are best friends.'

Rachel was trying desperately to hide the horror she was feeling at these revelations. Hiding the panic that was growing in her she spoke to him with all the control she could muster.

'This is very serious, Laurent. Does he know that?'

'He said to me it was all right. That the dog was only in his room, and only with him.'

'It's still against the law. There's still the risk . . .'

'*La rage*, I know *madame*. But there is more. She has bite me a little. Not much. Here on my finger.'

On Laurent's index finger was a faint pink toothmark. The skin was just broken. There was a corresponding mark under the finger where the jaw had closed.

'She was frightened, I think, and she bite me.'

'Did she seem well, Laurent? Apart from being frightened.'

'Yes, *madame*.'

'And you feel well yourself?'

'Yes, *madame*.'

'Do you know if Paul's dog had been vaccinated against rabies – against *la rage*?'

'I think not *madame*. Paul had to buy for the dog everything she needed. His father would not.'

It took Laurent some time to find all these words, and while he searched for them Rachel's mind was racing, ordering a course of action that she had gone through time and time against the dreaded encroachment of rabies: the emergency drill one hoped never to use.

'You should have told someone at once,' she said, sharply. She was acutely aware how she had kept the child waiting. If only he'd said. She could imagine, though, all the turmoils of his mind; in a strange country with a language only half understood, having to explain a predicament so extraordinary, and so certain to bring down trouble upon his friend's head. Childhood's honour, not to tell tales, could not be broken unadvisedly, lightly or wantonly. There was fear, too, to lend confusion and dismay to this appalling situation: the possibility, however unlikely and remote, of '*la rage*', painful in prevention, horrifying and fatal if not prevented. If the dog were infected, if it had had contact with any other mammal, domestic or wild, had licked the least scratch or abrasion . . . if Laurent himself were infected, and had scratched, in play, some member of his host family . . . The chances were unlikely, the chances were remote; but they were possible, and it was that possibility of the unleashing of so appalling a disease that made Rachel's voice and legs begin to shake.

What to do first? She must inform the police and the Divisional Veterinary Officer, and get the boy to hospital. The boy first then. Rachel telephoned the hospital casualty department. When she had explained the problem she could almost hear them shift into overdrive.

'Send him at once. Can someone bring him in a car?' Rachel glanced out of the window. Mrs Bird's Alfred, a sensible man, was waiting in the car park.

'Yes, that'll be O.K.'

'I'm sending you to the hospital, Laurent,' she told him. 'They may want you to have treatment. Do you understand?'

Laurent nodded. He understood only too well.

'It will hurt?'

'Yes, a bit I'm afraid.' She wasn't going to lie to him.

He straightened himself up, bravely.

'They will be angry with Paul?'

'I don't know, Laurent. I hope not, but he has to be told how serious this is.' Rachel was remembering a case not all that long ago, where a ship's captain at Sheerness Docks was fined several hundred pounds for allowing a rat to escape from his ship onto the dockside. How would the authorities react to a child who had deliberately broken this strict regulation – stupidly, understandably, but still, in law, criminally?

'He will be angry with *me*,' said Laurent, in deepening misery.

Mrs Bird, alarmed and anxious, went trotting off with Laurent held firmly in one hand and Rachel's explanatory note to the hospital in the other. Rachel made her other two telephone calls, and then a further one to the house at Nether Laybourne. Maybe she should have left it to the police, but she wanted to get a word in for Laurent with Paul before official wrath broke over Paul's head.

She had scarcely put the telephone down on the fluttering anxiety of the Parsons' household, when Tom came into the surgery.

'Wow,' he said, when she told him what had happened. 'This won't do much for Anglo-French relations.'

'Could we go to Nether Leybourne? I'd like to talk to the boy,' said Rachel.

'I suppose we could. As long as we don't get in the D.V.O.'s way. On the other hand, someone ought to be here in case anyone needs more information from you. Give me every detail you can, and then leave me as telephone watcher. Go and see the boy if you like.'

'Thanks Tom.'

'And don't go near the dog. Leave that to the D.V.O. Promise?'

'Promise.'

When Rachel arrived at the house, however, a police-van was just driving away, with flashing light and bleeping siren. On the steps of the house stood the D.V.O., Miles Preston, and a tall man with his hand on the shoulder of a drooping, weeping child of about eleven or twelve. As Rachel climbed out of Jessica she could hear the sobs – great roaring gasps of air, an animal noise, hot and tearless.

Rachel introduced herself to Mr Parsons and explained briefly how she had become involved with the incident. Mr Parsons looked anxious and bewildered. He was holding on to Paul as if he were not quite sure what to do with him. At least he did not seem angry with the child, and that was a relief to Rachel. The boy was going to have enough to contend with without the wrath of his hosts. Not that Rachel would have blamed the Parsons for being angry. Paul had involved them in a real mess, and in the chance – however small – of danger to themselves. So that Mr Parsons could at least take heart that the danger had been prevented, she said:

'Laurent would never have told me if the dog had not bitten him.' At this, the anger that had been thus far avoided fell out of the sky from a different source. A wave of furious French, naming Laurent in every breath, flowed from Paul, and he shook and sobbed the more.

Mr Parsons continued to hold him, much as a brave man might continue to hold some explosive device that is building up to a

155

final eruption. The D.V.O. looked totally embarrassed. He looked at Rachel. 'Perhaps you can get through to the boy,' he suggested. 'I've had to have the dog impounded, of course, and I have tried to explain to the boy that he has committed a serious offence, but he is so agitated about the dog I don't think he has taken it in.'

Rachel turned to Mr Parsons and asked him to take the boy indoors.

'I'll have a word with my colleague, and then I'll come and speak to Paul,' she said.

Mr Parsons took the boy indoors, but all the while Paul's head was turned and he gazed towards the gateway through which his dog had been driven away.

'What will happen to the dog?' Rachel asked.

'Normally it would be sent straight back to France,' Preston said. 'It's not had any contact with other animals. It's spent its whole time in the boy's room, except that he took it into the garden at night, on a piece of string.'

'No contact with wildlife?'

'He swears not. But now the other child's been bitten it's a whole new ball game, I'm afraid. The dog will have to be quarantined. The parents will have to defray expenses, of course.'

'But the father hates the dog. That was one of the major reasons the boy smuggled it here.'

'There's only one answer then, isn't there. Destroy the dog. Test for rabies. Then with luck we can clear the boy Laurent and he'll need no further treatment.'

'Should we 'phone the father?'

'We'll need to do that anyway. Speak to the boy. Get the message through to him if you can that this is serious. I'm sorry for the kid if his dog has to be destroyed, but nothing like as sorry as hundreds of people would be if we had a rabies outbreak. I've a copy of the Rabies Contingency Plan ready to hand in my desk. Maybe I'll have it translated into French and let the boy read it. He has no real understanding of what he might have unleashed.'

Preston sounded angry: was angry. Rachel entirely understood his anger and knew it to be justified; but Paul was only a kid, and the immediate threat to his dog was bound to mean more to him than the remote possibilities they had told him of. Even the prospect of his father's wrath could not overshadow the importance, to him, of this one small dog.

Rachel went in, and directed by Mr Parsons found Paul's room, where he sat, silent now, as if all his fearful anger had been wrung out of him. She did her best, within the limits of her feeble French and thwarted by his determination not to understand her in English, to explain what he had done that was so serious, and why it had been impossible for Laurent to keep the secret, not to 'split on him'. What was the French equivalent to that?

Perhaps something of what she wished to say got through, but one thing was certain. The friendship that had existed between Paul and Laurent was damaged beyond repair. They might, in time, become friends again, but this would always set them at a distance. It could never be the same friendship.

'Would you like me to telephone your father?' Rachel asked, making dialling motions with her finger.

'*Pourquoi?*' He knew quite well why. The question was only to put off, for a few more blessed seconds, the moment of her 'phoning.

'He will need to know about this. There will be expenses.' She did not add that there might be a whacking great fine. Enough was enough.

The boy nodded his head, but reluctantly and slowly, as if it were a great weight.

All kinds of foolish hopes flitted through Rachel's mind as she went to ask to use the telephone, bright, butterfly hopes – like the father turning out to be nothing like the unreasonable creature Paul obviously believed him to be, like a petition going round Milchester to pay the little dog's quarantine expenses, or some rich relation of Paul's in France coming forward to help.

Short-lived as butterflies, the hopes crumbled and died in the fury of the voice that crackled and fizzed down the line from France. God help the lad when he got back home. Rachel learned from the voice that the dog had been given to Paul by his mother. Paul's mother had then upped and left to live with another man. This information Paul's father gave to Rachel as bald fact. He did not say, 'That's why I hate the dog,' but it was obvious.

He did not say 'Paul would rather be with his mother than with me,' but that was obvious, too. She wanted to say to him, as he seemed to understand her words without difficulty, that you can't make people love you by getting angry with them: you can't divert love to yourself by destroying all other objects of love. She could not. Now was not the time. All she could hope for now was that he might, just might, change his mind and be helpful about repatriating the dog.

She did her utmost, but she knew within moments that she was not going to win. He blamed the sheer expense, and justifiably, for it would cost him a great deal of money even if there were no fine involved; but Rachel knew that, were he as rich as Croesus, he would not lift a finger to have the dog returned.

Paul needed no telling. He had known there was no hope. He sat dejected and unresponsive to Rachel's offered comfort. She offered to telephone his mother. He looked at her as if the suggestion were ridiculous.

Rachel had not tried further to make the boy realise how wrong his actions had been as Miles Preston had requested her to do. She could see no point. Instead she left him, still bitterly grieving for his dog for whom there could now be no reprieve.

When she spoke later to the D.V.O. it became clear to Rachel how fortuitous had been the small dog's entry into England. A bomb scare had caused the party of children to be pushed swiftly through customs and the vigilance of the staff had been diverted; otherwise it was almost certain that the dog would have been discovered, or that Paul might have seen and read the Rabies Prevention notices and realised the extent of his foolishness in bringing Minou with him.

If nothing else the incident would heighten watchfulness, tighten up security. That was as well, for probably even now some idiot was planning to smuggle in Rex or Fifi or Tiger or Tiddles, to keep them out of quarantine kennels. There was always someone stupid enough.

The extraordinary incidents of the day, the adrenalin-draining swiftness of action required from both Rachel and Tom, brought them home exhausted, to find David Stratton from the other veterinary practice in Milchester where Tom had been a partner before he married Rachel, busily doing evening surgery for them.

David was a good friend of Tom's, and an expert on small animals. He was also a very handsome man.

'I knew you'd be late back,' Vi Partridge told them. 'So I rang Mr Stratton and asked 'im to come, 'oping you wouldn't mind, knowing what a day you'd 'ave 'ad.'

'That's fine,' said Tom. 'He'll give the girls a treat, and we can take our time. Any tea in that pot?'

The pleasure of sitting down, feet stretched under the table, relaxing, was something to savour.

'Imagine how much the idle rich must spend to titillate their jaded fancies,' Tom said. 'And never know the sheer pleasure of sitting still after one heck of a day.'

'Not for long though,' Rachel said.

Tom groaned. 'Surely to heaven, nobody's rung for us?'

'No, but David, Peter and Alan are coming to supper. Had you forgotten? Peter's off on Thursday. We asked them to come, and Melanie, and that young woman of Peter's. Oh Lord, I've forgotten her name. I'm so tired I'm not sure I can remember my own.'

'It's Samantha. Not yours, thank God. Peter's young woman. Can you imagine a Samantha among the desert sands?'

Rachel was aware that Tom was playing the fool, hamming up his antipathy to Samantha to take her mind off the day's events. She must try to rise to him, to enjoy the evening and be sociable, and put out of her mind all the extraordinary happenings of the day and thoughts of young Paul packing miserably for his return to France. The Parsons would have let him stay, but his father was adamant. Already the D.V.O. would have put the needle into the little dog. The brain would be sent for testing for the presence of rabies, and within a week or so the results would be known.

Nothing now could change any of that, and at least if the dog were clear there would be no more painful injections for poor Laurent.

Rachel found a smile for Tom and said she thought Samantha would look rather fine on a camel. Imagination created a splendid picture of Peter's young woman on such an unlikely beast.

Peter Wilmott was off to some exotic Arab Emirate: a plum job among the horses of a stud belonging to a little tubby man whose oil-riches were uncountable. He was worth a good many times his considerable weight in gold, and looked, from his photograph, like an extra from a film of 'The Red Shadow'.

Peter and Samantha were to be married quietly at the Registry Office, and would then fly out to the kind of life Rachel could scarcely imagine. She knew so little of the world, except by report and hearsay. She knew they existed, the far continents, the countries on the other side of the sphere, but they had no reality for her, and she felt no passionate desire to visit them. She glanced at Tom and wondered if he did.

'What a dull, insular and thoroughly unadventurous person I am,' she announced.

'Are you?' replied Tom. 'I hadn't noticed.'

Rachel went back to drinking her tea and did not expand on her remark, though Tom looked quizzically at her. Still, she continued to wonder if he was as content with life in Milchester as she was.

'Do you think he'll put Samantha in purdah?' Tom said, grinning, and Mrs Partridge slapped his wrist with a French loaf and tutted at him.

'She's a very pleasant young woman, that Miss Arkwright. She suits Mr Wilmott very nicely. Don't you go upsetting 'er when she comes to supper tonight.'

'All right,' said Tom. 'I wouldn't want to put her off your steak-and-kidney.'

'It's steaming away nicely,' Vi Partridge said. 'And I've done a fruit mousse, so all you've got to do is the veg., Mrs Adams. The water's 'ot. I should 'ave your bath now if I was you.'

Tom ambled off, singing a tuneless song to words that appeared to be 'I called for Samantha but she didn't antha.'

Mrs Partridge snorted, 'That man!' and clattered about setting saucepans ready for the vegetables.

'You'll manage then, will you?' she asked Rachel.

'Yes, thanks Mrs P.'

'You're all right, are you? You look tired. And you've been fretting yourself about that boy. It don't do no good you know.'

'I'm all right. Really. You go home now, and thanks.'

Rachel could hear, as she lifted one leaden leg after another up the stairs, the sound of Tom singing and splashing in the bath. The song had changed to a rousing Revival Chorus 'Come and join us!' She went into the bathroom and threw a sponge at him.

Melanie came out to the kitchen to help wash up. Samantha stayed with the men, her chair drawn up close alongside Peter's, her attention rivetted to every word he spoke. Rachel, despite her feeling that Tom's reaction to Samantha was somewhat unfair, could see the reason for it. Samantha was terribly well bred, like a racehorse, with a fine-boned thoroughbred face, long elegant legs, and a general air of careful, no-expense-spared nurture. Her pricey education had clothed rather than informed her, yet Peter thought her intelligence razor-sharp because she listened to him with rapt attention and absolute agreement, whatever the subject – though it was usually about veterinary work: Peter was a totally dedicated man.

'You've had quite a day, haven't you?' Melanie was saying as she stacked away dishes. 'I think David envied you all the excitement in a way, though of course it was rotten about that poor French kid. I don't suppose he realised . . . Anyway, you're a marvel to have given us a good meal on top of it all.'

'Ninety per cent Mrs Partridge,' Rachel laughed. 'Besides, we couldn't let the young lovers depart for darkest Arabia without some sort of celebration.'

Melanie grinned. 'Rather them than me,' she said. 'No

women's lib. out there, you know.'

'You don't think David would like . . . ?'

'To work abroad? I don't know. I don't think so. I don't think I'll ask him in case he says yes! What about Tom?'

'Well, what about Tom, you scheming females? What plots are you hatching against me in my own kitchen. Was there ground glass in the fruit mousse? Arsenic in the steak-and-kidney?' Tom himself was standing in the doorway.

'We were only wondering if you and David had any urge to move to distant places,' said Melanie. 'I know Alan hasn't. As far as he's concerned nowhere's worth living in that isn't Cotswold Hunt country. He won't go as far as Cheltenham except when it's Gold Cup week. What about you, Tom?'

Tom looked up swiftly at Rachel then, and caught her expression unguarded. It explained to him a good deal about the mood she had been in all evening, chatting too brightly about the experience and excitement of working in exotic places. It was more than continuing to ward off the shadows of their day's work. He had sensed pleading in her, but had not comprehended what she was silently asking: 'Do you long for such a chance? Do you want this kind of success?'

'A man once wrote,' Tom began, 'that he was like a cabbage: that where he was stuck, there he grew. When I first read it, I thought it a mite dull. But I've grown up a bit since then, and realised that it's not the sticking that's important, it's the growing. I'd rather grow in Milchester than wither away in Arcadia or anywhere else. You can only exist in one place at a time, and this is the place for me.'

Rachel felt weights lift from her head. She had not realised how important it was to her that he should feel as she did. Perhaps one day if they had the time and the money, they might travel and prove for themselves that China and Peru and Patagonia and the Kamchatka Peninsula really did exist, but Milchester was home. Milchester was sufficient.

'Of course,' Peter was saying as they all went back to the sitting room, 'it will be good to escape the stultifying, provincial atmosphere, the suffocating smallness of this country. I feel I shall be expanding my knowledge, using what I know to best effect.' Samantha nodded and smiled.

'I'm sure,' said Tom.

Alan had been dozing over a large glass of brandy and a back copy of *Horse and Hound* that Rachel had found for him from the waiting room.

'Will you sing for us, Alan?' Rachel asked.

He bumbled a little, pink with brandy and pleasure, saying they didn't really want him to did they, but pleased as punch to be asked.

He had a pleasant, brown-toned drawing room voice, and he played well enough to accompany the easy sound of his singing without need of music. 'Shenandoah', 'Jeanie with the light Brown Hair' and finally 'The Sunshine of your Smile'. They pressed him for more, but he returned to his brandy after that.

Rachel looked round at the friendly, familiar room, made untidy by the evening's entertainment, with coffee cups and wine glasses scattered here and there. It was all pretty scruffy really: nothing to lift it out of the ordinary but Tom's brilliant paintings on the walls. One was of Speeds Hill with all its thorny tangled brambles and field-edge flowers. The painting made clear to the eye all those small beauties that were there for anyone to see, but noticed by few. Rachel wished that she had such a talent: could explain in paint, or words, or any other medium known to man, what she felt for the place in which she lived and worked. She let her eyes rest on the painting, allowed the sound of pleasant conversation to wash about her ears. She was shamefully near the verge of sleep. She saw, half in the picture, half in the floating landscape of dream, the wildlife of Speeds Hill: voles, mice and hedgehogs, and the fleet brown shadows of hares, and a fox crouched under a bramble bush, and a pheasant, cocksure in the close season, parading his bright feathers across a green ridge. On all these creatures too one small boy had in his concern for his dog risked letting loose horrifying death. To their deaths they would all come, to be sure. Wild creatures seldom make old age and no creature is immortal, but she was glad to know them safe from that terrible and fatal frenzy. They would not go into the dark in a rage of madness.

Chapter Fourteen

After all the swift action and high drama of what the vets all began
to refer to as 'our rabies scare', the news that the dead dog's brain
showed no trace of rabies – while it was a very great relief – gave
them all feelings understandably akin to embarrassment, as well as
pity for the child whose dog had been destroyed. Rachel's feelings
were tortuous, her reactions ambivalent. Of course she did not
want a rabid dog to have been brought into the country, of course
she did not want there to be the least chance that Laurent might
have contracted such a disease, yet the shock of such a thing might
have brought home the terrible risks whereas now there was bound
to be the feeling that a great deal of fuss had been made over
nothing; that a creaking machinery had been oiled and set in
motion to win the first battle of a war that had not in fact been
declared. They all told each other what splendid news it was, but
Rachel was well aware how much the D.V.O. was dreading
having to write to inform Paul's father of the post mortem findings.

So for a day or so both she and Tom felt they were living in an
anticlimax. It was a flat dull place, and it brought out the worst in
both of them. They squabbled and were childish, until Mrs
Partridge threatened to set about them both with a hairbrush.

'You're neither of you worth living with when there's not
enough to do. I swear I'll go out and give something nasty to the
next creature I see, just to put a bit of work your way.'

She would never have done any such thing, but it seemed as if
she might have addressed the Lord on the matter, fervent Baptist

that she was, for after only a very few of these doldrum days business became brisk again, demanding of time and skill.

They were not the only ones to be involved in sudden unusual activity either. David Stratton came bursting in one evening to say he had just been operating on a camel. Rachel had seen the notices in Milchester advertising the coming of the circus, and had wondered if any of them might become involved with illness or casualties among the more exotic performers.

'I nearly called you both when the circus rang,' he said. 'You know me, cats and dogs are more my line. I'm far more at home with my nice clean table inside four good walls than in a tent in the middle of a field; and camels, I ask you! Alan was out and Peter was packing, and I could see they were anxious so off I went. It only had a sore eye, they said, but you should have seen it. New Forest disease it looked like to me. Never been near the New Forest they told me. They went very quiet when I said I'd have to use a general anaesthetic though, and I didn't feel too cheerful myself.

'Well, I went and rang Bristol, and they took ages finding anybody who could tell me anything. I hung on, and hung on, and several hulking great chaps from the circus who had followed me over to the petrol station where the nearest 'phone was stood outside the 'phone booth looking in. I began to wonder what they might do to me if anything went wrong.

'Anyway, in the end I found someone who had a message from someone else who said the vets had checked the proper dosage of Immobilon for a camel, and I went back to the tent with the information, all prepared to do the job. I kept those great bruisers busy putting straw down while I scrubbed, and the camel stood by sneering and grunting and spitting disgustingly at anyone who came near it.

'I didn't relish the thought of that creature staggering around for any longer than need be, so no intramuscular injection for you my lad, I thought. Straight into the vein for you, and out like a light.'

Rachel heard the whistle of Tom's indrawn breath.

'O.K.,' said David, 'O.K. Maybe you anaesthetise camels every day. I'd never even seen a camel that close before. Picture the scene,' he exclaimed, with gusto. 'A cliffhanger if ever I saw one. There's D. Stratton, M.R.C.V.S. on his mission of mercy to save this camel's eyeball. Hypodermic poised, he moves in to anaesthetise the poor suffering creature. "Stop!" calls a voice and in comes the cavalry. Well, the man from the petrol station, actually. "Urgent message for Mr Stratton" he says.

'Thank God the blessed man had written down what it said on that piece of paper. If those circus hands had realised how near I came to murdering their precious camel I'd have been mincemeat.'

'Well, what did it say?' asked Rachel, impatiently.

' "Intravenous Immobilon kills camels," I should think,' said Tom.

'Right you are,' David replied. 'Five thousand quidsworth of camel would have been catsmeat along with yours truly.'

'Maybe there's something to be said for a quiet life after all,' announced Rachel. The incident brought home to her sharply that for all she had done and had learned since she had first started in practice, there were still yawning chasms in her knowledge down which she could plunge without warning. She had learned that to be thanked for her successes was a rare luxury, whereas to be blamed for failure was only to be expected, and failure was always an awful possibility.

She could have killed that camel just as easily as David had come within a whisker of doing.

'We'd better all bone up on our exotic species,' she suggested.

'I'll stick to dogs and cats in future,' David laughed.

Harry Ellis, the old stud groom from the Ashton Stud, rang next day, shouting down the instrument as he always did as if it were a speaking tube. He hated using the telephone, so Rachel knew it must be important.

'We got that old mare of John Jacobs' 'ere,' Harry bellowed. 'In 'er foal 'eat, to be covered. Got 'er last foal at foot. Don't like the look of 'im. Didn't ought to put 'er in foal again anyway, not at 'er time o' life. Still, that's not for me to say.'

Rachel knew John Jacobs' mare. She had been a point-to-pointer, a very good sort that he had bought for almost nothing when she broke down. He and his wife, who ran the Faracre Kennels, had hacked her gently around the countryside for years, and when even that gentle exercise became too much had put her in foal to a stallion in Wiltshire, a big strong bay called Flying Colours.

No-one had been called to the foaling so it had presumably been uneventful, though someone who had seen the foal in the paddock said it was a great big colt. Highlight was not a big horse. Covered by him she should produce a smaller foal, which at her age would be all to the good.

When Rachel arrived at the Ashton Stud Harry Ellis had the mare and foal all ready in a well-strawed box.

'Told Mr Jacobs I'd asked you to come,' he announced. 'He said the colt was poorly for a bit when 'e was first foaled, but thought 'e'd be all right.'

It was a good big colt all right, as far as his framework went, but there was no flesh on him. He had not filled out and bloomed as a flourishing foal does, and there was no brightness to his aspect. He did not seem to be enjoying the sensation of being alive.

'Did Mr Jacobs give the foal anything when it seemed off colour?' Rachel asked.

'Kaolin and morphine mixture, 'e said.'

'Well, you can see at least part of the foal's problem, can't you Harry?'

'A great 'ernia,' Harry observed.

There was, indeed, a large umbilical hernia which would have to be repaired. Thank God for Harry, Rachel thought, who would give her operating space as scrupulously clean as she could possibly wish for. She told him what she intended to do.

'Right you are then,' he said. ' 'E's a nice colt. 'E deserves 'is chance.'

'Has the mare stood to Highlight yet?' Rachel enquired.

'Like a rock,' Harry said 'She won't turn, you can bet your boots.

Don't know what's good for 'er, that old girl. I told 'er, you wants to think again, I says, but she claps eyes on the stallion and you'd think she was a filly again. Never learn, women don't. Well, savin' your presence,' he said.

Rachel laughed. A more backhanded compliment she could not remember ever having been given. Harry felt flustered, and stumped away ahead of her to put everything in readiness.

She discussed the foal with Tom that evening, and they agreed that with the hernia repaired he should improve rapidly. Tom had had a similar case in the spring: a neighbour of his aunt, Lady Bramwell, had a hunter mare whose foal had a similar condition, and now he was strong and lively and getting decidedly coltish.

Lady Bramwell had complained bitterly to Tom because the young creature, having tired of playing stallions with his mother, had made unseemly advances to Lady Bramwell's new mare who grazed the paddock next to him. Tom had laughed, and assured her that the stout timber fence between them would keep the colt in his place, but the new mare had confounded everyone by jumping the fence herself and the two females had had a ding-dong battle of flailing hoofs and flattened ears and high hysterical squealings, while the colt looked on, quite overcome by the brawl he had instigated.

Fortunately neither of the mares was much hurt, but Lady Bramwell was cross with Tom for several days as if it were all his fault, and averred to Rachel that he should really have stuck to painting and left animals alone. It was a great source of frustration to Rachel that she had not been able to persuade Lady Bramwell of Tom's excellence as a vet, any more than Malcolm Halliday had been able to do when he was alive: in this opinion the fierce old woman would not be shifted and referred to Tom always as 'my nephew, the painter'. It was Rachel, and Rachel alone, whom she summoned to minister to her horses, and it was Rachel who had dressed the injuries of the two mares and had suggested they should be kept well apart in future.

When she went to visit the Jacobs' foal, which was by then back in its own stable at Faracre Kennels, she had a picture of that other bonny colt in her mind and expected to see a creature equally delightful and lively. What she did see horrified her. This colt looked, if possible, worse than when she had seen him before.

'He's not thriving, is he?' John Jacobs said. 'He couldn't have picked something up at the stud, could he?'

'I doubt it,' Rachel said. She could not think of anything less likely.

'He's scouring like anything.'

'Yes, I can see that. His temperature is well up, too.'

Rachel gave the foal antibiotics and continued on her rounds, but all day long she felt anxious about him. During her experience as a vet she seemed to have developed a sixth sense about those of her patients who were not willing to put up any kind of fight to exist. She had seen creatures come back almost from the dead, not only because of medication and nursing but from a real determination to go on living. This foal had no fight in him.

That evening, when Mr Jacobs telephoned to say the colt was dead, it came as no surprise. When she began to blame herself however, Tom grew angry, telling her not to be stupid; and when she continued to look unhappy about it he left the house, slamming the door behind him.

Rachel sat in the kitchen and wept. Nothing was right. She was hopeless. Nobody loved her. Go down the garden and eat worms.

When she had finished crying and had trailed upstairs in the empty house to wash her face, she began to wonder how it was possible to grow so much older and be still so little the wiser: still to be affected by the same hurts, to be grown up only on the outside. Inside, you could be back in the nursery before you knew it.

Tom returned and she heard noises from downstairs, but she did not go down. Sounds continued, the surgery door opened and closed once or twice, but Rachel remained in the bedroom. After a lengthy silence noise erupted again: there were footsteps on the stairs, and there was Tom in rubber gloves and post-mortem apron, looking revoltingly gory and grinning like an idiot.

'Multiple abscesses on the liver,' he announced, his large frame outlined, dramatically, in the bedroom door. 'Must have been infected at birth. Navel not treated, you see, so infection tracked up the cord to the liver. Nothing could have saved that foal. He was doomed from the moment he got born in a dirty stable. Pyaemia, death, it was inevitable and none of it your fault, you silly woman.'

Rachel stared at him. He was a quite extraordinary sight, and not one for the squeamish.

'Thanks, Tom,' she said at last.

He glared at her. 'Is that all you've got to say?' he roared. 'I drive over half the county, cart a dead foal through the night in my nice clean car, do a post-mortem in the small hours, and all she says is thanks!'

'Tom.'

'Yes?'

'Take off that bloody apron,' Rachel said.

Chapter Fifteen

Rachel had made Tom an early breakfast as he had to drive over to the furthest extent of the practice to vet a horse, and only by setting out at crack of dawn could he give himself time to make a proper job of it. It was a big bay that had caught the attention of Mark Purvis, the event rider, and he would need to know without a doubt that the horse's wind and heart and legs would stand up to the big galloping courses and huge solid fences it would have to face.

'It's just the sort you'd like,' Tom had told Rachel. 'I took a quick look when I was passing yesterday and called in to say I'd be along today with all my equipment.'

'I'll have him, shall I, if Mark Purvis doesn't?'

'At five thousand pounds? Of course, and another for Sundays!'

One day, Rachel thought, she'd have a horse. Not that sort; just an honest plodder. Maybe George would find her something.

When Tom had gone she began to make her own breakfast. She fried an egg.

When she looked at it, lying there on the plate, she thought it was the most repulsive thing she had ever seen. Veterinary practice produces many sights to make the gorge rise, and Rachel had grown accustomed and was seldom affected now. But this egg made her stomach cringe and her throat tighten. It looked at her with its yellow disgusting eye, and she fled to the bathroom and was sick.

She came back to the kitchen, green and shaky, her throat

scalded with acid bile, to find Mrs Partridge scraping the plate into the bin.

'Didn't fancy your breakfast I see,' she said, and gave Rachel one of her looks. It was the look that said, without recourse to words, 'Well, I know what's up with you, but I'm not saying anything until you see fit to tell me yourself.'

Rachel and Tom had arranged to meet at Tophill Farm. There were some ponies due for flu injections and the bull needed his feet trimmed. Rachel could have coped with this herself, but the bull had turned cranky ever since he broke his tail and found Rachel's treatment of it painful. He considered her totally responsible for the pain and was reluctant to allow her near him.

On the way to Tophill Rachel had to pass the glebe field in which Polo, Mandy's pony, was continuing his slimming programme. Mandy had set about his cure with real determination, walking him about daily to get his exercise, each day a little further, so that at each outing he hobbled less and walked more. She stood him daily in the stream to cool his feet. She groomed him and talked to him to keep his mind off his insatiable hunger for protein that had been his downfall. As a result, his neck was no longer a bulge of hot hard flesh and the true shape of his shoulders could be seen where pads of fat had once concealed them. He no longer stood as if he should be on wheels. His feet hurt nothing like so much, and as a result his whole temperament and demeanour had taken a turn for the better.

As Rachel neared the church and its attendant field she saw a small thin figure leaning over the churchyard wall at the point where Polo stood. His whole attitude, even at a distance, proclaimed eager anticipation. Miss Abby was feeding him on great swathes of cut grass from the churchyard. As Rachel drew Jessica to a halt and leaped out she could see the long green strands of one forbidden feast sticking out of his mouth like whiskers, and another bunch was already being offered to him.

'Don't give him that,' called Rachel, sharply.

'What's that, my dear?' smiled Miss Abby cheerfully, her head tilted to catch the sound. Rachel had by this time scrambled over the glebe gate and stood now before Polo, her arms outspread as if to protect him from his own greed.

There was an abundance of cut grass in the churchyard. Bill Saunders from Leaze Farm had left it to grow while he was busy with his own work, and a few warm showers had made it spring up as good as second-cut hay. Even so late in the summer it smelt delicious, and to a small pony weary of his sparse diet it must have been like ambrosia harvested from Olympus. Now he gazed at Rachel with reproach and snuffled at the bare turf of his paddock in search of the least blade of his feast that might have fallen there.

'Please don't feed him, Miss Abby.'

'But he's hungry, dear,' Miss Abby said, as if puzzled that Rachel should make such a request. 'There's no grass in this field. Mrs Gunter said it was a shame to keep the pony so hungry. She wanted to tell the R.S.P.C.A., but I said she should not get poor Mandy into trouble. It wouldn't be right, would it? I spoke to Daphne about it, and she agreed with me. No need to say anything to anyone, we thought. Just make sure between us that he had enough to eat. We gave him our cabbage trimmings and peapods and our stale bread. It's good bread Mrs Adams: we make it ourselves. Brown, you know, much better for the system than white bread. And when they cut the grass on the churchyard we thought we would give him some of that.'

That blasted Amy Gunter again. Rachel could just imagine the tone in which she would have spoken of the poor starved beast and the cruelty of its owner. And the owner's veterinary adviser, no doubt. It would not take much to wring the hearts of the two dear old sisters, and it would not have occurred to them to doubt Amy Gunter's sincerity in the matter.

As Rachel began to explain to Miss Abby the reason for Polo's strict diet and the real necessity for ensuring that he stuck to it, a new, disquieting thought crept into her mind. The churchyard yews overhung the long grass which had been cut down for Polo's illicit feast. They were handsome great trees, their trunks twisted and convoluted with age and their great bushy heads, which in Street's palmy days had been topiarised, now sprouted undisciplined and made deep shade for the quiet sleepers below.

'Have you fed him any grass from under the trees?' she asked.

'No,' Miss Abby said, and Rachel's spirits rose in thankfulness. 'I thought he would like the stuff that had had the sun on it a bit. It smelt so good. Just like hay, you know.'

Already the elderly face was drawing down with concern at her misguided kindness. Now the lines deepened as she realised what it was that concerned Rachel in particular.

'The yew trees,' she said. 'Oh dear, I had quite forgotten. My dear father always used to warn us of them when we took out the pony cart: never to let Toby browse in the hedge where they grew. But I am sure I would have seen if there were any twigs in the grass. Then perhaps I would not. My sight is not what it was.' Her mouth was quivering now, and she shook her head abstractedly. Rachel inwardly cursed Amy Gunter again for involving this nice old woman in what could so easily, one way or another, have been a tragic mistake.

'Never mind, Miss Abby. Polo's quite all right. There's no harm done that a little extra exercise won't cure. I promise you that once his weight is steady and his feet totally better we'll move him on to slightly less short commons, but it really is for his own good.'

'That's another thing father used to say,' remarked Miss Abby wryly. 'Usually upon the subject of cold mutton fat, I remember.' Her face looked a little less bleak now, but she sighed, for all that. 'I have to admit, I did enjoy feeding the little fellow. Animals always seem so grateful, don't they?'

Rachel thought for a while. 'Carrots,' she said. 'Do you grow them in your garden?'

'Indeed yes. We grow carrots.'

'Feed him a carrot or two. They'll do him good. And he'll enjoy them too, not like cold mutton fat!'

Miss Abby laughed then, to Rachel's relief; and Polo, having realised that no more grass was forthcoming, shook himself in disgust and turned away to sniff hopefully at the bare turf of the little field.

Rachel returned to Jessica and drove on, planning how she

would get Tom to go and speak to Amy Gunter. Her own dislike of the old woman was so strong that she felt she would only gibber at her in a fury. Anyway, Amy Gunter was afraid of Tom, and Tom would delight in her discomfiture.

'I'll set my husband on you, you old crone, you see if I don't,' she muttered to herself as she put Jessica in gear and motored on in the direction of Tophill. The sky was clouding over. One or two fat spots of rain splattered the road ahead.

Tom was just walking into the yard from the house gate when Rachel arrived.

'They've gone off and left us to it,' he announced. 'Note on the door: "Gone to wedding, horses in barn, bull tied in box." Darn it, I told them we'd need some help here. Can you imagine a doctor coming out on call and finding a note saying, "Gone shopping: the baby's in the end bedroom"?'

'Well, at least there's the two of us,' Rachel remarked.

'Not near that bull there isn't,' said Tom. 'You see to the horses. There shouldn't be any problem, not like that bay at Shipton Clive the other day.' Tom had bruises all down his back where a big bay hunter had gone berserk at the sight of the needle and had rammed him hard against the wall. Most horses accepted injections with resignation but occasionally, perhaps from some unhappy earlier experience, one would prove needle-shy in the extreme, reacting violently and unpredictably to the sight of the syringe.

'Let's get on with it then,' said Rachel. 'It's beginning to rain again.' The air was cooling rapidly. She would be glad of the shelter of the barn.

The horses were no problem. They stood unflinching to receive their protective injections, and Rachel gave them peppermints as a reward. They stood placidly crunching; and Rachel allowed herself a moment's reflection on life, her judgment seat a bale of new yellow barley straw which had toppled from a stack behind the place where the horses were tied.

It was as well the harvest was in, for the weather was certainly on the turn and there was little chance of more hot weather now. The long-distance forecast was bad and she was sorry about that for she found nothing more pleasant than that late, after-harvest sunshine, that mellow Indian summer, rich and ripe, golden-grape days, rare and lovely. The rain was a steady drumming now on the corrugated iron on the lean-to covered way that ran from barn to cowshed. Conscience stirred her out of her daydream to find out how Tom was faring.

She was scarcely out of the door when she heard him shouting. As she ran she heard too the rising bellow of an angry bull, its upper note high and hysterical. As she came closer she could hear stamping and pawing and the sharp exhalation of breath as the bull snorted, enraged.

'Tom!' she shouted. 'My Lord, Tom, where are you?'

Fear drained the blood from her. The noise of her heart's pounding thundered in her ears. She could not run fast enough to get to him.

He was spread-eagled against the wall of the loosebox. The bull, chain trailing from the ring in his nose, was shaking his head, threatening attack. At the other end of the chain Rachel could see the tethering ring which had pulled out from the wall, still embedded in a lump of plaster and stone.

For a long moment she could not think what to do. The bull had Tom trapped and would not let him out. There was nothing to hand with which she could drive off the bull or throw to Tom as a weapon. Then she saw the hayrack, high up on the wall.

'Tom,' she called. 'I'll try to get his attention and you climb up there. I've got an idea.'

'I hope it works,' Tom said. His voice shook. There was no doubting the bull's intentions.

'Hey,' Rachel shouted, rattling the door. 'Hey, to me, come on you old bull, come on.' She went on, her voice high and taunting, until at last it registered with the lumbering creature and he swung towards her, crashing his great head against the door so that the bolts bulged and juddered in their sockets. In that moment of diversion Tom sprang up into the hayrack so that at least he was out of the bull's reach, though still in some danger from the fact that the hayrack's hold on the wall was shaky. Used only to holding a few pounds weight of dried grasses it creaked and shook under Tom's twelve stone. Already the bull was looking to see where the man had gone, and lumbered about, lowing and muttering like a puzzled lunatic.

'And for your next trick?' Tom whispered to Rachel.

'Hang on,' she told him.

'Like a blasted limpet,' he said.

Rachel ran to the car. The rain had stopped for the moment. She found a syringe and an ampoule of Rompon. How she longed for some dramatic knock-out drop, some bovine Micky Finn that would fell the bull in his tracks like a blow dart in some wild-life adventure. However, no such wonder-drug existed in her pharmacopoeia, so Rompon would have to do. If she could get it in the bull.

She ran back to the loosebox, resisting the temptation to fill the syringe as she went. She had heard of more than one vet who had injected himself accidentally and fatally by stumbling onto a filled syringe.

The bull had discovered Tom, and was setting about dismantling the hayrack with loud and insane fury. This time he must not know she was there. She drew up the Rompon into the syringe.

The bull's backside was tantalisingly out of reach. She would have to go in. She did not want to go in. The idea sickened her. The bolt had been rammed home by the bull and was obstinate against her shaking fingers. When at last it began to give she did not know whether to feel relieved or even more afraid. Only the sight of Tom clinging to his rickety perch roused up her determination, and at the first pause in the bull's activity she whacked the needle home into his backside and pressed the plunger. The dosage had been a wild estimate, erring on the far too much. She hoped to God she hadn't killed him. Oh what the heck if she had. She'd kill a whole holocaust of bulls to get Tom safe out of there.

'Light the touchpaper and hang on for ten minutes,' Tom whispered. 'Now get back out of here.'

'Ten minutes should do it,' Rachel said, as she retreated hopefully. They waited. It was a ridiculous scene: Tom huddled in

179

the hayrack, Rachel once again on the safe side of the door, the bull still angry, and puzzled by the sudden stinging at his rear end but slowly beginning to feel the affects of the drug.

There was a creaking sound, only audible as the bull's bellowing began to quieten. It was the sound of the wooden plugs that held the hayrack beginning to draw from the wall like corks.

The left-hand ones drew out just as the bull's legs began to feel frail beneath him, and as the rack dropped askew the beast fell to his knees. He saw Tom spill out and made one enraged effort to fight the drug and renew the attack, but his muscles refused, his eyes closed, his brain sank into darkness.

Tom lay enmeshed in the hayrack for a moment or so, and then seeing that it was safe to get up began to do so, only to stop halfway up and cry out as he put weight on the ankle that the iron bars had trapped. Rachel saw sweat break out on his face as he shuffled to the door, supporting himself where he could. She went in to help him, and by the time they were both safely out of the loosebox he was whiter and sicker-looking than even his immediate adventures could justify.

'Blast,' he said. 'I think I've broken my ankle.'

On the roof of the covered way the rain had begun its manic hammering again.

Chapter Sixteen

'A neat and uncomplicated fracture,' Dr Mason called it, evincing from Tom the remark that he hadn't done his ankle in in any spirit of competition and wasn't expecting a prize for good workmanship.

He came home with a prize though, all the same. David Stratton had had the afternoon off and had driven Tom to and from his plastering session at the hospital, delivering him back to Rachel at Painters frustrated by his injury, yet obviously full of some unrelated triumph.

'Heaven knows why he's feeling so pleased with himself when he's stuck in that lumping great cast for a month,' David grumbled. 'You're married to an impossible man, Rachel Adams, and that's a fact.'

The cause of Tom's excitement was a Boyle's anaesthetic machine which he had discovered in a corner of one of the corridors when he was being wheeled to the Plaster Room. It was obviously not in use, and he had sent a very surprised nurse scuttling to ask if the hospital would care to sell it to him.

'I've got it Rachel. I've got it,' he told her in triumph, 'and I've rung Jo Spiers – you know, Jo Spiers from Raysbrook, who works for British Oxygen. He can get it reconditioned for us. Even with that bill it will have cost less than half a new one. It's a start, isn't it?'

Having made the start Tom launched himself, dot-and-carry-one as he was, into the equipping of the animal hospital next door.

Rachel worried about the lack of rest his injured ankle was getting, but it kept him from feeling tied by the leg because he could not drive: made him less concerned because of the extra work load on her, though David helped when he could.

Odd cargoes began to arrive on lorries. A mountain of old flock mattresses from a boarding school near Stroud that was buying more comfortable bedding, rolls of waterproof nylon sheeting, some overhead lighting, and a big old-fashioned instrument steriliser. Tom hobbled about, gloating over these things and displaying them to Rachel like a cock-bird displaying to his mate. He was quite insufferably pleased with himself.

'You've missed your vocation,' Rachel told him. 'You should work for *Exchange and Mart*. What the heck are all those mattresses for?'

'For the floor of our operating theatre,' he explained. 'We lay them on the floor of one of the boxes and cover them all over with nylon sheeting. Then an animal can go down under sedation and do no harm to itself.'

As Rachel rushed about keeping up with the work that Tom was not able to do, she felt ridiculously resentful of the fun he was having installing the equipment. It was as much her project as his and now, at the end of the day, she was too exhausted even to bother about it.

Work was made all the harder by the persistent rain. Great grey clouds, having established their position over Gloucestershire, seemed determined not to retreat and they hurled down rain with a sharp wind behind it: a cold, soaking obliterating rain that veiled every horizon, mired every field, set every runnel and gutter chattering with water and made the streams run high and wide so that often the little stone bridges could not contain the flow and everywhere there were small areas of flood.

Autumn seemed to vanish into instant winter. It certainly felt like it. Leaves lost their proud colours and fell, and lay in sodden heaps. Late baled straw stood in the fields and sprouted. Yards were treacherous with puddled mud and dripping gutters. No-one would have thought that a wetter autumn could follow so wet a spring.

The community gloomed and glowered, and brooded over their sick stock and swore at the unrelenting sky. Everywhere farmers gathered, their talk was of the weather.

One Monday Rachel found Jan Kingsley huddled up in the market office, red-nosed, streaming with cold, and swearing she never wished to set eyes on sheep or farmers again. She had not long finished overseeing the last of the year's sheep-dipping, which had had to be done in appalling conditions for the weather would not ease and dipping must be completed by the due date. Rachel had seen her in the highest, bleakest yard of all at a remote farm beyond Claybridge, dunking already soggy sheep in a circular dip bath while the heavens poured down. No wonder she had a cold. Rachel commiserated with her.

'Ah well,' Jan said, 'I had one less sheep to do than I thought at that farm. I found their ram dead. I told the D.V.O. and he said it was tetanus. The ram had only stood on a nail. The hole was so small between his cleats I'd never have seen it if I hadn't been shown it. All the ewes had been vaccinated O.K., but no-one had thought to vaccinate the ram.'

'Expensive mistake,' said Rachel.

'I'll add it to the pep-talk I give to my new flock-owners,' Jan said, 'but it's no good talking to the established ones, or not many of them anyway. They think I get all my advice out of a book, so it's bound to be no use to them.'

'Leave them to their mistakes then,' Rachel said, 'until it hits each of their pockets. Then maybe they'll listen.'

'Maybe,' said Jan. Then, smiling ruefully, she said, 'If nothing else, I'm a good source of amusement. Did you hear about Bert Reeves?'

'The one you told to clean out his lorry?'

'That's him. He was in again last week. Drove up to the unloading bay, got out of the cab and left it, tailgate up, when he saw me standing there. Made up all sorts of tall tales he did, to get me to go away: said I was needed in the fat sheep section, said there was a beast down in the cull-cow shed. "Pull the other one," I told him. "Show me the inside of your lorry."

' "Lorry?" he says. "You don't want to see in there, do you?" Face as innocent as a newborn lamb. Polite as a choirboy on a Sunday. He could see I was busy, but he wouldn't open up. He didn't refuse point blank: just kept making silly excuses and delays. In the end I told him if he didn't open up I'd climb in and see for myself. "You do that," he says.

'So I did. You know how big that cattle truck of his is. Climbing up on the wheel to get in at the side-door was like going up a mountain. I'd just started this cold and my head was swimming, and I thought any minute now I'm going to fall off here and break something. Then I got the door open and looked inside.' Jan paused, her face a picture of remembered aggravation.

'Well?' Rachel urged.

Jan looked at Rachel for a long moment, as if she could hardly bear to complete the story.

'It was as clean in there as my mother's kitchen,' she said (Mrs Kingsley was known to be houseproud); 'you could have eaten your dinner off the floor. I could have killed him.'

Jan glowered at Rachel, and snuffled with cross sinusy misery. Rachel, heartlessly, began to laugh, until at long last Jan joined in with a watery giggle.

'Men,' she said. 'I hate 'em. Especially farmers.'

Rachel drove home from the market in continuing rain, Jessica's windscreen wipers patiently clearing a looking-space that was instantly blurred again. Cattle she visited on her homeward journey were muddied to hock and knee and their yard was a revolting sea of mud and muck through which she had to squelch in her wellies. Were those hot and lovely days of harvest only so few weeks in the past? This rain seemed to have obliterated summer and all its loveliness. Water was finding weak places in the seams of her supposedly waterproof jacket, and trickling down her neck and wrists. The cattle vented their misery in the way they knew best.

Then she remembered that this time last year the sun had been shining. A year ago tomorrow she and Tom had been married, and

184

there had been grave doubts as to the suitability of having a marquee on the gravel by the side of Stapleton House in case the weather should turn evil, but it had not. It had been the last glorious day of the year, for weather, anyway.

A striped tent and flowery-hatted guests on a sunny lawn seemed the least likely thing in the world on such a foul day as the one she now stood in, but the memory of them kept a little further from her the wet and cold of her present surroundings.

The year continued to weep its way towards winter into a good-for-nothing November that made everyone feel the gods had turned against them: were working out some grudge for unknown and unwitting failure to placate them.

Animals were fractious and bad-tempered. Rachel ached with bruises and had a sore arm where a horse had nipped her, so that her sympathy for Tom, his ankle still in its plaster shell, was not always all that it might have been. The cold and wet made the newly-knitting bone acutely painful, and the plaster hid from the possibility of scratching devilish itches that could not be relieved. Added to that, he was frustrated by the incessant wet from going outside, except by shrouding the plastered foot in a large black plastic bag to protect it. With this water-proofing he would hobble about, grumbling and cursing, his injured foot proclaiming itself to be the property of Milchester Rural District Council (Do Not Deposit Hot Ashes).

Mrs Partridge complained at the lack of bags in which to put the household rubbish. Rachel complained that if he had been patient with the injury in the first place it would not have taken so long to heal. Work was piling itself into a backlog of frightening dimensions, made longer and more tangled by the crop of illnesses the weather itself brought on. Sometimes Rachel felt she could murder Tom for choosing just now to be incapacitated. David helped where he could but they were short-handed themselves, in that practice, while they awaited a replacement for Peter Wilmott.

Everyone seemed so miserable that Rachel could not find a time when it seemed to be just right to mention that she thought she was pregnant. She almost did not want to mention it; and neither did she wish to purchase from the chemist the means of instant confirmation or denial. The feeling that she had about this possibility was something akin to waiting to open a present, a mysteriously wrapped parcel, or a letter arrived through the post in an unknown hand and with a strange postmark. She wondered if her strange reticence in the matter were in itself a symptom.

There was one point when she felt the moment had come, when for a brief time, like a sullen brat suddenly turning winsome, the sun came out from behind the solid grey cloud and set a soaked world gently steaming; but then the telephone called her out to a sudden emergency and the opportunity was lost, for when she returned Tom had shut himself away to paint for an exhibition in Cheltenham, from which he hoped to sell enough to defray a good deal of the cost of the animal hospital.

Sometimes Tom would paint landscape as it lay before him; or at least would translate it, through his own vision of it, direct from the original; but opportunities for this with his busy professional life were rare, so that more often than not he would compose his landscapes from things that he had seen at different times, but which, to his eye, married well and pleasantly together. His crowded sketchbooks provided much of this material, and held safe for him the atmosphere, the feeling, the light, that he would need to recall within four walls at some quite different season.

It was in this way that he had made his portrait of George. He had used the sketches he had made in secret of the old man where he sat in the Painters' kitchen, but he had set him in a landscape, for George was happiest out of doors. The little leathery man was seated against the wall of a limestone quarry, at the place where the sheep-turf spills over onto the slabbed, tipped planes of angular stone. The angles and contours of the landscape reflected those of the old man's face, so that he and the landscape were one.

Rachel had seen the finished painting, and recognised its brilliance. It had not the same meaning for Rachel as the woodland Tom had painted, the bluebell wood, his particular gift to her, but she was convinced that, as a piece of work, this picture

186

of George was the best thing he'd ever done.

When she went into the studio later that evening, however, and he showed her what he was going to send to Cheltenham, that painting was not on its easel.

'Where's the picture you did of George?' she asked him.

'I gave it to him,' Tom replied.

Suddenly, she felt very angry. He had no business giving away such a piece of work. It was bound to sell. No-one could fail to recognise the quality of it. She came near to telling him he was a fool.

Her mind harped all night on the idiocy of giving away a picture which could show the world what a painter her husband was. The dirty thought that the money would help fund their hospital she tried hard to bury under this first and nobler reason.

When, a few days later, she had occasion to call on George and was asked up to the flat, there was the painting hung up among his faded framed photographs of himself with the heavy horses that towered over him, peering out from their winkers, wearing their brass-hung breast-plates, their coats gleaming, their manes beribboned, so that the future should not forget what fine beasts they were. George named them for her, as he always did: Blossom and Damsel, Ebony, Jacob, and little Dinah, who was little at seventeen hands, the others all being at least a hand taller.

'All dead now. All dust. Lovely beasts them were,' said George. There was warmth in his voice that only this one subject ever called up in it.

So among these, in total obscurity, hung Tom's most brilliant painting, to be seen only by this old man and his rare visitors. Rachel wondered if Tom himself had recognised how good it was. She was far prouder of his talent than he was, and had learned not to speak much of it to him for she had sensed from the beginning that it was something over which they might quarrel: his singular lack of conceit over this particular ability had on numerous occasions irritated her to the point of anger.

She had once gone as far as saying that it seemed to her his attitude was that anyone could do it if they tried. 'But they can't, you know,' she had chided him, 'and you can. You see the essence of things, and the balance of shapes and colours, and you can recreate what your eyes have seen and your mind has interpreted. Most of us can't begin to do that.'

But he had only grinned at the intensity of her speech, and spoken teasingly.

'It's a knack,' he had replied. 'A trick. Taught by the gods, if you like, but a trick, for all that.'

'For heaven's sake!' she had expostulated. 'You make it sound on a par with sea lions playing "God Save the Queen" on motor horns!' But Tom would be drawn no further and had shrugged out from under the argument.

It did become clear to Rachel, however, as she talked to George that morning, that he was tickled pink to have been given the picture: pleased as a dog with two tails; and the more she realised this, the more churlish seemed her reluctance that he should have it. After all, it was George who had made possible for them at least the beginnings of their dream. And anyway, she began to reason with herself, it was his face in the picture. Fair enough it should hang on his wall: the old man as he was now, looking out from among images of himself as he had been in his prime, with teams of horses in his charge and the whole work of a busy farm dependent on his skill with them.

Chapter Seventeen

When a request came for a lecturer for a branch of the Young Farmers down in the vale, it seemed only sensible that Rachel should go. Tom's ankle, only just out of its plaster, would not take kindly to a longish drive, though he might manage a mile or so in an emergency, or if necessary have himself fetched to a case if the circumstances warranted it.

Anyway he was in no mood to be asked favours. After all his work, and to thwart so much he had hoped for, the Cheltenham exhibition had had to be postponed until spring, and the news had dropped Tom right down into the dumps. He was not a man to sulk but it was the nearest Rachel had seen him come to it. His anger was usually a noisy business, but this was a bitter disappointment to him and not relievable by roaring.

So for this reason too, Rachel felt it would be best if she took on the job, though she was not a willing lecturer. Under normal circumstances she preferred to leave that side of their work to Tom, who seemed to enjoy it enormously and who had undoubted talent to entertain and instruct at the same time.

November meant, of course, that it was dark after tea, and pitch-black by the time she needed to set out for the meeting. It was also raining again. She had planned her route carefully, for in certain places in the vale the floods were out and the Severn was running high. What a miserable back-end to the year they had had, with scarcely a chance to enjoy the brilliance of autumn before it was all snatched away and hurtled down the wind. Only in the most sheltered places did a few sodden leaves cling to the trees, and everything seemed drab and austere.

No wonder that by December humanity needed festivals of fire and light to revive the spirit for the long halting progress into spring. Spring seemed unimaginable as Rachel hurried the few yards from Painters' porch to the car, with the wind flapping the hem of her coat against her legs and her face and hair immediately wet. She spent so much of her existence in trousers that her legs, even in tights, felt exposed and vulnerable and decidedly chilly. She slung her notes onto the back seat and arranged the wet hem of her skirt so that the heater might dry it before she arrived. Rain pattered on the windows and drummed on the roof. She drove out, leaving the gates wide ready for her return – no point in getting soaked unnecessarily – and set off towards the vale rehearsing what she intended to say, wondering if anyone would be foolish enough to come out on such a night to hear her say it and rather hoping they wouldn't.

'The Life of a Vet' was her brief. She had worked on it, made notes in the approved manner, and found at the end that she had conveyed nothing that she really wanted to say. The notes had been consigned to the dustbin and she had started again. 'The life of a vet . . . is a fight against odds.' She had heard that somewhere before: a piece of silly verse. What was it? She teased it out of her mind at last: not a vet, but a snail.

> *The life of a snail is a fight against odds*
> *Which is fought without fever or flummox,*
> *For you see, he is one of those gasteropods*
> *That have to proceed on their stomachs.*

Rachel murmured the idiotic words to herself again as she drove round the roundabout and headed towards Dursley, and chuckled to herself, remembering several occasions when she herself had lain prostrate on the floor of some shed or cowstall trying to sort out the entangled limbs of unborn calves, or once, in pursuit of a reluctant sheep who had fled into the corner of a barn and taken refuge under a workbench.

But in general she did not proceed on her stomach in that her job was not a meal-ticket, not just a means to earn money to exist, a means to escape from the means of earning. Her job, like all the best jobs, was her life, and for a good ninety per cent of the time she did it because she wanted to do it. The other ten per cent of the time she would with the least encouragement drop all her qualifications down the nearest drain, but that was only to be expected.

Perhaps she could put this across to aspiring farmers better than to many: their possible jobs, too, might well be as demanding, as rewarding, as life-consuming, as her own.

She would also try to explain to them about the oddly privileged relationship that the vet has with the owners, the 'family' of each patient, those whose cooperation must be sought, prejudices overcome, anxieties soothed, hopes bolstered, and grief, occasionally but inevitably, understood and comforted.

Rachel herself loved this involvement, this being part of the rural community. It suited her particular nature, whereas to Malcolm Halliday it had been a necessary but painful intrusion on his private self. Had it been possible, his discourse would have been only with his patients with no intervention from humans. However, he was professional enough not to let this show, and his austere manner had not prevented his customers from seeing his true worth and regarding him with affectionate respect. People continued to speak of him to Rachel as a man they would never forget, and whose death they still mourned. 'Never be anyone like him,' they said, meaning no slight on Rachel or Tom. They were right. He had been unique. She would never forget him, and his acceptance of her into the established pattern of his life.

She wondered what private discomforts her presence had at first caused him which his impeccable courtesy would not have allowed him to reveal. She was glad that over the months they had worked together he had begun to seem pleased that she was there; had come nearer to warmth in his feelings for her than he had ever allowed himself to do. Rachel swallowed against the ache in her throat that she felt remembering him. So many, it seemed, that she had loved, in the wide sense of the word: her father, Miss

Blanchard – the fierce old woman vet who had first fired her enthusiasm – Malcolm, Mrs Kyle . . . all gone, vanished like drifting smoke. They would appear sometimes in dreams, called up by no conscious effort of her brain, and their faces, their turns of phrase, something of the essence of them would drift often across her conscious mind in the full light of day. And there was that other, too, that small life whose loss had so changed her. Well, Rachel thought. Well, perhaps . . . She glanced at her watch, saw the time and accelerated a little, bringing her thoughts back more closely to the road ahead for the rain, which had slackened a little a mile or so out of Milchester, was building up again to a relentless drumming on the windscreen and on the road ahead, each fat water-drop bouncing back from the surface to collide with others descending. Saturated trees and bushes cascaded down further water-drops, and the lane-sides were running streams full of gravel and whirling mud. The headlights probed the wet darkness like the lights of a diving bell, shimmering off all the gleaming surfaces ahead.

On the main road the driving grew worse, for every oncoming car brought its own brilliant blinding light, real and rain-reflected, to dazzle her eyes and a spray of splattered mud to obscure her vision further. Her eyes ached, every muscle felt tense with concentration. Her hands were cold from gripping the wheel, and her feet from being poised for instant action over the pedals. It was cold, anyway, in the car. The heater had been temperamental for days and now seemed to be throwing a fit of sulks so that her skirt-hem still clung to her legs.

However, she drove doggedly on, wishing the Young Farmers had never been thought of and that she were safely home and dry and warm.

It was a great relief to arrive at last, and she forgave them at once for existing when a friendly group of young men and women ushered her into a well-lit hall and commiserated with her on her appalling journey and the atrocious state of the weather. They dried her off and gave her hot coffee and sat her by the radiator with tender solicitude, as if she might otherwise think they had done this to her on purpose – which at the worse stages of the journey she had half begun to feel.

Ten minutes of being treated like an ailing granny was quite enough, though. Rachel, having given many assurances that she was fine, thank you, and not about to die and leave them lectureless, was led to the platform, introduced formally, and began her talk.

They listened while she spoke to them of what a vet does, and is, and should be. They were interested to hear of her first incentives to train, and what that involved, when she had qualified and how she saw practice, and why she had chosen Milchester. Her marriage and continued work in a new practice drew approval from the young women in her audience: she could feel it, and was glad. But what really brought them to the edge of their seats and made them listen most intently was the casework she told them about. She could feel their mood, moving with and matching hers, as she told them of particular triumphs and disasters, failures and successes, direct from her own experience so far. She forgot her nerves. She began to enjoy the responsive laugh and the sympathetic murmur, and the centering of their attention on what she had to say. At last she was able to understand what it was that made Tom enjoy doing this sort of thing.

'The old show-off,' she thought to herself, chuckling.

She told them about Trojan the horse, from whose head collar she had dangled in a hair-raising gallop around his field when he had become scared of having his teeth attended to; about the Gunter's pig, long since become ham and sausages, whose eye she had reluctantly treated; about the Fowler's haemolytic foal which had so nearly died; about Tom's terrifying adventure with the Topend bull. They lapped it all up and asked for more, and it was far later than she had intended when she eventually set out for home.

She had been provided with a flask of coffee and a couple of woollen travelling rugs by the president when it was realised that her car heater was not working properly, so at least she would not be so cold on the way back. The rain was only light now, but the huge puddles on the roadsides showed that it had only recently relented. She took a route which they all assured her should keep her out of the areas that might be flooded, and set off, feeling very pleased with her evening's work.

When she stopped for petrol she telephoned Tom, but there was no answer. She hoped he had not been called out far on such a night. She considered asking the garage man to look at the heater, but she wanted no delay in getting home now.

She was thwarted, though. Only a mile or so on the road was closed. A lorry had jack-knifed, spilling its load of drainpipes and blocking both carriageways. The long black cylinders were all tumbled askew like giant spillikins and a huge puddle of spilt diesel gleamed in sinister rainbow-colours on the wet road, but a policeman to whom Rachel spoke said no-one had been hurt. Since that nightmare time dealing with the trapped horses in the collision to which she and Tom had been called earlier in the year, such scenes brought instant anxiety to her: a need to offer help and a terrible fear that it might be accepted.

Diverted down a road she did not know she must have missed a turning, for soon Rachel realised she was lost, and that the way she was now on led back down into the vale.

Chapter Eighteen

Lost though she was, and in spite of the darkness, Rachel began before long to have that odd sense of having 'been here before', and as she drove the conviction became stronger and more compelling. For a long time she could not remember when, or in what connection, but she knew for certain it was in reality and not in dreams that she had come along this particular road between these particular hedgerows. Then some tall grain silos on her left confirmed what she had already begun to suspect, that this was the road past Joe Burge's house.

From time to time as she drove, her headlights caught the gleam of water where the floods were out. Water had no business to be this side of the high banks that protected Joe's fields. Suddenly anxious for him, she pressed on towards his old farmhouse, hoping she would remember exactly where it was in the dark.

But outside Joe's house it was not dark. There were lights flashing and the sound of an engine and voices, as Rachel drew Jessica to the side of the lane and hurried to see what was amiss. The house lay below the lane, and she realised at once she would need her boots on to go down there: the house and yard stood in water – only an inch or so, as it turned out, but floodwater for all that. She put on the boots that she always kept in the car, and walked towards the lights and the voices.

'Is Joe all right?' she called.

'Who's that?' someone asked.

The vehicle was an ambulance. The driver was leaning out of

the cab, peering into the darkness in Rachel's direction. She explained that she knew Joe and had come to see if she could help.

'He's all right,' the ambulance man said. 'Just exhausted, I think. He'd spent all evening getting his horses up onto high ground when he heard the water had breached the banks further upstream. He's got a few fields up the top there it seems, where he keeps his cattle in the winter, and there he was, back and forth like a shuttlecock, and no-one knew about it until someone found him collapsed in the gateway here. Silly old fool. Anyone would have helped him, if he'd asked.'

So they would, Rachel thought, but Joe was an independent old cuss and the welfare of his horses was his greatest concern. 'May I speak to him?' she asked.

'Just a quick word then. Maybe you can stop the old boy worrying. The stables are all empty and we've checked all round. The livestock's all safe, but he's still fretting and fussing. You won't get much out of him, though. He keeps drifting off. We had to sedate him.'

In the back of the ambulance Joe lay amazingly small under the blankets. He took a while to register that Rachel was there at all, and she had to prompt his memory to know who she was.

'The horses are all safe, Joe,' she assured him, 'and the man who found you will make sure they're fed, and the cattle, too. Now you must try not to worry.'

He stared at her as if she were quite stupid, and shook his head and murmured about 'the old boy. Make sure . . .' before his eyes closed and he faded into sleep or semi-consciousness, she could not be sure which. In any case it seemed to Rachel that she should not delay his journey to hospital any longer.

When the ambulance had gone, the driver and his mate urging her to get on home as soon as she could, Rachel began to wonder what 'old boy' Joe Burge had been talking about. Perhaps it was the neighbour who had charge now of his animals. She would drive up and check that all was well, so that she could telephone when she got home and reassure Joe.

She climbed back into Jessica, but as she started the engine and tried to move forward she heard the wheels spin in mud and felt the little car lurch to the side. She had parked too near the ditch, and was now well and truly stuck. She revved the engine, but the wheels could get no purchase. She got out again, thankful that the rain had stopped for the moment, and tried to remember how far it was up the road to the next farm and a telephone. She took a torch, and was just about to set out to walk when she began to realise who it was that Joe Burge meant when he spoke of the 'old boy'. Had Hector been taken to the higher fields? Could he possibly be somewhere here? But the men had checked the farm buildings; the driver had told her so. She tried to persuade herself of this, but the feeling grew in her that this was what Joe had been trying to say. It would not hurt just to check the stables again. She had her torch and her boots, and the water was not deep.

She walked down the bank, past the house and across the yard, swilling through the shallow water, feeling each foothold carefully, and checked every stable. It took a long time by torchlight, but each one she found empty was a kind of relief. She pictured the placid horses ambling up to the safety of the high ground, swinging their great quarters, nodding their heads, trusting Joe to do what was right for them. But had Hector gone too? Was there anywhere else he might be?

Across in the darkness Jessica's sidelamps made a comforting landmark. If you had any vestige of sense, Rachel told herself, you'd set out now and get someone to help you with your car and forget about an old man's wandering words. Yet she felt there were still places to look, dark or no dark. Was she just standing further down the slope, or was the water rising?

She called out into the darkness, 'Hector! Hector, are you there?'

The situation was quite ridiculous. It would be like looking for a black cat in a cellar even if he were there to be found.

She had taken three steps towards the lights of the car as common sense began to prevail in her, when she heard a sound, high and unmistakable: the abrupt and trumpeting call of a stallion. She called again, and again he answered. Where in the world was he? A final shout, a final answer, and she knew where the sound came from. Yes, now she remembered. Joe had told them when they had visited his horse all that while ago. He had said that on the far side of the paddock behind the farmhouse was a small barn, one end of which was partitioned off as a stable for Hector where he could in peace and quiet be introduced to his visiting mares, whose reactions were not as predictable as those of his resident wives. Rachel remembered now that Joe had said he sometimes shut the old boy up there when the yard was busy.

Hector was there. It was no use denying it. If she was to get the horse out before the water trapped him and drowned him she must walk across the lake that had once been a paddock, and she found the idea so frightening that it was an effort to move at all. Lurching along round the edges of the yard in the shallow had been bad enough. To set out across that wide space, by torchlight and in deepening water, with no way of knowing what lay beneath her feet, was a daunting prospect; and her mind raced and filled her head with such conflicting decisions and counter-decisions that she felt it would burst.

If only she could drive away in Jessica and fetch help. Well, she could not, and anyway the flood was rising. She must get Hector out somehow by herself. Then came the thought that she should not put herself at such risk for a horse, it was irresponsible. She could not be expected to risk herself, and her baby, whose existence she no longer doubted. But it was her job to care for animals; they were her responsibility, too. Even as she debated she began to move, taking up a rope halter that she had found in one of the stables – and it was not in Jessica's direction.

It seemed to take several hours to negotiate the paddock, although it was scarcely more than a hundred metres across. As she went she continued to argue with herself. She spoke aloud, as a kind of comfort in the darkness, to herself, to the baby – if it was a baby, and not just a hiccup in the system, a group of symptoms with some other cause than that first amazing division of cells that leads to another life.

'Look,' she said to it. 'If you are there – and I'm sure you're there

– I'm your mother. But I'm a vet too, and I've got a job to do, and I'm not enjoying it very much. Not to put too fine a point on it I'm frightened out of my wits, for myself, and for you too. Perhaps you think it isn't my job anyway. Nobody's paying me, are they? Nobody's asked me to, have they? Well, only Hector.'

She splashed on, and the water was over the boots now and went coldly down to her feet. 'Your father will think I'm mad,' she said. 'No, no he won't. He'll be angry, but he'd do the same himself. Later on, when you know me better, you'll understand. You aren't going to be the sort of person who'd walk away and let the old man's horse drown, are you? No, I thought not. Well then, baby, you just hold on tight. It'll be O.K. We're nearly there.' A madwoman. Talking to herself, talking to a foetus.

Torchlight showed her the wall of the barn, no distance at all, and in sheer relief she quickened her step, forgot to check her foothold and went down on her knees in cold creeping water. Under the surface the torch gleamed for a moment, lighting the underwater grass to a ghostly green, and then it went out, and Rachel was swallowed up in darkness.

Panic hit her again, and she could scarcely make herself stand up. The weight of her soaked clothes dragged at her and the cold she felt was so sudden that she began at once to shake. It was all so very stupid. She had come all this way, and now she had no light by which to finish off the job. She was almost as trapped in her situation as Hector in his. Well, she must make the best job she could. No point giving up now. Finding the wall of the barn was no problem: darkness under the sky is never totally dark. But once she had found the door and opened its top section to peer in, it was like looking into a box full of black cotton wool. The darkness seemed solid.

She knew he was in there, though he did not call now. She could feel the large warmth of his presence in the stable, was aware of his quiet breathing. What she did not know was his exact whereabouts in that blackness, or what end of him was nearer to her. She might walk straight into his back end in the darkness, and in his fright he might smash her with his great hoofs. She would have to hope that if she spoke to him he would turn towards her, would trust her not to be any kind of enemy, any threat to him. Half a ton of shire horse resisting a threat, even if it exists only in his imagination, is a powerful and terrifying force, and not to be faced lightly.

She called his name and he answered softly, an enquiring whicker. She heard the squelch of his feet on the soggy straw. The stable door fitted snug and sound, and only a little water had got in. Trusting that he had turned himself towards the sound of her voice Rachel climbed in over the half door, still talking quietly to the invisible horse and then stretched out her arms in the blind dark, feeling for him.

He was closer than she had realised and the sudden touch of his warm skin was a shock of surprise in the apparent emptiness.

'Well now, Hector, there's a boy. Good lad, now. Good boy.' Her voice shook, in sympathy with her shaking hands.

She had forgotten the vast size of him: eighteen hands, and built like a battleship. If he did not like the idea of wearing the puny rope halter she had brought with her, there was no way she could persuade him otherwise: her hand could reach scarcely higher than his withers, and the great crested neck rose high above as he gazed out over the flood. She could see the outline of his head now, silhouetted against the lesser darkness of the doorway.

Then she found in her pocket a small piece of magic – a symbol of luck, perhaps: a grubby peppermint that had fallen out of the packet she had put in her pocket for the drive home. She proferred it, palm outstretched, and the great head bent to examine the gift. She felt the brush of huge lips and the whiskery touch of his nose and chin. The rope slipped over his ears as he crunched the mint, and there he was haltered and ready to be led. Well, she hoped he was.

Rachel had almost forgotten until now how cold and wet she was. Her brain had centred on the search and its attendant problems, cutting out peripheral discomfort. Now she began to shiver, and more and more the coldness brought home to her the nastiness of the situation she was in.

For a start it was raining again: heavy, drumming rain that would swell the flood even more and would make it even more difficult to see than the darkness alone – and Lord knew, that had been enough. However, the sliding back of the bolt on the stable door had revealed a worse problem than that. The door could not open because of the pressure of water from the flooded field. How could she get him out? She felt panic behind her eyes, beating, beating.

'Oh, this is so silly!' she shouted into the darkness, and the voice and its echo shook with a growing fear. This is ridiculous, Rachel thought. I'm no heroine. What am I doing here? If this is adventure you can keep it. 'What on earth are we going to do, Hector?'

He looked at her mildly, and splashed with a huge forefoot on the squelchy straw.

'Stupid horse,' she said, her voice anxious and sharp. 'Think of something, can't you?'

She leant and heaved on the door again, but it would not budge. He ambled after her, and leaned to snuffle at the water swirling past. With his weight against it, the door moved fractionally, and water spurted in along its edge. Rachel watched it and knew that his unthinking action had given her an answer. That was it then, wasn't it? If he would lean on the door again and let more water in, the weight of water on either side of the door would equalise and it would open. But Hector had seen enough. His interest waned and he backed off a step. The door shut firm.

'Come on,' Rachel commanded him. 'Shove!' He merely looked at her, curious to know why she was pushing at him and looking so cross. He swished his tail at her as if she were an irritating fly.

She lost her temper with him then. She forgot he was five times her size and ten times more powerful. She pulled and tugged at him until he came alongside the manger which she knew lay along the back wall of the stable. In the blackness she felt for it, and scrambled up and from there onto Hector's back. In that state of high recklessness that comes with desperation she drummed her heels into his sides and shouted: 'Walk on, you great stupid oaf. If you don't want to be rescued that's up to you, but I want to go home. I want my husband, and I want a good hot cup of tea, and I don't want to get drowned and I don't want to lose my baby; so walk on, darn you, and shove that door!'

Perturbed by the fury of her voice, Hector lurched against the door. More water gushed in. Again and again she drummed him with her heels, urging him forward, until at last, when she was on the point of thinking it would never happen, the door surged open and they were out in the flooded field. It was frighteningly deep now: soon it was up to Hector's elbows as he plunged forward. She clung on and kept his head turned towards the tiny beacon of Jessica's lights in the distance. She soothed him now, her fury gone. From now on she must keep calm and not let him panic as she had done. They waded on. The whole situation was so ludicrous, a child's storybook adventure. If she weren't so wet and cold and scared it would be good for a laugh, really. What an idiot she must look, soaking wet, her boots swilling with water, riding a shire stallion through several feet of spilled-over Severn in the middle of the night. She tried to laugh, and fear came up and quenched it.

A wind had got up, quite suddenly, flinging the rain harder into her face. Somewhere in the darkness great trees began to heave and sway, and Rachel could hear the crash of their branches like the sound of the sea; and the flood water itself made more sound now, swirling and sucking past them, greedy, like a creature that wished to pull them down, to drown and devour them. Rachel would not look down at the dizzying water but gazed ahead at the car's lights and tried hard to overcome the fear that rose up on her, faster than the flood. She swallowed hard, and thought she might try singing.

'Onward Christian soldiers,' was the only tune that came to mind. She sang it, very loud, and Hector flexed his ears to the sound and continued to plod, large and determined and somehow totally safe, beneath her, like St Christopher at the ford.

'God bless dear old Hector
Marching through the flood,' she sang to the tune;
'Doesn't mind the water
Doesn't mind the mud.'

She sang the words over and over again, and was so busy with her singing that she did not at first see the headlights come sweeping towards her, beaming across the water, searching. 'Is that you, Mrs Adams?' A voice called, still thin and distant. It was near enough though for her to know on the instant that she was not alone, and to relieve her sufficiently to bring her irritability flooding back. Who did they think it was? The Loch Ness monster? Or were there likely to be several people having a jolly paddle in the floods in the middle of the night?'

'Yes!' she called. 'Yes, it's me.'

After a moment or so an engine sounded, and the headlights were swung again until they caught the two of them in the double beam of light. It was worse then the darkness. Hector stopped, snorting with surprise.

'Switch off!' she shouted. 'I can't see!' With sidelights only lit the car became another usable landmark. On plodded Hector, until at last they rose up out of the water like some creature of mythology; one of the centaurs perhaps, or Jupiter in one of his better disguises.

'Good Lord,' said the driver of the car. 'What have you got there?'

And cold and wet and tired as she was, the relief of being safe poured through her like wine so that she laughed aloud, and praised and patted Hector. Her rescuer looked alarmed, as if this might be the beginnings of hysteria, but she slid down to the ground looking quite sane and rational, if extremely wet, and he had the good sense to give her brandy and a blanket on the instant.

He introduced himself as Bill Stevens, the farmer from up the road, the one who had charge now of Joe's horses. He had flagged down the ambulance as it passed to see if Joe had any particular instructions, and the old man had murmured incoherently of Mrs Adams and 'the old boy'. Not being able to make sense of this he had decided he had better go and double check at the farm to see that there was nothing else that could be done there. He had found Jessica, apparently abandoned, and had been searching round for Rachel in the darkness when he had heard the sound of splashing and seen a sight he would not forget in a lifetime. A young woman coming up out of the water on a great shire stallion. Her wet hair was plastered about her face; her wet skirt and coat hems clung to the horse's sides so that she seemed moulded on to him as he streamed with water like a ship breasting a wave, his great crest of mane spangled with water-drops.

Stevens had stood for a moment, awe-struck, hardly able to believe this vision truly human, truly equine, but then he had seen how Rachel shook with cold and had acted at once.

When the brandy had reached the spot and stopped the chattering of her teeth, Rachel told him that there were more blankets in her car.

'Still cold?' he asked.

'For the horse,' she replied, and he fetched the rugs from Jessica and spread them over Hector, where they lay looking small and inadequate.

'I'll give him some brandy too, if you like,' Stevens offered.

'Better not,' Rachel grinned. 'Thanks for your help.'

'I'm only glad I found you. I've got a tow-rope in the back, and I'll pull your car out later, but for the moment I'd better get you home to my house. It's only just up the road, and the missus'll look after you while I come back for the horse. You shouldn't drive after all that wet and the brandy and all.'

'I'm going nowhere without Hector,' Rachel said obstinately. 'Nowhere at all.'

So she climbed back onto him again and rode him ahead of Bill Stevens' car, in the lights of the headlamps, until they arrived at the Stevens' yard and Hector could be safely left in a cowshed, well furnished with straw and sweet hay.

The warmth of the farmhouse kitchen was like a blessing fallen on her. Her cold limbs stung and ached as the blood came back to them. Mrs Stevens fussed pleasantly over her, put soup to heat on the Aga and went off in search of dry clothes. Being so looked after, so cared for, was a treat to beat anything money could buy after the large and hostile dark in which she seemed to have wandered for so long.

When she had Rachel dressed in dry things Mrs Stevens explained that her husband had not worried about Hector for the simple reason that he did not know he was there. The stallion had gone on loan to a stud in Wiltshire earlier in the year and had not been due to return until Christmas, but it seemed Joe Burge could no longer bear to be without him and had gone only the previous weekend in his lorry to fetch the horse home.

'If it's all right I'd like to ring the hospital and ask them to tell Joe that Hector's safe,' Rachel said, 'and then, if I may, I'll ring my husband.'

A message was promised to Joe at once. He had been making a great nuisance of himself, it seemed, demanding news of his horse when they had none to give him.

When Rachel telephoned Painters, however, the bell rang and rang at the Milchester end until she was about to put the instrument back in its cradle and begin to worry about where Tom could be. Then the tone stopped, and a breathless voice said, 'Hello?'

'Tom? It's Rachel. Where were you?'

It was instantly obvious he had no idea how late it was, or how many hours ago she herself ought to have returned. He began at once to tell her, excitedly, where he had been, and with whom, and why! He had been called up by Abel Cash, saying it was something important, and had managed to drive himself cautiously to the garage, to find a most incongruously dressed gentleman, dinner-jacketed, very clean and correct, sitting in Abel's room waiting to meet him.

'Only stopped for petrol, Rachel. Saw that metal sculpture of mine. Said he wasn't leaving without it and how much did Abel want. Abel said he didn't think I'd part with it for less than five hundred. I ask you! It's only old bits of junk I was mucking about with. I'd have let him have it for a fiver. He said he never haggled, and would a cheque on Coutts' Bank do? He took it away there and then Rachel, wrapped up in plastic and strapped to the roof-rack of his Mercedes. The man must be insane. God bless him.'

Tom was so amused, so delighted at the happenings of his evening, and so intent on telling her every last detail that it was a long time before he registered how late it was.

'Good Lord, Rachel,' he said, suddenly. 'I've just looked at the clock. Why aren't you home? What's been happening?' His voice was instantly full of concern for her.

For a moment, while he was speaking, she had longed to interrupt, to say, 'Look, for heaven's sake, I could have died tonight. I've been cold and wet and half-drowned, and anyway I'm pregnant, and in the face of that what's a bit of old sculpture to get excited about,' but she couldn't; and now, with his sudden anxiety for her, how could she tell him all these things at a distance and then leave him alone and worried until she could get back to Milchester? She could tell him in her own time, in her own way.

'It's all right,' she said. 'I'm quite safe. I called in at a friend of Joe Burge's. I'll be home in an hour or so. Don't wait up. If you're awake when I come in, I'll tell you all about it.'

'Come back soon,' he said. 'I'll be awake.'

Rachel set the 'phone down and turned gratefully to the kitchen table where the hot soup was waiting for her.

'My Bill's gone to get your car out,' Mrs Stevens said. 'But you'd be welcome to stay here the night if you'd like.'

'That's kind of you,' Rachel said, feeling the pervading warmth of the food inside her. 'I'm very grateful, but I really must go home.'

She sat down again at the kitchen table. Her aching, weary body glowed gratefully with warmth and nourishment. She looked down at it, draped in borrowed garments – at a guess three sizes too big for Mrs Stevens was a large-boned woman and substantially made. Rachel smiled. The blurring of her outlines was the least of the things she was going to have to get used to.

Bill Stevens came in then and announced that Jessica was out in the yard and none the worse for being towed from the mud.

'And that horse of Joe's is stood in my stable eating my hay as if he owned the place. I hope he understands what he owes you, young woman.'

Rachel never supposed, or expected, gratitude in any of the creatures for whose welfare she worked. The relief of distress, the abatement of illness, the mending of wounds or bones was enough in itself. She had seen the great horse safe in his straw bed, snatching good hay in imperious mouthfuls, and had been glad that her probably stupid action, her unwillingly dragged-up courage, had got him out of that barn which now stood deep, as Bill Stevens reported, in the sullen, swirling Severn flood.

For a little while longer Rachel sat and chatted, but all the while she was thinking of Tom and imagining his face when she told him what she now knew without any doubt to be true. Fatherhood would suit him, she was convinced of it, and she felt a giddy rush of pleasure at the prospect of his own delight at her news.

Back once more flooded that old elation. It could not set her dancing, she was too bone-weary for that; but it carried her spirits up and began to wash away the horrors of the darker flood. Her whole night's adventure would take some telling, once she had told Tom what was most important for him to know; but she would emphasise the triumphs of it and the more ridiculous moments, rather than the terrible power of the dragging, spinning water and her panic in the darkness of the stable. That was all in the past now.

It was pleasant in the farm kitchen, with its homely muddle, its warm stove, the Gloucester Market calendar on the wall, next to the milk-yield charts and some down-hung bunches of herbs that smelled like summer.

The chair upon which she sat was a big old wooden Windsor, battered with age but well made to take the body comfortably, and that comfort, together with the warmth of Mrs. Stevens' welcome and the weariness of her own bones, lured her to stay; but now that her thoughts had turned towards home, she longed for her bed, and Tom, and a quiet night, and no demanding bells.

With such thoughts on her mind, Rachel grew increasingly restless to be off and away, and in spite of Mrs. Stevens' protests, she insisted on climbing back into her own clothes, which were still dampish and smelled strongly of river water.

She walked out into the yard, to discover that the rain had stopped at last and between rags of cloud a dull moon splashed light onto the puddled cobblestones. As if sensing Rachel's urgency, Jessica started up sweetly for the journey home, and they set off across the yard and through the gate, with farewells called after them from the lighted doorway, and Hector trumpeting from the stable.

Rachel drove towards Milchester in that state of high elation that comes with dangers well past. As she drove she occupied her mind with reciting aloud all the trite phrases with which she might announce her pregnancy to Tom, but this exercise made her giggle, and she had to recall her attention swiftly to the road ahead. Perhaps she should wear the mantle of motherhood with more dignity, she chided herself, yet she revelled in the lovely weightless excitement that had taken all the weariness from her.

The homeward journey seemed a matter of moments, and there was Painters, with the bedroom window lit, welcoming her back.

Quietly she let herself in and went up the stairs softly, but two at a time, to find Tom sprawled out asleep on the bed, his arm flung protectively across her empty space.

Rachel watched him for a moment and then knelt by him, touching the hairs of his beard until at last he stirred, and woke, and looked at her. At the moment his eyes opened, he began to open his mouth too, perhaps to say that he was sorry for having been asleep when he had sworn to be awake, but she bridged his lips with her finger to hush him.

"Hey, old Noah," she said, "I've got news for you." For a moment he continued to look at her. Then he stretched up his arm and encircled her neck, drawing her down against him. She had seen the smile of delight that lit his face from brow to beard, and knew she need not spell out the news to him. All the stilted phrases she had tried out on the night air during the journey home evaporated. She would use no words, for there was nothing that needed to be said.

CHRISTIAN HERALD ASSOCIATION AND ITS MINISTRIES

CHRISTIAN HERALD ASSOCIATION, founded in 1878, publishes The Christian Herald Magazine, one of the leading interdenominational religious monthlies in America. Through its wide circulation, it brings inspiring articles and the latest news of religious developments to many families. From the magazine's pages came the initiative for CHRISTIAN HERALD CHILDREN and THE BOWERY MISSION, two individually supported not-for-profit corporations.

CHRISTIAN HERALD CHILDREN, established in 1894, is the name for a unique and dynamic ministry to disadvantaged children, offering hope and opportunities which would not otherwise be available for reasons of poverty and neglect. The goal is to develop each child's potential and to demonstrate Christian compassion and understanding to children in need.

Mont Lawn is a permanent camp located in Bushkill, Pennsylvania. It is the focal point of a ministry which provides a healthful "vacation with a purpose" to children who without it would be confined to the streets of the city. Up to 1000 children between the age of 7 and 11 come to Mont Lawn each year.

Christian Herald Children maintains year-round contact with children by means of a *City Youth Ministry.* Central to its philosophy is the belief that only through sustained relationships and demonstrated concern can individual lives be truly enriched. Special emphasis is on individual guidance, spiritual and family counseling and tutoring. This follow-up ministry to inner-city children culminates for many in financial assistance toward higher education and career counseling.

THE BOWERY MISSION, located at 227 Bowery, New York City, has since 1879 been reaching out to the lost men on the Bowery, offering them what could be their last chance to rebuild their lives. Every man is fed, clothed and ministered to. Countless numbers have entered the 90-day residential rehabilitation program at the Bowery Mission. A concentrated ministry of counseling, medical care, nutrition therapy, Bible study and Gospel services awakens a man to spiritual renewal within himself.

These ministries are supported solely by the voluntary contributions of individuals and by legacies and bequests. Contributions are tax deductible. Checks should be made out either to CHRISTIAN HERALD CHILDREN or to THE BOWERY MISSION.

Administrative Office: 40 Overlook Drive, Chappaqua, New York 10514
Telephone: (914) 769-9000